Acc
South

"If you only read one book this year, make it *South of Cincinnati*. Hits all the right notes in a narrative to have you renew your faith in the sheer joy of a great book."

—Ken Bruen, bestselling author
of the Jack Taylor series

"Scumbag addicts, dirty cops, savage brutality, and the price of a broken heart. My kind of people. My kind of book. In his latest Jon Catlett novel, author Jonathan Ashley tackles the toughest question facing a junkie: what's harder to kick—the dope or the girl? *South of Cincinnati* is a thrilling head-first dive into the dirty drug underworld as we watch a hero trying not to drown in pursuit of his humanity."

—Joe Clifford, author of *Junkie Love*
and the Jay Porter Thriller Series

"Jonathan Ashley is elbowing his way to the front of the crowd of crime writers with his crisp dialogue, edgy characters and relentlessly gritty action. *South of Cincinnati* is a razor-sharp slice through the mire of the Midwestern drug underworld, allowing us to peek from a safe distance."

—Joe Ricker, author of
Walkin' After Midnight

SOUTH OF CINCINNATI

ALSO BY JONATHAN ASHLEY

Jon Catlett Series
The Cost of Doing Business (*)
South of Cincinnati
The Last Fallout (*)

Stand Alones
Friends in Low Places (*)
Out of Mercy (*)

(*) – coming soon

JONATHAN ASHLEY

SOUTH OF CINCINNATI

A JON CATLETT NOVEL

DOWN&OUT BOOKS

Down & Out Books
3959 Van Dyke Rd, Ste. 265
Lutz, FL 33558
www.DownAndOutBooks.com

Cover design by JT Lindroos

ISBN: 1-943402-89-2
ISBN-13: 978-1-943402-89-2

To Coolee Jean,
for finding me
when I was lost south of Cincinnati.

"Show me the man who invented the human heart then show me the gallows where he was hanged."
—Lawrence Durrell, *Justine*

PROLOGUE

The low evening sun half-sunken behind the upward slope of pavement and skyscraper rendered downtown Music City rife for pillage in the dusky gloaming. I knew these streets. I'd lost a lot of weekends here, the bulk of my youth ardently forfeited to drink and lechery. The abysmal avenues of this broken suburb remained eclipsed in the faint shadow of the Parthenon's irradiant arches. The Athenian wonder had been replicated to the last detail, reflecting not what crumbling ruins still stand in the birthplace of democracy, but that baronial resplendence that died with the ancient Greeks.

Since my return to the bent life, I'd barely noticed the seasons changing. This town lacked Kentucky's suffocating humidity. Back home, when came the harsh drudgeries of summer that lingered far into September like a teenager's first heartbreak, the murder rate always tripled. But the weather was not the only cause this time. Usually there was a peak in shootings when the equatorial temperatures grew too taxing on the poor and marginalized and potentially murderous. But there were other factors that had contributed to this particularly awe-inspiring increase in killings. This streak had started long before the heatwave. When our product hit town in late March, the West End turned

1

into a war zone over night. Low bottom junkies and competing corner boys now ventilated each other with impunity, all over the mahogany kilos my friends and I had begun transporting across state lines last Spring.

The year before I entered the game, there'd been seventy-five suspicious deaths in Louisville. Since January, we'd had a hundred and twenty-eight, rivaling Memphis and Nashville in violent crime.

And I'd compounded the problem more than I'd ever care to confess.

This run would mark my first hands on drug deal since I'd thrown back in with my psychopathic sidekicks. I'd stayed away from the dirtier side of the business since the morning my best friend and I survived a shoot-out that would've made Sam Peckinpah proud and wistful. In a last-ditch effort to save our own lives and dethrone our former employer, we strapped on Kevlar vests and armed ourselves to the teeth, determined to, if not survive, at least ensure that our adversaries perished with us.

The crooked detective leading us into battle, a brooding country gentleman who ranked prominently among my long list of criminal confederates, had pilfered an array of weapons over the years from dead or pleading suspects. Many of the smaller calibers I'm sure the sergeant, at one time, intended to use as "drop guns." These token street pieces were perfect for squeezing into the grip of an unarmed suspect shot to death mistakenly or, depending on the officer involved, for motives more sinister.

For our purposes that bright spring morning, such lady guns would hardly suffice. From the sergeant's extensive arsenal, we chose Glocks affixed with foot-long suppressors, Armalite AR-15 assault rifles manually upgraded to fully automatic subjoined with night vision scopes, and massive pump-action shotguns, Ithacas and Remingtons that could, and did, cut men clean in half with single discharges.

Clad in dark overcoats and knit caps, we could have passed for the poorly aged star attractions of a high school shooter reunion tour. We crossed the city limits, the rural route buttressed by fallow fields of grazing cattle eyeing passing traffic with a gaze as lifeless as that of the killer cop steering us to our fate on Dog Hill, Luther's farm east of town where three trench-coated gunmen with nothing to lose would make Kentucky history. Some ambitious and surprisingly street-wise crime reporter would entitle the bloodbath, "The Dog Hill Dog Food Massacre." The writer's headline I found particularly impressive as most drug-culture laymen are justly unaware that "dog food" is a street name for heroin.

Taste the stuff after it's been broken down with water and you'll understand the reference.

Why did we have to kill Luther Longmire?

I'd made the lanky loudmouth Eastern Kentuckian stupidly rich with my connections in the Cincinnati and Chicago heroin trades. Don't get me wrong. Luther was wealthy before I came along. The man had, for nearly a decade, been considered by both the police and concomitant criminals the most successful marijuana cultivator and distributor in Kentucky. But when we started raking in the kind of money to be made peddling dog food, Longmire, almost overnight, succumbed to that paranoia so common among the powerful, and began murdering anyone who might *someday pose a threat to his freedom and finances.*

"Can you start loading?"

I blinked twice and turned to face the woman who'd summoned me from my deathly reverie to the rear parking lot of the Sweetwater Music Club where I'd escorted this unsuspecting icon of alternative country music. On the way in, Catherine had treated me to a derelict Nashville street tour, pointing out the Batman building and, as we passed by, Printer's Alley. A few blocks from the venue, while she performed her honky-tonk ballads, I planned to unload to the local chapter of the Dixie mafia several kilos of Afghanistan heroin. Our mysterious supplier who brought the dope into the country paid less than a grand a kilo. We were reselling them at eight a brick. Tonight's exchange would net a hundred grand in profit and it was only one of five conducted this week. My cut: just shy of thirty K. Multiply that by twenty; we shipped five days a week (we'd take two off for debriefing), four weeks a month and weren't planning on slowing down.

"You okay?" Catherine asked from the passenger's side where she sat with the door open.

Rock 'n' roll anachronisms of all types lined the club's sun-bleached adobe walls. Hippies, greasers, mods, plastic men and painted women.

"Yeah," I said. *"I got it. Go do your thing. Socialize. Network."*

"'Network?'" Her tongue hung limply atop her bottom lip and she feigned a few dry heaves. *"Don't ever use that word around me again."*

"Then why do I have to unload your guitars?"

"Because I want some of these people to think I'm more

of a rock star than I am and having a gofer perpetuates the mythology."

"I think I'm in love."

"There are just a few people I need to speak with." She peered past me, through the driver's window, at two stooges in nudie suits and J.C. Stetsons staring at us like we were the Beatles fresh in from Liverpool.

While Catherine doffed her cowboy hat and rounded the hood of the van to greet the two suits, I closed my eyes and continued to relive the worst moments of my life, the week that Luther Longmire died.

I began with Irina, the woman I'd loved for years then lost because I couldn't quit using heroin or instigating bar fights or, in the more expansive stages of my addiction, threatening strangers with castration on Facebook, Irina, who I had tried foolishly to win back with money and pomp. I should have known that she'd never be swayed into the arms of the kind of man I'd become.

I never thought I'd get away with all the things I'd done. I never once believed I could forever hide my worst sins from the stubborn and precocious Irina. I simply convinced myself that, after I'd wooed her back, she'd forgive, that she'd look beyond the drug dealing and the unapologetic ruffians with whom I'd surrounded myself. She had for-given worse. The woman had nursed her dying father to a comfortable end despite what he'd done to her when she was a little girl and the lasting damage the molesting and beatings had left.

A few days before we turned Luther's farm into the OK Corral, I lost her.

I'd always considered myself impervious to easy detec-

*tion, at least by Irina, since I conducted most of my busi-
ness during the day while she was at school or busy looking
after her misanthropic, alcoholic mother. We were also es-
tranged and, like most men in their flagrant failure to understand their women, I equated frigidity with unloving. I
vastly underestimated her heart.*

One afternoon, Irina skipped class.

*She was studying to be an elementary school teacher.
When she had gotten sober, she'd moved in with her
mother to go back to college. She'd aced all her papers and
tests and never missed a lecture, that is, until the day she
couldn't stand the worry any longer, wondering what
trouble her degenerate junkie paramour had brought down
on himself.*

*She followed me from the Highlands to Anchorage
where Luther lived.*

*The day she realized why I had been missing so often
since our last falling out, why I never called or answered
her texts, Irina was shot to death, gunned down to a pulp
right in front of me with a massive .357 hand cannon in the
middle of Luther Longmire's dining hall. Luther's courte-
san cousin held the gun and laughed while Irina bled out.*

*Later, when we decided to kill the hillbilly kingpin, the
bent cop who served for years as Luther's bodyguard and
first lieutenant explained why he'd saved me from the
boss's goons, why Sergeant Mad Dog Milligan had chosen
to betray his master. "He does this every few years and I
can't watch anymore. People who didn't need to die have,
all because of Luther's madness. This time will be worse.
The heroin has him spooked. I knew we should have stuck
with weed. You can sell that shit for a hundred years and*

never have to take a life." I wondered how the detective had kept his day-job since he worked twice as hard brokering assassinations and coordinating cash drops and heroin re-ups as he did interrogating suspects, serving warrants, or conducting sting operations.

We cornered the old man where he had holed up in his Dog Hill compound.

We let the Mexican farm hands go free. Those unarmed, that is.

We killed everyone else, all except Amara, who we tied up and threw in the back of the van. I don't know why we didn't shoot her on sight. I suppose, despite her trespasses, executing a woman was something we all still considered beyond the moral pale.

"We'll figure out what to do with her after we clear out," the sergeant had said.

I already knew how I'd cast my vote.

We cracked the safe in Longmire's office and found nearly one and a half million dollars, which we divided evenly between the three of us. We loaded up as many kilos as we could fit into the van. Then, with a lot of gasoline and what was left of the C-4, we leveled the place, hoping that the burnt bodies would stall the police in identifying Longmire and buy us some time to get our stories straight.

We didn't anticipate how quickly the KSP could pressure the lab boys and coroners from Frankfort to rush the process.

We drove to an abandoned rest stop a few miles east where I handed over the keys to my business to Paul Frank, my longtime manager, and told him the place was his.

In the cab, we briefly discussed the woman's fate. Then the decision was made.

I pulled Amara from the van, let her cry and lie and beg a little.

Then I shot her in the face.

Now, a season later, here I was in Music City, U.S.A., still free, peddling heroin twice as strong as the batches I used to bring down from Illinois.

And for the first time since I cradled Irina's dead body, I was close to a beautiful woman, one I had long desired with an earnestness and innocence I thought I'd long ago forfeited to the loose, whiskey-swilling hussies of the Highlands, to South Louisville juke joints and West End Jones men.

Before she went inside, Catherine leaned into the van and kissed me, a last loving gesture offered to a broken man dying of some undiscovered and wasting disease. "Don't miss the first song." She dropped the Bobby Bare Stetson onto her crown and disappeared into the cavernous dark of the Sweetwater.

While she proceeded with her sound check, I found a better parking space. I loaded her extra guitar and various sound pedals through the back entrance reserved for bar staff and entertainers.

The star attraction bent down from the stage as I set her equipment off to the side and asked me if I was all right alone, after all the unfortunate half-truths I'd confessed on the ride down 65 from our bloody Ohio River home. "I'm better now," I lied and formed my millionth fake smile.

While I'd never seen the light that Hank Williams Senior

sang of as he helped build this country-western Athens, I had certainly felt the heat.

The star's faded pupils peered through the neon twilight that crept in from the open doorways and I stared at Catherine with a poor man's eyes. I'd probably die long before I could get around to letting her down.

Two men in a rented Honda Civic with Ohio plates watched from the parking lot of the corner drugstore across the Nashville thoroughfare. The cornrowed Californian in the passenger bucket brought his work to a close, fitting 9mm hollow-point rounds into the two banana magazines that fit the submachine pistols hidden beneath the back seats.

"He's leaving," said the passenger's partner from the driver's seat. The elder snorted, swallowing his spit.

The younger said, "We been followin' him since Louisville. We shoulda taken him there but the client didn't want it done near the business and the motherfucker has been holed up in that bookstore all day. We coulda ran them off the road and done 'em on the side of the highway. Why the hell did we have to follow him all the way to fuckin' Nashville?"

The elder scratched his gray-flecked goatee. "We didn't get paid for two. We got paid for one. We do the girl too, we're gonna have us a conflict with our man in West Louisville. He's a cheap son-of-a-bitch and he won't want to pay extra. We ain't got the book man away from the store and by hisself yet. But it looks like we're about to get our chance"

"*I say we pull up on him now. Light him up in the parking lot and then head downtown so I can challenge some of these cracker motherfuckers to a karaoke showdown. Show 'em what real singing sounds like.*"

The elder reminded his squire that there were too many witnesses.

They watched Catlett enter the van alone and pull out of the bar's backlot.

The Honda's engine turned over.

"*Guess little corn fed bitch got lucky.*" The younger popped his knuckles and glared at the white bread nightclub they'd allowed Catlett's date to enter unmolested. "*Lucky she dealing with some cheap-ass niggas.*"

"*She got lucky for tonight,*" said the elder. "*She wants to live to grow old, ofay bitch better start making better relationship decisions.*"

1

I was back in town at the behest of my old partner and the two police detectives investigating a recent rash of related killings. Fortunately, the LMPD homicide division only solves one out of every four of the average seventy-fifty plus murders committed within the city limits every year.

Essentially, you had to be a real stupid asshole to get caught clipping someone in Louisville.

I'd rehearsed my story a dozen times on the three-hour car ride back from the Appalachian Mountains where I'd been laying low with my extended meth-head family since the Dog Hill massacre.

I practiced aloud to the mutt puppy my cousin had given me, one of about a dozen half-Chihuahua, half-Jack Russell terriers to survive his bitch Dragona's litter. The dog closely resembled a baby golden retriever, blonde with floppy ears that, when something caught her interest, rose like antennas and betrayed her south-of-the-border birthright. Her eyes were outlined in black, as if she'd been provided a lifetime supply of naturally reapplying mascara at birth. She lay on her side, curled up in the floorboard, her sad brown gaze fixed on her strange new caretaker. Back in Cumberland, my crotch-scratching cousins offered only free packs of crystal meth and hard liquor as an alternative to my malaise, offers I repeatedly turned down to the great amusement of my hellion hosts: "Johnny'd rather have him one of them foo-foo drinks them fag bars in the city serve." I'd decided long ago that if I were to commit suicide, this time I'd do it quickly with a gun or a hand grenade, and not prolong the process by diving head first into active addiction again and hoping for an overdose. Without the little dog's companionship, I would have likely gone the way of the self-inflicted hollow-point wound. She was more precious than most of what I'd lost to find her.

"Detective," I said as we left Jackson, Hazard, and the rest of Eastern Kentucky behind for the city where I'd begun my larcenous learnings. "Detective, I only know what I know." I spoke in a lilt that I'd drop when going through the motions with the cops, affecting the lisped tone of a lower registered Truman Capote. I could say anything to the puppy and she'd invariably wag her tail at the strange sound of this inflection. "Irina, she had so much life left. Detective, she...I loved her so fucking much. I'm a lesser man without her in my life." Saying her name caused me a hard, bitter swallow, the image of my beloved with half a head, crumpled like a drunkard's suitcoat in the trunk of a muscle car. "Irina, listen, wherever you are." I stopped talking to the fictional cops and spoke instead to the bitterest of my many dead. "I'm sorry."

"Irina," I said to the dog.

Then I realized, I had finally provided the mutt with a name.

"Irina. That's it. The prefect name for a little angel. She would have been your mother, you know, and it stands to reason that you *should* have her name, by God. She would have adored you too, you vexing little minx." I patted the passenger seat and Irina hopped up for me to scratch behind her ears.

At least I knew now what to call the precocious little creature. I think even she was tired of hearing me yell, "Little doggy" or "Hey, shithead." I'd have to be sure not to call her by name around the investigators lest they question my soundness of mind. I wasn't in the mood to fight a mental inquest warrant.

As I exited off Route 15 and hit the Mountain Parkway, phone reception returned and my cell began ringing. After leaving Louisville, I'd tossed every burner but one, the number to which I'd texted a few old Louisville friends, in case someone died or the city sank into the Ohio River.

"Fuck you, Scotty," I answered.

"Surprised this number still works." Scott Morgan cackled like a consumptive brothel keeper. He had once considered himself a proud addition to the shiftless procession of dope fiends and inebriants wandering the streets of Louisville seeking truth and misadventure. We together enjoyed the low life of modern boulevardiers until the day Scott's marine general daddy ordered him to straighten up or expect a complete and swift severance from the family and the millions papa had accumulated leading poor young men to their violent deaths.

Scott, despite his juvenile criminal record—strictly misdemeanors—and his near religious adherence to anarchy, applied to the state police. He passed all the physicals and psychological exams and begun pursuing a career in law enforcement, abandoning his rowdy friends to settle down with a pretty wife and a picket fence and, hopefully, some tow-headed children to complete the perfect American family portrait. For two years, he'd been working plain-clothes with the KSP. He was assigned to cover any armed robbery or murder that fell within the jurisdiction of a county that couldn't handle the case's scope and magnitude. If an investigation involved multiple related homicides spanning across the state, the boys in Frankfort would call in Scott and his team. For all I knew, he'd been one of the staties assigned to make sense of Dog Hill.

"I'm surprised you're calling me," I said. "I texted you my number in case you needed an alibi for some police shooting, you know, if you blew away an unarmed black kid and needed me to bring you some crack to sprinkle on the poor little bastard before IAD arrived. Should I purloin you some grade-A freebase and a decent drop gun to place at the feet of some unsuspecting and underprivileged housing project resident?"

"Thanks anyway," he said, "but the worst projects are out of my jurisdiction. You might want to consult the LMPD, if you think you have a knack for those services. Those Louisville cops are always shooting unarmed suspects."

If only he knew, I thought.

"What can I do for you, then, Corporal?" I asked.

"I'll be in town next week. We need to talk."

Shit. I wondered if he knew. I mean, he knew I was a junkie. That was why he'd cut me out of his life years ago. Even when I called and told him I'd quit—a lie, I had just snorted a fat line of China white before I dialed his number—he said, "That's nice," and found an excuse to get off the line. Kentucky State Police detectives couldn't afford to be associated with drug addicts.

"Last time I talked to you, you couldn't be seen with a known junkie. It'd be bad for a statie's career," I said to Scott.

I doubted he suspected my involvement in the Dog Hill killings. He was probably in the middle of a divorce or an alcoholic nervous breakdown, a third-life crisis. Scott could drink on duty and pop prescription painkillers with impunity, but introduce needles and his repressed scruples reared their smug, self-righteous heads.

"You said you'd cleaned up. You told me that, remember? You said so in the message. Was that another lie, Jon?"

"I'm clean." It was the truth. I hadn't used in months. I'd just killed a lot of people. "Now that I'm not a liability, what can I do for you?"

"I'm at work right now," Scott said. "I don't have a lot of time to talk."

"Then why are we talking?"

"I'm just making sure I can come to you. That you're straight."

"I'm straight, Scott. I swear. Haven't had anything in months. I know that's not exactly long-term sobriety, but it's the truth. Do with it what you like."

"Then expect a call mid-week." He hung up.

The sun winked above the Appalachians and spread a ruddy glow over the mountaintops and again, for a K-9 audience of one, I recited the version of events I would confess to the two irksome Louisville detectives who had ordered Paul to find me and rein me into the investigation.

Now I had an answer for any inquiry regarding all the

missing and murdered people with whom I'd been publicly associated.

The detectives' first round of questioning had been in a tiny interrogation bowl on the third floor of LMPD headquarters on Jefferson Street, across from the courthouse and the city jail. The police were investigating each of my alibis. I'd told them that James O' Hearn, whose execution was authorized solely to assuage Luther Longmire's bottomless bloodthirst, had not contacted me for nearly two months prior to his death. Jimmy was a friend, but a shameless drug addict from whom I'd distanced myself over the years. I said I'd heard he was involved with some undesirable sorts and that—it was just my opinion—he may have been the one to drag my ex-girlfriend Irina back into the drug life. I played the victim well, always have. After the initial inquisition, the detectives, a dipshit pair by the names of Longbow and Hertz, had ordered me not to leave town until I heard from them again. Longbow, the old one, grizzled, bald with a clown helmet of white hair at the sides of his temple, cussed frequently and awkwardly, mixing expletives in nonsensical couplets—*cockfag*, *shitfuck*, and my personal favorite, the painfully redundant, *pussy cunt*— and verbally flailed random accusations, most unrelated to the matter at hand.

"Tell me you've never sunk so low you turned to eating Chinese food for breakfast, you little dickfag." While Longbow asked me if my taxes were in order and how many grams of cocaine I ingested daily, his younger partner sat across the short, narrow steel table, attempting to incite a staring contest. I couldn't get a read on Detective Hertz. He resembled a young Robert Redford, a handsome, stoic ginger, more collected than most boys of his generation.

I refused to make eye contact with either of them unless asked a direct, pertinent question, keeping my gaze affixed to the two-way mirror, wondering who was watching. A DA? A fed? Probably just a menial higher-up, some sort of city police sergeant or lieutenant making sure these idiots didn't molest me or beat me stupid with a phone book.

Finally, they said I could leave. The afterbirth brothers seemed to find my ignorance believable.

They had more questions and declared that they may, in their background check on me, discover cause for at least one more line of inquiry. My mandate to remain in Louisville for any prolonged period left me crushed and sobered. One lesson I'd learned from my recent and tragic misadventures: the longer you're in one place, the harder it is to leave.

Apparently, they discovered something quicker than either the inspectors or I could have predicted. I got a call before I'd even placed the key in the ignition of the red Crown Vic my cousin had sold me.

The homicide detectives had more questions and would be at the bookstore in a few hours. They wanted Paul present for the next round.

"God fucking damnit." I punched the wheel twice and started the car.

* * *

"Thanks for watching the dog while I suffered those two morons," I said to Paul Frank.

"More suffering of said fools is closer at hand, my friend." My former manager turned around in the swivel chair from where I once ran Twice Told Books. The act incited within me an indescribably profound sense of loss. "You must've really made an impression on them. They just called and said they're on their way."

"From what I understand, these cops like to drag things out."

"You're probably right." Every so often, when he moved to retrieve a book or rose or sat, he'd grunt and clench his fists, frustrated at the rate at which his broken ribs were healing.

"I assume you didn't go to a doctor?" I said.

One of Luther's men had shot him in the chest at the tail end of the Dog Hill gunfight. The Kevlar had saved his life but the impact of the bullet had left a bruise the size of a basketball.

"Of course not," Paul said. "Mad Dog taped me up. He showed me how to do it myself since, as he so eloquently put it, he didn't sign on to 'play Twice Told's bitch boy nurse.'"

"I love that guy," I said drolly.

"I'm lucky a lung didn't puncture."

"Try not to move around a lot when those cops show up. We don't want to provide them with any more ammunition."

"They probably didn't discover shit but want us to think they did so that we're more likely to spill something. They're looking for a weak link."

"They won't find one."

"Let's hope."

"See no evil, hear no evil," I said. "Keep that in mind and we'll get rid of them quick."

Irina, the K-9 incarnation, lay on her side with her snout touching the bottom of the display window that faced the hippy record store whose derelict owner Paul and I used to terrorize. We'd make a weekend out of prank calling the shameless and slow-talking Grateful Dead fan. We engaged in this sophomoric chicanery more often than any sane person would care to admit. Paul had somehow acquired every phone number where we might hope to reach the contemptible jam band expert. Years after we'd ceased and desisted, the man admitted to nearly committing himself to Eastern State Psychiatric Hospital just to escape the merciless recurrence of a voice that sounded not dissimilar to a daytime soap opera's token Mexican maid offering rim jobs and religious advice.

"She pissed on the floor." Paul shrugged. He wasn't angry, just stating a fact. "It was in the bathroom on the linoleum, though. An easy clean."

"You'll learn to love her."

"I'm just glad it's a dog and not a child. A dog might survive you." The bastard laughed at what had become of Jon Catlett. How easily he forgot that if it hadn't been for me, he'd be surviving on government cheese or doing a county year down at the city jail for overdue child support payments.

"Have you decided on a name for her?" he asked. I'd avoided the question when I'd first dropped the dog off at the store, hurrying to get out of the Highlands and beat five o'clock traffic, maybe make it to police headquarters punctually.

Paul asked after her name again. He could tell I was avoiding answering and my impishness clearly concerned him.

I decided to forego any deception and said, as if a question, "Irina?"

Paul slowly hissed, "What is the matter with you?"

"What?" I acted like it was perfectly normal to name a puppy after your dead lover.

"You're long due professional help."

"Come on, man. A shrink? That's a little much, don't you think. I mean it makes sense, the name, if you think about it. She's cute."

"The dead girl or the dog?"

"Well, the dog, obviously. I mean, I doubt Irina's cute right now, even if her family used the best undertaker in town."

"Jon..."

"She barely had a head the last time I saw her. You should think about what you say before—"

"Are you even listening to the words that are coming out of your mouth?"

Paul extended his index finger and made an invisible circle, mouthing the word "Feds."

"Really?" Oh, Paul. With the paranoia already. We weren't on any federal radar. We were too small time, at least as far as anyone who wasn't dead or working with us knew. Maybe soon. But not yet. "You really believe the cops are listening to us?"

"No. Not cops." Then he mouthed the initials, "FBI,"

his lips dramatically shaping each letter as one might silently verbalize to a child with a severe learning disability. "Not that it matters now that you've returned. We're sure to wind up sodomite cell buddies at some federal penitentiary now."

"Better you and me than you and O.J. I bet that guy has a rod the size of—"

"O.J. is doing fed time? Goddamn. I hope I don't get sent wherever they shipped him. He scares the shit out of me."

"Your fears are focused today on O.J. and the feds? Sounds like two entities you have a reasonable possibility of avoiding."

"Anyone that can put us in a dungeon scares me."

"That's not a repressed childhood memory rearing its pedophiliac head or anything." Before he could construct a worthy comeback, I continued, "Were you speaking to the same two police detectives who interviewed me today? Because if anything, they, with their astonishing ineptitude and idiocy, gave me a lot of hope, hope that we might just pull through this alive and with rectums of average circumference. They're as compromised and limited as the system they serve."

I'd been appraising the rows of bookshelves, overcome with discontent over the anal-retentive rearrangements Paul had implemented. I now stood between two new cases poorly constructed of unpainted two-by-fours, all editions alphabetized and divided into sections, from Medieval times to September 11. When I ran the place, I'd labeled the Civil War shelves *The War of Northern Aggression*. Offensive, I know, but a choice I'd consciously made to run off the smug hipsters so fond of wandering in hourly, always neglecting to purchase a single item.

"You raise a legitimate point," Paul said. "I did some digging online and, you know what? Our overgrown river town does have a pathetically weak closure rate when it comes to homicides, especially those drug-related."

"Closure rate? You're beginning to sound like ol' Mad Dog," I said to Paul from between shelves of dog-eared paperback mysteries and thrillers. "Closure rate?" I laughed. "This time six months ago, you'd barely fired a gun."

"A lot can change in six months." Paul kept typing on the book listing he'd been creating, an addition to the store's online inventory of obscure rarities and first editions, the bread and butter of the business prior to our violent and abrupt entrance into the dope game.

"So, you and Dog have become quite the unhinged little odd couple since I left town?" I asked. "You invite him over to check out your Criterion Collection? You two watch a few Bergman flicks together? What's his take on Kurosawa and his samurai films? I always liked his better than the American remakes, but I figure Dog would be a *Magnificent Seven* man since they talk so much macho bullshit before they ride off to gun down the antagonists."

"Mad Dog saved our lives." Paul retrieved a large hardback art catalogue from the stack of similar editions at his feet, opening to the first page and checking the other side for the ISBN number as I'd taught him years ago; he remains the only employee I ever trained who fully grasped the methodology behind turning a profit at spotting, pricing, and listing rare and used books online. I felt as if I were Ebenezer Scrooge, face to face with Christmas future. Another man sat in my chair doing the specialized kind of work, the skilled trade I'd prided myself in mastering, what had kept the store open until Kindle and ebooks. People could now download any novel they wanted for half the price of a hard copy without suffering burnout bookstore clerks. Why would someone order a book and wait two weeks to receive their purchase when, with the click of a button, they could begin reading immediately? To compound our economic crisis, even without the impact the ebook revolution had on our daily sales, my monstrous heroin habit alone had nearly bankrupted the business. Before I switched sides of the drug trade, trading a habit in for a 9mm, some scales, and partnerships with perhaps the deadliest men south of Cincinnati, I had stooped to offering my most precious possessions to competitors at an embarrassing markdown. A week prior to my first murder, I had sold a first edition of *The Grapes of Wrath* to Wiley Cobble, a book dealer here in town who, after handing me in cash a third of the book's worth, couldn't help but comment, "That's why I got rid of the storefront. I'm making a killing just selling out of my basement, shipping my orders media mail. I got ZERO overhead minus the packaging and postage." He couldn't have been happier at the hard times that had befallen the Twice Told crew. A few months later, Wiley walked into the store to find that we'd expanded, installing new cases and adding several sections. He also took obvious and drooling notice of the shapely brunette stocking the western section.

I just grinned and told Wiley to go back to his basement. There's nothing like enjoying the facial contortions of a man who has just realized he vastly underestimated you.

Now the brunette was dead and I no longer even owned a business to defend.

Paul, as I'd sadly learn soon enough, was ever the adroit chameleon. He had adapted the cadence of his speech, his hand gestures, even his wardrobe to better suit the esteemed position of self-made entrepreneur, a role he'd rather deceptively adopted. The man had stolen the personality I had developed near the end of my reign as, what Paul himself drunkenly nick-named, "The Dog Food King of Kentucky." Once, when I lived in a truck cab and ate out of dumpsters, back before I entered the used book business and joined the working week, I resorted to devouring the contents of a can of Alpo someone had left in a shopping cart outside of a Kroger. I can attest, with the experience to back it, that real dog food tastes notably better than that which sells for twenty dollars per tenth of a gram in most Kentucky towns.

"That crown on your head doesn't seem to weigh so heavy," I told Paul. "Maybe you should have been running things all along." I didn't mean a word of this but it served as decent bait. Give Paul half a chance to talk about himself and you better not have any other plans for the weekend. I wanted to hear just how far gone off the deep end he'd allowed himself to venture with the minor power a small city drug importer possesses.

"I'm not just the proud owner of a used bookstore, Catlett, but the MC of a misanthropic mecca, a starving artist's salon in the tradition of Stein and Hemingway and, later, Andy Warhol."

He was repeating, nearly word-for-word, the exact same

speech I'd made him the day he'd hired on when the place opened. I'd explained what a celebrated local institution we'd become, carrying on the tradition of the shop where I'd worked throughout my vicious early twenties, when Paul and I had first met. For decades, the old man who ran the place had educated those who could not afford formal schooling. He had employed the unemployable, making witty and confident smartass clerks out of homeless and shiftless Highlands punk rockers and psychopaths. Without the store, we all would've wound up incarcerated indefinitely.

Paul remained joyfully attached to the delusion that we had carried on the torch. All the blood we'd shed in the name of pride and profit had not cheapened or sucked dry the business's integrity, not according to its new owner.

Herein we examine the duality of Paul's self-aggrandizement. Not only did he fancy himself the Gertrude Stein of the Highlands. He would restore the credibility of the counter-culture by educating the lost teenagers of the Highlands. He would save us all from Twitter and Instagram and hashtags.

I'd created a monster and handed him the keys to the laboratory in which he'd been created with instructions listing the ingredients essential to replicate the horrors the retiring mad scientist introduced to an unsuspecting world. Who would ever—especially accounting for the kind of men who'd died at our hands, Russian mafia goons, ghetto dope kingpins, dirty cops—fear a skinny white boy with bad nerves and an extensive vocabulary, one he did not repress even when engaged in business deals with illiterates? The thugs we'd outmaneuvered never saw us coming. They considered us unfit for the underworld, weak, all because we knew a few polysyllabic words and possessed a glaring lack of ebonics cogency in an era when hip hop culture reigned supreme, when even some of the most privileged Caucasians from the affluent East End knew how to communicate effectively on the deadliest of Louisville streets and walked around with their cargo shorts sagged so far below their ass cracks, more of the little mush-mouthed shits should've tripped on their drooping waistbands and broken their necks.

I didn't know how much longer I could hold my tongue. I longed to openly mock Paul's strutting bravado. He'd convinced himself somehow that he was the reason there remained a bookstore inside which our ilk could whine and bicker and decry the foolish world we were cursed to suffer until our bruised hearts finally and thankfully imploded. He believed this despite the financial sacrifices I'd made to keep Twice Told open the first few years we were in business. I'd sold every personal belonging a pawn shop clerk would buy and stooped to shamefully decreasing the prices of my most beloved first editions just to keep the lights on and prevent the printing of an eviction notice. He'd employed the same psychological tools of self-deception he used to proclaim his fitness for fatherhood. He'd traded in his Levi's 501s and paint-stained punk rock tees for a sport coat and a black dress shirt.

At least he'd kept the rockabilly ducktail, resembling a less bloated, longer aged Joe Strummer, the likeness allowing my resentment momentary dissipation. For a moment, I forgave him, fondly recalling the lines of coke and pints of Kentucky Gentleman we'd shared as we lamented the unheralded genius of "London Calling," our faithful sound-track spun so often on the store turntable we'd worn out four copies.

I wanted to ask Strummer's look alike, "Should I stay or should I go," the quote maybe breaking the ice we'd both navigated so poorly since I'd entered the store.

"Mad Dog should've been here five minutes ago," Paul said, checking the time on his phone.

"Mad Dog..." I muttered a few hushed blasphemies. "To think someone gave that maniac a badge and gun. Not only that, but they promote him to head a narcotics squad."

Paul placed the book he'd finished listing onto the desk atop a near tumbling stack which he, upon finishing the day's internet work, would store in a locked glass case at the back of the shop that I'd never labeled. Why would I have bothered? We accepted early on that none of our walk-in customers would pay the high-end cost of the first editions and such obscure rarities for which the case had been reserved.

I glanced toward the back, at the shelves in question, squinted to read the label. I recited it and felt physically re-pulsed, "Something Rare, Something Different."

Well good for goddamn Paul.

He'd really assimilated effortlessly into the mediocrity of millennium popular culture.

"Seriously, Paul..." I read aloud again the label he'd printed for the first edition case.

Paul ignored me. "Mad Dog very covertly weaseled his way into this next interrogation." I heard a rusty squeak. Paul must've turned toward me in my old swivel chair. I still refused to face him for long, even though he likely expected undivided attention. I remained fixated and murderously enraged by the changes he'd made to my precious bookstore, the refuge I'd constructed for the emotionally crippled, for out-of-date punkers and chronic malcontents for whom anti-social behavior had become more than just a post-adolescent phase, glory days to be enjoyed then, upon college graduation, cast aside in favor of PTA meetings and minivans, fidelity to a sexless spouse, an unfulfilling career, and children who would doubtlessly succumb to the growing idiocy of American popular culture.

"Why did you have to turn this place into yet another hipster fart factory?" I spoke slowly through the pain of gritted teeth. "And why are you even wasting your damn time listing 'Something rare' and 'Something different' when we both know how you're making enough money to afford such lush greenery?" I jerked a thumb toward one of the many potted plants hanging from ceiling then ran my index finger along the Civil War label, which Paul had laminated, professionalism we couldn't afford in the days before Mad Dog and the Russian mafia. "And why the classy promulgation? I thought you desired to maintain a low profile. If anything is going to attract unwanted attention from federal law-enforcement types, it'll be on you for classing up the place with your lamination and fancy suits. Those cops might well start wondering, 'Why the sudden widening of the profit margin?' At least you kept the sandwich board. I bet you had to fight the urge to construct a neon marquee."

Paul rose from the chair. He trudged closer. The man now standing before me had bucked up and now proudly wore the title of owner and boss. I anticipated an ass chewing for discussing the true source of our bill money so recklessly and in a semi-public forum.

"I took a cue from you, Jon." Paul, contrary to my prediction, spoke cool, matter-of-fact, like a player explaining the end of an affair to one of his many lovers. "You always said that we never stop pretending like we're busting our asses to keep this place afloat. The minute we start thinking the sailing is smooth then we're sure to drown. The place is empty almost every weekday and half the annoying Highland fucktards that come in on weekends just want to browse and have someone who can't walk away with whom they can have coffee shop discussions about books no one with half a set of testicles would ever bother reading. How's it gonna look if I don't keep up the only kind of work that kept the store open before we turned to more unseemly business concerns? It's a good thing for all of us if customers walk in and see me listing online. And as for the improvements, anyone who knows me won't be surprised that I cleaned up once I was left in charge. I don't know how I stood the dump you made of this place when you were running things. You know how hard I had to work to get this building properly dusted? You know what we've been breathing? Did you even once change the filter on the furnace?"

"Exactly," I said. "The place looked like a total shit-hole. It made sense. We're broke. We can barely afford the rent. We can't find the time or resources to dust and mop and shit. Now what are people going to think?"

"The adjustments I've made to the ambiance cost next to nothing."

The bell sounded and in walked Albert Delancey, hobbling up the stairs and whistling "Dixie," literally. Albert had retired from engineering twenty years ago and had watched his wife die of colon cancer. His children had, in favor of a good fundamentalist Christian life in the suburbs, abandoned the old bastard to the care of an assisted living facility on Cherokee Road, a few blocks east of the store. He was about five-foot-three with a head of thick white hair that many a man half his age would covet. He wore leisure suits seven days a week, believed that aliens walked among us, and, since our first day in business, hadn't made a single purchase. He'd been coming in for years and would sit for hours talking our heads off, discussing, in equal detail, his conspiracy theories and begrudging bowel movements.

"Jon," Albert said. "I thought you was done with the business."

"I just can't seem to stay away from this place, Albert. Now's not really a great—"

"I'm glad you're back. Paul never has time to talk about all the new discoveries I've made at the library. Did you know that in 1957, in Stockton, California, two scientists at the institution—"

"The fucking closed sign is up, Albert," Paul said.

"I saw that, but I figured since we're buddies..."

"Get your ass out of here, Albert. We're having a business meeting. And besides, didn't I ban you?"

"Well, Jesus, Paul." Albert sighed dejectedly as he disappeared down the stairs.

"You banned Albert?" I asked Paul when the door slammed shut.

"He's lucky I didn't shoot him."

"So, you've gone all Rudy Giuliani on me, huh? You're gonna only sell books to rich housewives and business-men."

"Albert never bought anything."

He had a point.

"I'm just trying to clean the place up a little, yes. But it's not like I'm spending a fortune on renovations."

"So far," I said. "But I foresee some leather sofas and a download station in this place's future. You won't be able to resist." I didn't appreciate being talked to like a dolt by a man I'd made rich, a man who, for the first few months of our heroin import business, regurgitated often when dirty deeds needed doing. "And as for your little speech, thanks for taking a dick year to recite the obvious. That's three minutes I'm never getting back. Jesus, did you say all that shit just to practice sounding like an adult for a change? Yeah, Paul. I know why we keep up the online business, or at least list shit while there are customers present. My point, a response to which you have com-pletely skirted in favor of your incoherent babble, is that you're listing items while the place is empty. Kind of defeats the whole fucking purpose."

"I got enough shit on my mind without having to massage your wounded ego." Paul cracked a blind, peering out onto the street, at the shop faces across Highland Avenue, probably to see if any unmarked LMPD units had parked in front of the sandwich place or record store. "If we don't shake these pigs, and I mean soon, we risk losing our already diminishing favor with the Russians. They're wondering how we're gonna make shipments without

Luther, without the horse trailers and bankroll."

"See." I grinned wolfishly. "Had you idiots consulted me, we'd already be copasetic with the Russians, up and running, free of any police probes, under the auspice of a completely brilliant and legitimate business endeavor that would also explain any ventures we might need to make into the lower economic areas of our fair city. In fact, it's a fantasy we used to float when we both had ideals and hopes, and some vague wish to do something important with this store. Man, were we stupid."

"Care to enlighten me?" Paul finally asked.

Then the bell rang above the front door again. Mad Dog entered, his inclusion in the imminent interrogation a mystery, and something for which Paul had neglected to fully prepare me.

"We'll see how the talk with the murder cops goes," I said. "Then I'll explain in detail how I can save your asses from bankruptcy, jail, and even increase the ridiculous cash influx from the side business I began. Anyway, what's Porter Wagoner doing here?"

Mad Dog hung his head at the sight of me. I predicted he'd be disappointed my sabbatical hadn't lasted longer or that I had not been somehow permanently exiled from the roughneck river town none of us could seem to escape for long.

"Porter Wagoner never grew facial hair, at least not for the public to see. It'd have been more appropriate for you to compare me to Vern Gosdin. I get that a lot."

"I don't care. Why are you here?"

Our open hatred for one another carried with it an eerie sense of familial comfort. I welcomed the feeling in these uncertain times. I suppose your worst enemy could seem like an old friend when you're as lost as I'd become, lost like an old country sinner humming "The Kneeling Drunkard's Plea" at the arbitrary gods that had so often deserted him, far from the reach of even the north star's guiding light.

"I thought I might be able to assist you with your murder interrogation," Mad Dog said. He'd let his hair grow out since I'd first met him, two streaks of gray running along the sides of his temple, a matching handlebar moustache immaculately groomed. He wore a bolo tie over a flannel dress shirt that matched his mohair suit and allowed him, as I'd already pointed out, an endearing resemblance to an aging country star of a peculiarly dignified and regal carriage, impervious to the whims of the record-buying public. "See. I can explain how I've had Longmire and his incestuous cousin under investigation for years. How you two contacted me when Longmire started threatening you over Jon's affair with Amara who worked at the store to draw customers with her curves. From now on, we don't discuss what really happened. Not even in private. Jon never fucked Amara. No matter how much he liked it, it never happened and he never mentions it or brags to his dope-fiend friends about her."

"I'm right here," I said, tired of Mad Dog talking about me in third person.

"You two never shared a word with Luther Longmire," Mad Dog continued. "Do you guys understand me?"

"Were the judgments really necessary?" I asked him.

"No. I suppose they're not. But I hope you haven't forgotten that because of your blindness, because you got sprung on some holler cat gash, you got the woman that loved you killed."

I stepped toward the mad detective and reached to the small of my back where I'd holstered the snub-nosed .38 I'd bought off my cousin in Cumberland before I made my way back to the world.

"Irina was in the wrong place at the wrong time." Paul got between us.

"Bring that hand where I can see it," Mad Dog said.

I kept my fingers tightened around the grip of my gun. "I loved her," I said. "How was I supposed to know these maniacs you introduced us to would start killing innocent people? That they'd come after our families and lovers? And Amara..."

I quieted, remembering Amara collapsing like a building after the demolishing detonators had been activated, after I shot her perfectly between the eyes. "She got Irina killed. She was playing us, relaying every tidbit of intelligence she could gather to that bastard Longmire, probably knowing he'd kick start a mass-murder rampage, one that was unnecessary. We were making money. We had the perfect transportation front. And because he believed Paul and I might someday threaten his empire, he started killing everyone."

"He also wasn't pleased to learn you were fucking his cousin," Mad Dog said.

"Then he shouldn't have been plowing her himself," I said. "He wasn't doing wonders for Kentucky stereotypes carrying on with his own blood kin like that."

"Let's just all agree," Paul said, "all this considered, that Longmire had to go. It was an inevitability."

We each nodded in silence and Paul said, "Good. Now, Detective, it's your turn to explain to us how to get out from under this heat."

Mad Dog went on: "I can explain how while I was investigating you two, I considered the possibility that you might have had something to do with Longmire's drug empire but dispelled the notion after I realized what morons you are. As far as Irina goes: collateral damage. They started with her and Jimmy, both of whom may have known too much because of Jimmy's association with Luther, to which I can attest. I have photos of Jimmy and Luther. I took them for insurance. I'm not stupid. I knew the day would come when I might have some explaining to do, so I built dossiers on everyone involved with Longmire."

"You have a file on me?" I asked.

"Sorry," Mad Dog said. "It's not my problem you didn't build your own blackmail portfolios. That's criminal ethics 101. You get as much dirt as you can on as many players so that you're hard to kill."

"I'll keep that in mind," I said bitterly.

"You're welcome."

"I don't remember thanking you."

Paul mouthed the words "wire" and "tap," pointing again upward toward the shop's lofty ceilings as if somehow a surveillance expert snuck in while the store was closed and hung undisguised boom mics from the rafters.

"You think they got this place wired?" Mad Dog laughed in Paul's face. "Who the fuck do you think you are? Tony Montana? El Chapo? At most, these half-wits might suspect that you laundered money or something for Longmire and his crew. You fellows are far too nonthreatening to arouse suspicion of anything more devious. I've known these two homicide assholes for more years than I care to admit and if every murder investigation were left up to Longbow and Hertz, this city would have a crime rate as high as Detroit. I'm sure Lieutenant Powell over at Homicide chose these two because the mayor wants to wash his hands of the city's link to the case. He wants the staties to handle this mess since, thankfully, most of the bloodshed occurred outside the city limits. These are formalities you're suffering, gentlemen, and I'm here to expedite the process."

"Sounds good to me." Paul shrugged as if we were designating a sober driver for some meaningless sporting event.

"And don't ever do that again," Mad Dog said to Paul.

"What?"

Mad Dog mimicked Paul's dramatic mouthing of the words "wire" and "tap," the old cop's eyes rolled into the high corners of their sockets like the victim of a recent seizure. He straightened up and added, "You treat me like a moron again and I'll sodomize you with my Glock."

Paul mumbled an apology.

"Problem is," I said, "I already told them Jimmy and Irina were having an affair and Jimmy might've been the one that got Irina killed."

"All the better. A little inconsistency and vagary only proves none of us were sure of the real story."

"Basically, a bunch of dopers got killed by a psychotic dealer?" I said.

"Pretty much."

"Then said dealer fell out of favor with his suppliers," Paul said.

"That's what I hear the KSP suspect anyway," Mad Dog said. "Longmire killed a bunch of junkies who may or may not have known too much about him only to suffer execution at the hands of his less-emotive northern business partners. And no one has a lead on where Luther was getting the heroin. Had we known that he had more dope on the premises, buried shallowly beneath the horse stables, we may have prevented investigators from ever knowing Luther had been peddling dog food. Cops all over the state are speculating who he was getting such high-grade product from. Greeks in Atlanta? Armenians in Detroit? No one's said bupkis about the Russian mafia."

"One of those 'junkies' was a friend of mine. And one was a woman I love very much. And I introduced them both to that homicidal maniac."

Mad Dog nodded as if expecting a better-made point, then something across the room caught his eye and he grinned like a rabid Alsatian as he noticed the newest addition to the Twice Told family, my vicious little Jackahuahua. I'd never seen Mad Dog so happy as he sauntered across the room to rub behind the puppy's ears and mutter sweet-nothings to her. I whispered to Paul, "Now's not the time to get into the whole 'dog named after dead girlfriend' issue with Milligan."

"That's the first reasonable thing you've said all day," Paul whispered back out of the side of his mouth.

"You've yet to hear my plan to save the business," I muttered.

"What's her name?" Mad Dog spoke in that irritating

baby voice that I only used in private with the dog.

"I haven't decided yet," I lied.

"Well it needs to be something pretty, something that suits this little angel. This may be one of the prettiest fucking dogs I've ever seen, boys."

"An astute observation, Officer," I said, proud of my girl.

"You need to get my rank right, smart ass."

"Can we get back to business?" Paul asked.

"Let's get a few things straight here." Mad Dog snapped back into cleft-asshole mode. He stopped petting and scratching the dog's belly, stood up straight, and shifted his gaze back and forth between me and Paul. "We're all in this too deep to quit now. The people we're dealing with up north don't walk away amicably when business deals dissolve. They aren't good with goodbyes, especially when it comes to money. And the kind of retirement plans they offer their employees aren't anything the three of us would be interested in. So, to keep the Russkies happy, once we're through fabricating some fiction for my two homicide colleagues, the three of us need to have a meeting of the minds."

"I was thinking, Sarge..." I raised my hand to speak. "See, Paul and I were just talking and—"

"I know, I know," Mad Dog said. "I know you want out, Catlett. Just help us through this mess with the homicide detectives."

"Mad Dog, I think Jon has decided to come in for the big win." Paul stepped over to the mirror above the fireplace filled with ash and hollow starter logs and straightened his collar. "He never was suited for modern civilization." He checked his look, lightly straightening his oiled pompadour. I'd seen another man strike such a pose, Luther Longmire, the mobbed-up pervert we'd put down like a rabid dog nearly a month ago. And here he was again, plaguing me in his celestial vanity like a bad case of scabies.

It's funny how we take on the sensibilities of the dead after we've killed them.

"So, what's it gonna be, Johnny?" He only called me Johnny when he needed my unwavering loyalty, like when I used to lie for him to the now ex-wife about how he was spending his late evenings. I'd tell the former Mrs. Frank that, the last I'd seen Paul, he was studying at the old bookstore and taking breaks to chain smoke and list first editions online. He was probably, while I spun tall tales for the ball and chain, deep dicking a U of L freshman with toxic, tragically unaddressed daddy issues.

He met my eyes in the mirror. "Are you back?"

"I think we need to burn that bridge once we've crossed it." I stood next to Paul, examining his profile in the mirror. "We have a bigger beast to tame right now and other such clichés."

I'd bought my brown and faded suit at the Salvation Army on Shelbyville Road when I first got back to town. The rose print tie and the peeling ostrich-skin cowboy boots belonged to my father who'd drank himself half to death in Lexington last I heard.

All the clothes fit well.

I resembled a marginally successful southern insurance salesman and no one could easily mistake me, by my measly fashion sense, as a drug-pushing murderer.

The bell above the door chimed for the third time since I'd begun my reinvolvement with the business I'd founded.

"You ready?" Paul whispered to me.

2

Detectives Neil Hertz and Robert Longbow, or as I liked to call them, Kneel and Bob, arrived an hour after they'd told me to expect them. "Kneel and Bob," I held my arms open as if ready to embrace both policemen in a communal hug. "Those aren't just your names, but your favorite pastimes, right?"

Neil ascended the top step of the entrance, his partner below, closing the front door. Neil nodded to Mad Dog who stood with his arms crossed, leaning on a support post behind Paul manning the desk.

"You don't think we've heard that one before?" As Neil stopped at the corner of my old command station, tilting his head to read the titles on the spines of the stack of books Paul had been listing online, the detective continued, "And if I had been linked to four people killed in drug related homicides over the past month, I wouldn't be getting smart with investigating officers, Catlett."

"Four?" I said. "What the hell are you talking about?"

"We got a call back from one of your old business associates we'd contacted last week." Neil crossed his arms. "And just in case you were confused, by 'business' I mean this book bullshit, not mainlining drugs and covering for kingpins and their kissing cousins."

Associates? I thought they were all dead, save those standing silently and in firm and united denial alongside me now.

Then I remembered Wiley, that white-bread rat fuck. Of course, he'd call the cops and offer observations and testimony.

"Said associate remembers seeing a man fitting Luther Longmire's description exiting your front door."

"Like I told you," I said, "his cousin worked here. Amara. And Amara watched the shop while I was out. So, if he was ever here, chances are he was here to see her. And if she was working, chances are I wasn't."

"Amara," Neil said. "All due respect, one of the loveliest corpses I've ever seen laid out on an autopsy table."

Except her face, I thought. After two hollow points to the mug, Amara's dreams of someday working as a magazine cover girl were probably over. But my thoughts remained briefly burning on the broken memories of her masochism. She'd sold me out, gotten Irina and Jimmy killed, and she would've forever displayed herself like a grateful Gaelic slave, on auction to the highest bidder. Killing her was one of the smartest decisions I'd made in years.

"Except for the face." Detective Bob took the words right out of my mouth then stood next to his partner and hung his head in reverence for my dearly departed.

Paul shot me a furtive glance. I nodded. I knew when to keep my mouth shut, contrary to popular opinion. Well, sometimes I did.

"Yeah." Neil grinned, making no attempt to fake any respect for the dead. "Except for her face."

"Neil and Bob." Mad Dog surrendered a slight bow sans the arm along his waist. He showed no other sign of fondness for his two co-workers. "Still got a hard on for me, Detective?" Mad Dog sneered at Neil. The sergeant had informed us before the detectives' arrival that Hertz had worked internal affairs and had tried several times with no success to catch Milligan dirty.

"Milligan?" Bob seemed to just notice Mad Dog.

Of the two, I detested Longbow the most. He'd been the one who'd threatened to involve child-protective services in Paul's life: "Adam seems like a good boy. Handsome. Smart. Probably rocking a 3.8 or even a 4.0. Be a shame if some social worker happened to stop by when that drunk mother of his was on one of her benders. You know what happens then? He belongs to the state. Kind of like slavery except it ain't just the girls the foster families have their fun with."

"I want to kill the son of a bitch," Paul had said of the pedestrian-minded homicide cop on the phone when he'd made first contact to tell me it was time to come back to town and stand the heat.

"The state couldn't take Adam," I'd said. "You're now a successful business owner with a thriving operation that's more than paying your bills. Worst case. You'd get custody. Remember that social worker I used to screw, the blonde with the stove pipe legs? She told me that whenever they could find family to place the child with, they did. You got no worries."

"No worries, Jon? You really want social services looking at our income for proof that I can provide for Adam?"

Paul was right.

Now Bob, the swine, stood here slack-jawed, finally revealing his true character, primitive and perpetually confused. His beanbag of a beer gut stretched preposterously his coffee-stained suit-shirt, his tropical tie riding high above his navel.

I'd known the first time I laid eyes on him that he would be a prick, and, if I allowed it, would take a giant piss in the bookstore's proverbial water cooler. He had to be shut down, lest he decide to do more digging.

Which brought us to the looming question the interrogation would inevitably raise, the answer for which I'd thoroughly prepared: Why did I sign over my bookstore for free to a man who'd never invested a penny in the business? There were never any records with the IRS indicating I'd paid Paul anything or that he'd ever worked for me. He'd been employed under the table. To those who weren't in the know, the question made sense: Why would I give this man my shop, now of all times? Ostensibly, I'd rendered myself unemployed and without income in the middle of a personal holocaust.

"The best lie is always the one containing a decent grain of truth," Mad Dog had once advised. I trusted the sociopath, he himself a genius at the subtle arts of interrogation.

It's true that dogs always know. Irina's Chihuahua ears had perked up at the sound of the front door opening when the two dicks arrived. She was now circling them, smelling intently, examining the motley two from ankle to eye.

Neil smiled, and, for a split second, almost resembled a human being. "Look at that dog? Jesus. She's fucking gorgeous."

His partner glared at him.

"What?" Neil shrugged. "The dog's gorgeous. I don't care who owns her." Neil looked at me. "She yours?"

I tried to hide my excitement, nodding *yes*, as I realized that little Irina was following the family tradition. She had been my dog less than a week and was already assisting in my criminal pursuits. Considering her keenly cynical instincts, I saw this moment as the true beginning of a very fruitful friendship.

Irina had shown me which cop might have a heart, and, consequently, which one our crew could more easily compromise and manipulate.

We might just have to kill the wonderful Detective Bob. I'd ended more meaningful lives and couldn't foresee losing anymore sleep maligning my soiled spirit slightly further.

"Thanks, Irina," I thought, winking at my pride and joy who'd abandoned the friendlier inspector to come sit at her wayward daddy's feet.

"Fuck the dog," Bob said. "You need to be taking this more seriously, Mr. Catlett." Bob addressed me while still gazing disgustedly at his partner. "This is life and death, freedom and lack thereof. You can't feed a dog from a cell at LaGrange."

"Boys, there's simply no need for anyone to be discussing prison." Mad Dog stepped behind me and placed a hand on my shoulder. For a moment, I forgot that the man despised me. "I'm no homicide detective," Dog said. "But I know that time is crucial in homicide investigations, so allow me to save you some. I've already questioned these two men."

"What?" Bob was livid.

"Mr. Frank here—" Mad Dog patted Paul's shoulder too, "—well...he called me for help before the killings began. I'd braced him a few weeks prior to his call, trying to suss out any intel on Longmire the little hipster might have. After I put the fear of God into him and was convinced he didn't know shit, I gave him my card. When he contacted me, he feared for Mr. Catlett's safety because Catlett had become a little too fond a certain high-assed cousin of a known drug trafficker, a pervert who, it turns out, had been diddling said cousin since she was a little tyke."

"Did you know Paul had called Milligan?" Neil asked me.

"Not until earlier this afternoon," I lied.

"Far as I can tell," Mad Dog said, "these two were completely oblivious to the mechanics of Luther Longmire's drug empire. Did they know he was shady? Probably. But anyone who ever heard of the man knew that much. But in case they're involved criminally with that murdering hick son-of-a-cocksucker, I'd like a heads up, and I mean immediately. The narcotics squad still has an interest in this case. Robert, I called your office, and you know your lieutenant couldn't keep a fixed fight to himself if it meant his mortgage."

"I hope that moron chokes on his Beef Lo Mein today." Neil moved toward the stairwell that led up to my old office and dragged out one of the chairs we kept beneath for readings and book signings. Bob followed suit, asking if Mad Dog wanted one.

"I prefer to stand because it puts the suspect or victim— whichever we're dealing with here—at a disadvantage, mentally and physically." Mad Dog hatefully eyed me and Paul so convincingly that I reconsidered his true loyalties, but only for a moment.

The two homicide detectives took a seat near my old desk and Bob said, "Start from the beginning."

So, leaving out a few key details, such as the *other* reasons I'd decided to leave town, I explained, in front of Paul and our silent sergeant partner, that upon hearing the news of Irina's murder, I'd had a complete nervous breakdown. Nothing false about this. I'd wept like a heart-broken eighth-grader who'd been texted pictures of his first love going down on the entire football team. I'd screamed like a man who'd accidentally committed patricide. Then when Jimmy died, my friend who I told the detectives I had reason to suspect had been having an affair with the late Irina—this part was pure bullshit—I'd packed some bags and headed to Eastern Kentucky to regroup and avoid suicide. "I figured there was nothing here for me anymore," I told the two suits.

"So...you just signed this place over?" Bob asked. "Free of charge."

"And you—" Neil wagged an index finger in Paul's direction, "—you knowing your friend wasn't firing on all cylinders, that he was under severe duress, you accepted?"

"Actually..." I said. "Mr. Frank here has since called and graciously offered a very fair percentage of sales." I looked at Paul, both of us grinning, both hearing in our heads Thin Lizzie singing "The Boys are Back in Town."

"I knew Jon wasn't thinking clearly." Paul plucked a cigarette from his pack of Pall Malls sitting on the desk next to the laptop keyboard. "I also knew if either of us

wanted to eat, if I wanted to make my child support payment, the show had to go on. So, yes, I took over, gave him
a few weeks, and now we're regrouping."

"I'm seriously considering re-involving myself. Too
much time on a grieving man's hands is not a good thing."

"There's no smoking in here," Bob said.

"Well, that's news to me." Paul inhaled deeply, grinning
at the first draw, a similar expression to the one I used to
wear when I'd see the blood plume toward the flat end of
the needle's plunger. "Which is funny, considering I am the
proprietor of this business and I thought this business
existed in America, a free country founded on bloodshed,
slavery, small pox blankets, and tobacco."

"That's why we're patriots," I assured the detectives.

"It is illegal, you know, to smoke inside a business."
Bob crossed his arms, self-satisfied.

"Business is closed actually," Mad Dog said. "And since
this building also serves as a residence—Jon has been living
in the apartment upstairs—I think any kind of legal action
against the bookstore and its owners might be tricky. Look,
this is an interrogation. You work the room. You want
answers. You throw the suspects or victims or whatever a
bone. Let the man smoke up."

Bob and Neil shared a frustrated glance, both rolling
their eyes on cue, a habit I'm sure they'd formed years ago
when questioning smart asses like Paul.

"And if that doesn't get the stick outta your crawl,"
Paul said, dramatically enjoying another drag, "fine me."

"There's still the small matter of Amara Longmire," said
the younger detective. "Luther's cousin who used to work
for you two. A lot of connections between the Longmire

clan and Jon and Paul here. And why are we just learning of Paul's alleged phone call to Sergeant Milligan?"

"Alleged?" Mad Dog approached the investigator slowly until the two men stood with not a half a foot between them. "Are you suggesting that I have somehow been derelict in my duties to the narco bureau? I was billy clubbing project pipe-heads in Clarksdale when you were still jerking off to re-runs of *T.J. Hooker* out in Oldham County."

"Sergeant—" Neil started.

"No," Mad Dog snapped, poking Neil's chest with an index finger to the rhythm of the senior policeman's words. "You talked smart to me, son. Big fucking mistake. And in front of civilians. Who do you think you are? I've got more favors owed to me by more ranking police than you'll ever hope to meet, in this city and across several states. I make a phone call—" Mad Dog snapped his fingers, "—and you very well may find yourself knocked down back to uniform or worse."

Neil blinked a few times, probably imagining a career spent writing traffic tickets and risking his life settling trailer park domestic disputes. He stuttered and finally got out, "I apologize, Sergeant. I'm sorry—"

"You most certainly are." Mad Dog turned away from the homicide detective.

With this, Bob took over the questioning while Neil recovered from the embarrassment his partner had done nothing to prevent or shorten. "Let's get back to the matter at hand. Mr. Catlett, one of your own employees was related to Longmire, correct? I find this a little too coincidental for comfort."

I thought on my feet, remembered Mad Dog's coaching. "How do you think I met Amara? Jimmy brought her in. And if you'd seen her—"

"We did see her." Bob said. "But I guess I just don't go for chicks with missing faces."

Thank God he wasn't speaking of Irina. I'd shot Amara myself since she'd sold me and Paul and Jimmy out to Longmire then tried to slither out of any retribution by doing her femme fatale number and trying to use her bust to weaken my decision-making. I finally responded to the cop's crude comment: "I'd imagine that would've been a problem. Had she survived, I may have had to fire her since her favorite book was *A Million Little Pieces*, and her main sales technique involved bending over to help customers search for authors, even the ones on the very top shelf."

"You don't seem too torn up about her untimely passing." Neil grinned, thinking he'd found some splindly link in my story, something he could break.

"No." I stared at my feet in feigned regret. "She did her best. She helped bring in customers. Maybe not for reasons some would consider ethical. But shit, Hooters has great wings but would anyone know it if it weren't for the servers?"

"So Twice Told is now the Hooters of the used book trade?" Neil said.

"We've been called worse," Paul said. "And by better."

"She helped turn this business around," I said.

"Did you ever personally meet Luther Longmire?" Bob finally asked.

I looked over at the sergeant who nodded then spoke before I could. "No reason to tell a lie, Jon. First off, you already spilled your guts to me and I told you I would share anything I learned from you with these detectives. Secondly, and despite how much I'd like to send you to LaGrange where you could become every cell block bubba's favorite punch, I honestly believe that you got nothin' to hide."

We'd planned for Mad Dog to interject, to assist the two homicide cops in applying pressure and make it look like he was helping rather than hindering the interrogation. While his animosity toward me was genuine, the sergeant had skewed its context for the sake of authenticity.

If Neil and Bob only knew how masterfully they were being played.

I sniffled a few times, even thought of Irina to produce a few tears. "I walked in on them fucking."

"What?" Neil stood from the chair he'd pulled up, his face white as a Klansman's sheet.

"I'd been out most of the day buying books and trying to convince a few collectors into purchasing this first printing of *Dune* I found at a library sale in Newport. Believe it or not, even book club first editions of that piece of sci-fi shit go for two grand. Anyway, I didn't have any luck with these two particular assholes and Paul wound up unloading the item online later. After wasting an entire workday and turning not a penny profit, I returned to find that the store's closed sign was up, which I found weird since Amara was told not to leave her post. It was a Friday night, one of the week's biggest moneymakers. I walk in, and right there..." I pointed to where Paul was sitting, my old swivel chair, "Amara was riding her cousin." I wiped the tears from my chin where I'd allowed them to descend. "I didn't want to tell anyone because, you know, she was a good person. She was always really sweet to me and Paul and the customers. And Paul here had fallen in love her. It would've killed him." Paul placed his face in his cupped palms and operatically convulsed. He then looked at the desk in question and abruptly stood, backing away, mimicking dry heaves.

I took a deep breath. "The next week they were all dead. Our friend. The woman I loved. The woman Paul loved. And, sorry for saying it, but that cocksucker Longmire, may he be tortured in hell for all eternity."

There was a long silence before anyone spoke.

"See boys," Mad Dog said. "You can't make this kind of shit up."

Yeah, you can.

"I guess it figures." Bob closed his notebook and dropped it in his coat pocket. "The incest. I mean Longmire and that sick twist were both from Corbin, right."

"Perry County, originally." I said. "And most of my people are from Eastern Kentucky, you ignorant prick. The Brown family here in Louisville, the richest, classiest shitheads this side of the Mississippi River, have been accused dozens of times of incest. So watch your cockscuker when you run it about people from Appalachia. It's sort of a sore subject for me."

Bob's pallid jowls reddened and he pushed himself up from the chair and stepped toward me. I made fists at my sides and prepared to knock the son-of-a-bitch into intensive care.

Neil intercepted his partner and placed a hand on the older cop's chest.

"We got what we came for, Bob." Neil grimaced, then shifted his shameful gaze my way. "I mean Robert."

Bob cringed. His nostrils flared and he asked his partner, "Really? 'Bob?' You too, now."

"Sorry." Neil said.

"Let's get out of this shithole." Bob stormed toward the stairs that led to the exit.

"Shithole?" Paul yelled. "But what about the new lush greenery?"

3

Just in case the bookstore, as Paul had suspected, was the subject of a more covert investigation, we adjourned to the Chinese place around the corner to discuss the future of Twice Told Books.

"Wish I could've gotten that on tape." On this rare occasion, Mad Dog had lightened up. I'd never seen the man elated, his expression soft and whimsical rather than a scowl that betrayed chronic constipation. "You two should've been on Broadway, especially considering your true sexual proclivities. For a second, you nearly had me fuckin' convinced."

"Now what?" Paul asked me.

I turned around as if he might be speaking to someone behind me, then looked back at him.

"What?" he said.

"I just couldn't believe that the great Paul Frank is humbly asking his inferior for business advice." I pinched my forearm. "Just making sure this isn't some kind of a hallucination, like maybe I relapsed and someone spiked my drink with LSD."

"Are you finished?" Dog asked. "Because we have unsatisfied clientele and a Russian share holder who we can't afford to further disappoint."

I gave the two a brief, vague summation of my plan to save the H business and, consequently, our lives. Then I told them, "Fuck the feds, I need a computer to give you two the full effect. It'll help the rest of the explanation along. Plus, these egg rolls are shit."

I'd effectively inveigled Paul the Paranoid away from his obsession with Big Brother and we retired back to the office/apartment above the bookstore, where I planned to stay until the heat died down.

First came the matter of avoiding death at the hand of those psychotic Eastern Europeans who had made us all millionaires and, rightly, expected us to keep up our end of the workload.

The idea that I could never quit, that there was no retirement from the trade I'd chosen, was something I went great lengths to avoid mediating upon for too long.

"Why are we shopping on Craigslist?" Mad Dog paced the carpeted floor behind the swivel chair where I sat, the king returned to his throne. Paul was back where he belonged, sitting at the edge of an oak desk, awaiting direction.

"I told you I had an idea that can keep our distribution networks up and running that may draw even less attention from the cops." I clicked the mouse again on the third link I'd considered. I memorized the phone number associated with the ad; the seller was local, probably somewhere near Churchill Downs on Southside Drive. I closed the browser. "Found it. So, whose car are we taking?"

* * *

We stood in the backyard of a brick suburban one-floor reminder of the days when the middle class comprised a notable portion of the country's population. The fenced-in driveway had been padlocked shut and the beer guzzling, shirtless homeowner—the laid-off GE employee had inherited the house from his mother, he'd offered for some reason I didn't understand—led us through the inside of his home. Much like the front yard jungle of dead trees and fallen branches and weeds taller than a Doberman Pinscher, the house remained in a state of abject neglect. Dirty clothes were strewn all over the floor. Styrofoam gas station cola cups filled with putrid soda dirtied by cigarette butts and ash covered the glass coffee table. The kitchen smelled of death and feces and as we entered I gagged. The cat litter box probably hadn't been cleaned since the homeowner had been gainfully employed and dirty dishes and pans overflowed onto the linoleum counter from the sink clogged with rancid water as thick as syrup.

"We're not here to judge," I whispered to Paul who made no attempt to hide his repulsion. I could barely open my mouth without fighting the urge to wretch all over the filthy floor.

Once we made it back outside and enjoyed a few easier breaths, I looked up to feast my eyes on what had been displayed in the color photo on the Craigslist ad.

"Used to be an ice cream truck." The laid-off GE employee pointed to the white vehicle in the drive, its front bumper almost touching the garage door. For a moment, I wondered what possible use this weirdo could've had for this thing, a single man who'd once lived with his mother and had never started a family of his own and lived like a hermit. I thought of the images of missing children they used to print on the sides of milk cartons when I was growing up.

At least, if that were the case, the sins we'd perpetrate with the truck were of a lesser caliber. At least that's what I told myself then.

The owner handed me the keys and stood aside for me to enter the cab.

The white sides were faded though you could see that there had once been a logo painted there, the faint traingular outline of an ice cream cone. I hoisted myself up on the metal platform, swung open the door, and peeked inside. There were only two front seats. Several metal shelves ran along the sides of the aluminum storage area.

"Does it still have some sort of cooler?" Mad Dog asked.

"It busted," Beer Belly said. "The AC in the front works just fine, but anything you're thinking of hauling in the back ain't gonna do too good if temperature's a concern. Is temperature a concern?"

"It's not," I said to Paul, stepping down and opening my wallet to pay the owner. "Books don't melt."

So utterly dissatisfying had been our first attempt at lunch, I insisted that, on our way back from the South End, we stop at yet another Chinese place downtown, one for which I could vouch.

To this day, I believe soy sauce and MSG make men more aggressive and lessen moral fiber. It seemed that Paul, Mad Dog, and I conjured our most hideous designs when weighed down by Peking duck and fried rice. China Dragon was on Broadway just across from St. Francis High School, a good halfway point between our neck of the woods and Myron's dirty old side of town, mostly housing projects and section 8s, neighborhoods that, much like Mad Dog's PTSD-plagued mind, one wouldn't want to travel through alone.

The place was a touch classier than most local take-out joints, but had only achieved a B rating by health inspectors as advertised on a city certificate in the front window. The restaurant always remained empty an hour or so past the downtown lunch rush, and solitude, for today's purposes, was our main concern.

"I wish this had been my idea," I explained the plan for the tenth time. "In Whitesburg, right near where my people come from, there's this guy...he makes a fortune driving all over the town with a van full of books. It's a roving bookstore. When some kids or adults even see the van, they motion for him to stop. The dynamic is quite similar to an ice cream truck. The guy opens the backdoors and they peruse."

"The dynamic also sounds similar to that of a roving child molester." Paul always had to dissect everything to the point of uselessness.

I continued, "The books are sectioned off and alphabetized. Granted, it ain't a big inventory, but there's no overhead besides restocking his books, most of which he accomplishes simply by making his rounds. If a customer runs up to the van with a bag full of books, he'll buy or trade."

"Not a bad little gimmick." Mad Dog, unconcerned

over my lifelong bouts with alcoholism and addiction, drank deeply from his glass of rum and cola.

"And no one's gonna wonder why Twice Told Books would try something like this?" Paul asked.

Mad Dog said, "For the minimal investment in that shit-heep we just purchased, you up your sales and advertise your storefront all day. It's a savvy business decision. No one will think twice about it. And, as I think I proved this morning, we're not dealing with Columbo here. Those two morons couldn't find their own dicks with a DEA search team."

"Exactly," I said. "Now, Paul, I need that van up and running, and the store's symbol on the side within forty-eight hours. Mad Dog promised the Russkies I'd be up there to put their minds at ease poste goddamn haste."

"Hold on a second." Paul leaned closer. He'd sat across from me, his shoulder to the red wall opulently painted with Geishas fanning their masters and dragons ready to devour tiny Asian villages. "You signed over the store to me." Paul extended his thumb toward his own chest. "And all of a sudden you're making plays again, running the show again?"

"Paul, goddamnit." I tired of repeating myself as if explaining time-out to a prepubescent. "The store is yours. But I didn't sign over this..." I stuck index finger firmly into the jade tabletop. "The dope trade will always be mine. Like you said, motherfucker, I'm the Dog Food King of Kentucky. Case in point: In one day I've managed to do more to resuscitate our golden goose than you have in two weeks. We've got viable transport—that van can cross state lines without suspicion and cruise the ghetto, charitably offering impoverished children the fruits of knowledge. Which brings me to my next idea; we're going to open a West End branch of Twice Told Books, show the community just what kind of goddamn multicultural and diversity-oriented pricks we really are."

"Okay," Mad Dog said. "You had me up until the part about turning the store into a chain. You're speaking gibberish now. No one's going to buy F. Scott Fitzgerald west of Roy Wilkens Boulevard."

"Detective Milligan." I crossed my arms and shook my head in over-dramatic disappointment. "That's simply ignorant *and* racist. Maya Angelou just passed away and you have the nerve to insinuate that black people don't read."

"Jesus Christ." Mad Dog leaned back in his chair and stared at the tiled ceiling.

"You better drop that bigot attitude before Myron shows up." Then I whispered, "Besides, if the IRS or any other such organization ever starts asking questions, that's exactly how we respond. The race card."

There was a brief beat.

Then three of us laughed like we'd just won the lottery.

"You had me at 'race card,' kid." Mad Dog reached across the table and tussled my hair like a proud father. "Whenever you accuse someone of being racist, you *always* put them on the defensive. That's how O.J. Simpson originally got off."

"Come on," Paul said.

"Again with the O.J.?" I said. "Aren't there other famous criminals we could use for examples?"

"Some auditor asks how we turn a profit in the West End and we come back with, 'What? You sayin' blacks don't appreciate the nuances and beauty of classical literature?' They will immediately leave us alone."

I'd never seen Mad Dog so inspired. It was like witnessing a resurrection. The dead had risen. A lifeless corpse was laughing and gesticulating before my very eyes. "They'll drop the case flat. It won't work forever, but it's worth the investment if it keeps the wolves away from the door even temporarily. Then, if they dare keep on, we'll organize a strike with that Reverend X and have him and two dozen other angry blacks marching in front of the IRS offices. And the media will have a field day."

Yes, we would be spreading one of the most addictive narcotics known the man throughout a neighborhood already decimated by drug violence and addiction. But in a country founded by genocide, it's difficult to integrate integrity or, for that matter, guilt, shame, and remorse into a profitable business plan.

The new shop would mainly serve as a central hub for transactions where local dealers—those within a sixty-mile radius—could stop by and pick up shipments, boxes of thick, Encyclopedia-sized books with squares carved into the pages where kilos could be hidden. It'd also ingratiate Paul and myself with community organizers fighting to make the streets of Portland and River Park safer for the innocent, the children yet to join gangs or start slinging independently, and the elderly who couldn't afford to move on up to the east side.

"One thing though," I said. "And this is not negotiable."

"That fuckin' tone." Paul shook his head.

"I'm with Paul on that," Mad Dog said. "You need to drop the emperor act."

"Emperor?" I scanned the Chinese restaurant. "Guys, what did we just say about being racist. Any other word would have sufficed in this situation. I mean, Jesus, I feel like Mr. Cotter trying to tame a classroom of juvenile delinquents. Have some decorum, my friends, and show some respect to our Asian brothers and sisters."

"You're an idiot," Paul said.

"Yes," Mad Dog said. "Remember that your hubris and your dick almost got us killed."

"Not to mention those who *didn't* survive," Paul said.

I breathed as slow as I possibly could, considering the pressure building inward from both sides of my forehead.

"I mean what about Jimmy?" Paul said. "Jimmy didn't do—"

I lunged across the table, wrapped my hands around Paul's neck and jerked him over to my side, the impact rocketing silverware, water cups, and soy-sauce dispensers onto the red-carpeted floor, which, luckily, saved any of the dishes from shattering. Paul lay on his side now, making every vain attempt to unlock my fingers from around his throat. His face had gone as red as the restaurant's main motif and his mouth flailed open and shut.

"Listen to me," I hissed. "And listen close, you fucking spineless metro-sexual. Your succubus ex-wife is never going to call you a deadbeat dad again or question your manhood because of your inability to maintain gainful employment. Yeah, asshole. You're welcome for that."

Mad Dog sighed heavily and removed his suitcoat before he reached to break us up. Then the hostess appeared, the ageless little Chinese broad who should have been in Hollywood playing Chow Yun Fat's love interest rather than dealing with downtown Louisville lowlifes ogling her. She began shifting from Chinese to English randomly while pointing at the scene I'd caused.

I pushed Paul back toward his seat. The top rail of the chair hit the table behind ours, then its legs wavered a bit before reaching a center of gravity.

"Ma'am." Mad Dog had his badge out, now speaking to both the hostess and an older woman who was probably the owner. "All apologies for the outburst but we are involved a very important and strenuous police case." Mad Dog wasn't lying. We were, all three of us, involved in a police case. I always found it interesting that Mad Dog, whenever possible, chose honesty over deceit. He seemed truthful, even when he lied.

Mad Dog told the owner, "We hate to use the term 'serial killer,' but suffice to say, patterns have emerged."

The young woman covered her mouth. Her mother said something in Chinese, probably asking the hostess to translate what Milligan had told her, which the younger Asian did. The older lady wobbled from side to side, blinked rapidly and drew a hand to her breast, breathing like an untreated asthmatic. She wavered in her stance like a drunk preparing to try and walk a straight line for the cops. Before she could collapse Mad Dog embraced her, placing one hand firmly at the small of her back, lifting her to upright like a fallen mannequin, telling her, "It's okay. It's okay. Breathe in very slowly through your nose, then let it out your mouth." Then he remembered the language barrier and asked the daughter to translate again.

The daughter barked orders to her fainting mother in rapid fire Chinese.

The older woman patted Mad Dog's forearm after she had gathered her composure. She said, "Thank you so much, Officer. Thank you."

"It's Sergeant, actually," I corrected her.

"Shut up," Mad Dog said to me. "And don't ever disrespect the badge again by losing your temper in public like that, Detective McCockiner."

"Detective McCockiner?" I mumbled. Perhaps the man possessed the capacity for humor after all.

The woman continued massaging Mad Dog's forearm, saying in her best English, "So sorry. So sorry. Please. Please..." Then the elder looked toward her daughter and spoke briefly and lowly.

"Please catch this man." The hostess kissed the back of Mad Dog's right hand. The gesture seemed to genuinely touch the grizzled copper. Had I not known better, I may have thought that the women's gratitude had come just short of moistening the old warrior's dehydrated tear ducts.

It was nice to know the man was human.

"Mama says we help anyway we can," the daughter told Milligan. "She says bring man to justice."

"No problem, sister." Mad Dog snapped back into game-mode, smiling slyly, a knowing expression that he'd mastered long ago when he'd been schooled on his first police beat in the subtle art of bullshit by some old hair bag like himself. "We're so close. In fact, we think we may have the bastard in bracelets before dawn. But we're waiting for our undercover man and it would really slow things down if we had to move to another restaurant for our rendezvous."

The hostess demanded, as per her mother's translated orders, that we stay. "We cooperate fully. We close for you."

"That'd really help us out." Mad Dog described Myron, the fellow who'd soon be joining us, and, as far as the Asian ladies were concerned, our "undercover man."

"Anything you need. You good men. You true protecttors." The hostess nearly glided over to the front door, locked it, and flicked off the neon OPEN sign. "Good men," she said again.

"We'll make up the difference for what you might have lost letting us have the run of the place," I offered.

The older woman, now back-peddling toward the kitchen, at first did not understand, pausing in her steps to cock an eyebrow my way.

"Reimburse." I raised my voice like a true American asshole, as if an increase in volume could breach the speech hurdle.

She still didn't get it, of course.

Mad Dog employed the universal language, removing a clipped wad of hundreds from his slacks' pocket and peeling a few off. The owner waved the cash away.

"We insist," I said.

The owner accepted, more out of fear than greed. She didn't want to further enrage the rogue Caucasians.

Mad Dog said over his shoulder as he reclaimed his seat at the table, "I'll make sure the chief hears about your assistance. No more random health inspections or heat from the INS for a while."

Tears gathered in the crow's feet at the corners of the hostess's eyes. She wiped them away, gathered herself, and turned her attention toward the door in preparation to greet the fourth member of our special police unit crusading to protect the vulnerable Asian community.

For some reason, our dishonesty to those hard-working ladies hit me harder than blowing off my ex's face. Maybe it had to do with who deserved what, but the deeper I plunged into a life of grand larceny, opiate distribution, and ultra-violence, I discovered that the rain fell on the just and unjust alike, especially in the heroin trade.

Lying to the elderly and the socially challenged.

Manipulating a minority sensitive to police neglect and injustice.

All in a day's work at Twice Told Books.

The door chime sounded, one of those clichéd Oriental ditties you'd expect to hear in a cheap kung fu flick. I looked over Paul's shoulder to see Myron, our main guy in the West End, entering. He scanned the restaurant until he spotted us near the restrooms in the back. Before he headed over, he turned left to check his look in the long mirror that ran the length of the foyer. He'd dressed in a brown leather coat, a scally cap of the same material, and seamless Hilfiger jeans tucked into his unlaced Timberlands.

"Kid has moved up in the world," I said. "How the hell's he been feeding the piggy bank if there's no supply coming in?"

"That's something we'll talk about here in a sec," Mad Dog said. "But for now, try and avoid using the term 'race card' again. Fuckin' wordsmith."

Myron took a seat next to Paul, closer to the exit, lifted

the white paper menu and began perusing. After a moment, he snapped his fingers, making eye contact with the good-looking hostess the three white men at the table had terrified earlier. "Get whoever's supposed to be taking care of us, baby, and tell them daddy here wants a Miller High Life and a plate of them pot-stickers."

I went bug eyed and looked over at Paul. Who the hell did this former corner boy think he was? Stringer Bell? And had he forgotten who'd put him in power, where he'd been when Paul and I found him, a couple of seconds away from a bullet to the temple? Now he's snapping his fingers at servers and dressing so loud he had to be attracting the attention of the entire narcotics bureau.

Myron looked over at me. "My man."

"Good to see you too." I accepted the young man's handshake. When Paul and I had first met the gangbanger, he'd been a running boy, or, to put it straight, an older kingpin's little bitch. He was abused daily by this sadistic old-school gangster. Slapped around, kicked in the ribs, spoken to like a dog that had strayed too far from the front yard. After Paul had rendered Myron unemployed with the help of a sawed-off shotgun, we made the kid part of our crew. Myron had shown both loyalty and foresight, taking over the entire heroin market in the West End, from Portland Avenue to West Broadway, a veritable junkie's paradise.

I asked Myron, "How exactly have you been getting fat while the rest of us are laying low, keeping the heat down, and having near zero contact with our suppliers?"

Myron's jaw nearly touched jade. He looked over at Mad Dog and said, "Why don't you ask Mr. Five-O here?"

Before Paul and I could begin yelling at him, Mad Dog said, "Calm yourselves, children." The old cop intertwined his fingers and rested his elbows on the table. "People gotta eat. The machine can't stop running over one whore and a gun-crazy hillbilly"

"Why are you waiting until just now to explain this?" Paul asked. "We've already started investing in our new—"

"It's a good investment." Mad Dog said. "Less talking and more listening, boys. It'll all make sense once you know the whole story."

I'd yet to be put at ease.

Mad Dog went on, "And, to help you change your tampon, Paullette, I wanted to wait for Myron to get here so that he too could assure you that what we had going on while Jon was away was strictly temporary. In fact, it's already finished. No more deals with this other party."

"As long as we get back to slinging something soon." Myron rubbed his hands together, a child awaiting a double-chocolate cake desert.

"Were you in on this?" I asked Paul.

Paul shook his head, and I could tell he wasn't lying by his locked jaw, his trembling lips and gritted teeth.

"Then where were you going for the supply?" I asked Mad Dog and Myron. "What new and mysterious psychopath, or paths for that matter, have you brought into our lives now?"

The white cop and black street thug shared a glance, one hard to read, which made sense, given the two men had poker faces as lifeless as the slickest Vegas card shark. Myron moved his eyes to the table, reached in his coat pocket for some rolling papers and a bag of Kentucky's

Best Menthol tobacco and began constructing a homemade cigarette. Mad Dog scratched his chin and allowed the quiet to linger, maybe hoping we'd accept his silence for an answer.

"This affects us," I said. "If you got in bed with some big players who can move the kind of weekly weight we used to deal in, I got a hard time believing they're okay with a one-time influx of cash, then letting you just walk away. There are no one-time deals in this thing. You said so yourself. And if we have two interested, competing suppliers, we have a problem. Have you gotten us caught in a crossfire, Milligan? Not to mention, they might think you're a cop, and they'd be right. They—"

"They know I'm a cop," Mad Dog finally spoke, barely a whisper. He began breathing heavily in and out of his nostrils, his mouth closed tight as he considered his next statement. "And you have a point. You need to know about this so you'll have one less thing to drive you back to the needle or the nuthouse, Jon. And, Paul, well, you got your son to worry over. I'd want assurances myself." Mad Dog took another deep breath and motioned the four of us to huddle toward the middle of the table. "An old friend of mine on the force took a leave of absence to do a few tours in Afghanistan. Do you boys know where some of the best heroin in the world happens to be produced?"

"Afghanistan." Myron said, proud of the information he'd retained.

"So. my boy and a few of his friends start smuggling whole bricks back to the states. They bring it into Fort Knox, right here into the commonwealth, forty minutes away from where we're sitting. But since it's been years since my guy's been on the street, he doesn't know any of the players. He's got no one he can trust to help him unload these kilos."

"So, he comes to you," I predicted.

"That's right."

"They unloaded it all?" Paul asked.

"The truck load we got from Luther's was gone within a week," Mad Dog said. "There was a vacuum. I couldn't have our boys in the wild West End taking fire and our customers out of state patronizing other vendors. I had to come up with something. Now, every corner dealer in the city, not just the West End, wants the Afghani fire. Same with all our partners south of Cincinnati."

"Whoa," Paul said. "I think it's a little too soon to drop word-bombs like 'Afghani fire.' Do we want Homeland fucking Security to take an interest in this? Jesus." He loosened his shirt collar and straightened a crick in his neck. "I thought we just had trafficking charges to worry about. Now we're fucking terrorists."

"I mean, not to take Mad Dog's side here," I said, "but 9/11 happened a decade ago."

"And the holocaust was several decades ago but it's still passé to make light of it," Paul said.

"Well, I don't know about that." I laughed. "I mean, in private, you've made a few holocaust jokes. Remember the one about the car and the—"

"Will you two shut up?" Mad Dog hushed as the server appeared, filling the table with huge platters of Sesame Chicken, War Su Gai, and a few large bowls of noodle soup.

"Is this stuff from Afghanistan as pure as what we

brought down from Chicago?" I asked Mad Dog once the china doll had left us.

Myron clapped his hands excitedly and nodded. Mad Dog reached across the table and clenched the leather lapel of the gangbanger's shiny new coat, pulling him closer. "What are you trying to do? Announce it to the whole city?" Mad Dog let go of the kid. "To answer your question," the cop said to me, "according to those who've been banging the Taliban—"

"Excuse me?" I asked. "Who is banging the Taliban and why? Some sort of new torture on Guantanamo Bay?"

"Are they retiring water boarding?" Paul asked.

"The Taliban is, I regret to inform you two, the more popular street name for what we've been pushing since we temporarily switched suppliers."

"It wasn't my idea." Myron showed me his hands like I was plainclothes man arresting him. "Name just kind of caught on."

"And it caught on," Mad Dog eyed Myron hatefully, "because someone let it leak where the dope came from."

"We're fucked." I placed my forehead against the jade and let my arms go slack.

"No one knows about Fort Knox," Mad Dog said. "I know the kid well enough to know he ain't that stupid. He's just young. He'll learn."

"Not another goddamn word about our sources." Paul pointed at Myron. "No matter where we're getting it, no one on the street needs to know. All they need to know is if the shit's good. Now, answer the original question, will you? How was the Taliban in comparison to what the communists have been sending down?"

"The Taliban?" Myron chortled. "It be just like sounds. It shows no mercy."

"But," I said, "unlike the Taliban and other terrorist organizations and batshit crazy religious sects, there isn't an endless supply of the Afghan dope. See, the great thing about those Muslim fundamentalists is that they're broken up into cells. It's nearly impossible to get to them all. The feds tell the public that if you cut off the head the body dies—I don't know where they got that symbolism. Fuckin' Bram Stoker?"

"Also," Paul said, "I think al-Qaeda would be a more proper street name. Just from a standpoint of truth in advertising. The Taliban were the actual government. Why would we name our illegal product after a goddamn government?"

"Great." Mad Dog slapped the table. "Perfect time for a political science lecture from the one-class wonder here."

Paul tilted his head over his shoulder, sleepily lowering his eyelids to respond to Mad Dog. "I've had to work for a living while I finish my college education."

"Work?" I said. "Why don't, when you're done analyzing the terms 'Taliban' and 'Al-Qaeda,' also explain to us your definition of 'work?'"

"I'm simply saying that if we're gonna have a street name for this product, it should be metaphorically sound."

"I didn't come up with it," Myron hissed through clenched jaws. "And besides, Al-Qaeda don't have the same ring."

"You do know you have to fix this," Mad Dog said to Myron.

"What you want me to do?" Myron shrugged. "They

gonna call it what they gonna call it."

"Then you're gonna get the word out that the next dope fiend you hear using that term is cut off for life," I said.

"You tell those unpatriotic, disrespectful pricks that if that word ain't off the street fucking *now*," Paul said, "those still implementing the term are gonna get stoned to death along with their women and we'll make their mommas wear burkas from now on. Shit, I'm so angry, I'm mixing my metaphors. I mean I'm not making any sense. If they're shooting the Taliban then how could they be punished for it? I'm sorry. I'm upset. We're not gonna stone anyone. I just don't understand how you let this happen, Milligan."

"We stop using terrorist terminology right now," I said. "We are on the ground floor of this city's most lucrative economic opportunity. We cannot afford to take risks."

"*You* are really gonna try and tell us about risks?" Paul said.

"I know I've made my share of mistakes."

"And if we don't smoothly navigate the crosscurrent of loyalties that we're right in the middle of," Mad Dog said, "if we don't find ways to please the Russians we may not get to make another mistake. *Ever. Again.* The Russians do not know about my side deal. That's a concern."

"Oh, I'd say so," I muttered.

"If it gets back to the cops that there's a drug on the street," Mad Dog said, "heroin or anything else, it don't matter, with the street name we've been arguing over all morning, the one that references a group responsible for the deaths of thousands of Americans, women and children, Homeland Security and the FBI will come down on

Louisville like Godzilla did on Japan."

I finally got around to mapping out our new business model for Myron who couldn't keep the smile from his face. After going over the book truck and the new store, getting our west end kingpin to agree to shop around his hood for anyone with a decent piece of commercial property they'd be willing to lease or sell for a lower cash price, like a six-year-old who'd been waiting his turn at show and tell, Myron barked, "You gonna let me run the second location, right?"

I made a poor attempt to conceal my shudder at the thought. Paul knew now that this one would be my baby. However, no one would patronize a business in the West End with just one white man misrepresenting the demographic. While my *race card* argument might go far to delay an audit or sting, at some point, some fed or IRS agent would find a legal loophole that allowed thorough investigation of a lucrative storefront that had long remained empty. And as much trust as I had in my own accounting abilities and creativity with numbers, it would be best if we avoided drawing attention to our drug front's financials.

I told Myron he'd be granted the title of manager and allowed some say as to which books we carried and which other products we might specialize in.

As if I'd just requested he deliver an impromptu speech at a White House summit for the progress of young African Americans, the eternally confounded street thug cleared his throat and began speaking of his various plans for the new Twice Told branch. "We should have a jazz section where we got biographies of the artists filed right next to the musicians' albums. Rhythm and blues. A shitload of jazz and soul books, records mixed right in. You ever seen shit arranged like that anywhere else? Oh. Oh. And the Black Panthers." Myron snapped his fingers, moving his head lithely as if dancing to the R and B he'd just cited. "Gotsta have all the Panthers represented."

"Like in person?" Mad Dog asked.

"Might be hard to locate some of those fellows," I said. "The ones the feds didn't massacre are either rotting in prison or keeping very low profiles that don't involve advertising for hick town ghetto record stores."

"Wait one goddamn—" Myron stopped with the gyrating.

"And I don't think anyone, black or white, is gonna appreciate us using men who helped shape our history as marketing tools," I said.

"You want us to resurrect Eldridge Cleaver and ask him if he'd stand out front with a sign displaying the week's discounts?" Paul said.

"I meant books about the Panthers," Myron said lowly.

We'd stolen the young man's vim. He stared glumly at his empty plate and his sodden red napkin like he'd just received a draft notice.

"We're just fucking with you, kid," Paul said to Myron after a few awkward moments of sterile silence.

Myron grinned again, just now getting a joke the rest of us had moved past. "Y'all need me because ain't no one shopping in the hood at no place run by a couple of nerds."

"Nerds?" I took genuine offense.

"He just means we buckle our pants at the waist and aren't preferential to puffy jackets with furry collars," Paul said.

Mad Dog reached in his wallet and threw a few fifties on the table, enough to cover our meal and any further offense caused by the noise and Myron's colorful language.

"Do what Jon said," Mad Dog ordered Myron. "Find us a building that ain't sagging, gutted, or in some other form of disrepair."

Paul and I stood with Mad Dog.

"Thanks for the meal," Myron said to the sergeant.

"Yeah," I told Milligan. "Thanks. But what gives?"

While Myron finished his meal, Paul and I followed Dog to the street.

"You're not exactly famous for your generosity," Paul said.

Mad Dog remained silent until we'd made it outside, then he stopped short of a bus stop on Broadway, looking both directions before speaking. When he was satisfied that our only eavesdroppers were the vagrants and grocery-cart pushers, he said, "Like I told you, I got a meet set with the Russians in Chicago." Mad Dog jabbed an index finger into my chest. "And you're accompanying me. You'll be able to better explain our new import and export system."

Then it hit me, his sudden disregard for the value of a dollar. "You don't think we're gonna make it back to Louisville alive."

The old detective didn't answer. He ran a hand through his gray-black hair and sighed. "You know by now the kind of people we're dealing with," he said.

I'd never seen the man scared. His anxiety was as contagious as his cool.

"Shit." I looked away, toward east downtown and the skyscrapers owned by careless and well-fed men of good

76

fortune, looming floors of commerce that towered over the streets below where the desperate struggled to survive.

"And you're sure that other thing," Paul said, "the thing with your Marine friends, it's over, right? They know they need to find someone else to help them unload their spoils."

"A deal's a deal," Mad Dog said.

"It'd sure be nice if that were true." I walked toward the pay-lot where Mad Dog had parked his civilian Town Car.

4

That night I watched Paul drink himself under the table while we listened to Bob Dylan and tried to recapture the spirit of better days, before the bookstore had become nothing more than a platform for betrayal and the massive production of random death. Our laughing ended in tears, Paul's for his own innocence, the men he'd gunned down to protect us, for his son, and, to my surprise, his ex-wife. I could've done without the sidebar involving how he would always love that superficial succubus, but I entertained him nonetheless.

Then I choked up for my own reason, I cried and confessed and looked over to my partner for a kind, forgiving word only to find him comatose. Paul was snoring with his head atop the front desk, spittle leaking onto the keys of the store laptop.

I slid the computer from under Paul's cheek, holding his head up with my free hand and slowly letting him down. I hadn't had a drink or a drug in months, yet I stared at the half-full bottle of Maker's that had rendered Paul legless and could think of only one good reason not to imbibe: blowback. If I broke down, the business would break down.

It's funny how tears can render palatable otherwise nauseating clichés.

Instead of turning to the bottle, I perused the literature section where I found a copy of *A Fan's Notes* by Fred Exley, a psychotically depressed, unemployable alcoholic. My kind of people. I took the hardback upstairs, opened the window facing Bardstown Road in all its resplendent Saturday night debauchery and sat on the gabled roof.

I found the passage; an elegiac goodbye to a dear friend Exley knew he'd never meet again: "I had finally reciprocated Bumpy's love by paying the abundant tribute of my tears."

I sat on the roof of my favorite place on this godawful planet, still lousy with tears, where I dedicated a psychic toast to absent friends and wept until I passed out.

The morning after I watched Paul get wasted then wept like a newborn on the bookstore roof, I was to meet Mad Dog in the alley behind the shop where he'd be waiting to drive the two of us to Chicago in either a stolen car or a rental procured under one of his fake identities.

I had moved out of my apartment about a month ago. Well, to describe what I'd done as moving out is not quite correct. I trashed most of my knick-knacks and movie posters, lugged what furniture I could carry into the alley, dropped the key in the mail box, and changed phone numbers, never to hear from my old landlord again, nor many friends like Scott, the tax-paying, hard-working, civilian types I'd isolated from when executions and Kevlar vests became staples of my working week. Since I now carried a murderer's burden, I didn't think twice of stiffing the old, frizzy haired Jewish malcontent on the thirty-day notice and the last rent payment I owed. He had my deposit and the futon I'd left in the bedroom. I doubted the old prick had even gone to the trouble of putting a black mark on my rental history.

At the time, with a hillbilly homicidal maniac and his ex-mercenary goon squad searching the city to relieve me of my mortal coil, the disappointment of the elderly and credit reports were not major priorities.

I do, however, regret that my disappearing act had made it more difficult for me to return to anything resembling a normal life. I should have paid the old landlord just so I had a place to call my own, to get away from work stress. I wasn't sure how much longer I'd be breathing and, if we survived Chicago, when I might need to pull up stakes and skip town again to dodge the police or the Russians or this mysterious ex-marine Milligan had brought into the fold. I saw no point in looking for a new place until things settled down. If I wound up in the trunk of a Cadillac this afternoon, I'd feel awful silly having spent some of my last hours on earth purchasing furniture and signing leases and bill agreements.

I awoke around four a.m. that morning and made my way back into the office from the roof, collapsed on the inflatable Kmart mattress where I tossed and turned for half an hour or so. I threw on the same jeans I'd worn the day before. My wardrobe as of late consisted of about four T-shirts, one denim snap-button, and three pairs of Levi's, all stored with such class in the two duffel bags that contained most of my worldly belongings.

I couldn't really complain. While I was technically homeless, in one of those duffels, beneath my shaving kit, I'd packed the seven hundred thousand dollars I'd earned in blood and dope money. I had money to spend but on what? I had nowhere to go, no one to call. I didn't even have a mailing address anymore.

If I spent the rest of my morning—Mad Dog wasn't due until nine or so—roaming the aisles of bookshelves and sitting around the dark office upstairs, I'd likely work myself into a state of catatonic despair.

I walked out into the wan morning and stepped to the west.

I was too emotionally hung over to endeavor even a half-mile drive to the closest locally owned coffee shop. So, crucify me, I walked across the street from the bookstore to the corner Starbucks.

Hey, at least they paid their employees a living wage and provided full benefits.

In my early twenties, I had worked for one of these "indie" chains as a barista for barely minimum wage and shitty tips. Just like all the workers there, I was not allowed full-time employment so that the silently elitist BMW driving owners did not have to fret over worker's comp and health insurance.

This taught me my first lesson in business—it's not about the principle; it's about the money. Not many people will admit that, especially if it profits them not to. So many of my fellow baristas refused to apply at Starbucks out of some misguided sense of integrity, some prejudice against the very word "corporation." What would you call the company we worked for? Samaritans? Charity endorsers?

We were living on starvation rations, me out of laziness, most of my co-workers out of self-defeating megalomania.

You don't want to see what happens if I've had a few drinks or am feeling the slightest bit irksome and some doltish hippie starts verbally eviscerating Starbucks and blindly praising the independents. As far as corporations went, there were far more evil ones to boycott than Starbucks. I wound up going back to school and working at a used bookstore. When I quit the independent coffee shop, I wrote the managerial staff a cruel and threatening letter, a savage indictment that left me banished from the entire chain.

Oh well, another good excuse to stay loyal to Starbucks, if you ask me. Their drinks were cheaper too and, like I said, it ain't about the principle. It's about the money. A dark ethos by which to live, I know, but one that had yet to fail me.

I considered bringing K-9 Irina for a walk, but she'd already pissed and shit in the upstairs bathroom and wouldn't get out of my blow-up bed for any amount of begging. Even shaking her dog bowl half-full of dry food yielded no reaction. She was a proud procrastinator, a lazy lout like her new father.

The outside of my nearest Starbucks lacked the folky ambiance of a lot of the smaller places in town such as those owned by the two greedy yoga enthusiasts I'd suffered for years. Once inside, however, I didn't consider my experience lacking in the way of pleasantries and service. I began fumbling through my wallet, scanning the massive chalk menu hanging above the counter. The woman in front of me had her hip cocked and faced away, toward the round counter at the end of the register cubicle where customers retrieved their drinks.

"One moment, sir," said the perky redheaded college girl I'd been trying to bed since they'd opened the store. Once she'd dropped by at the book shop for drinks after her shift. I put up the closed sign and we watched an episode of *Sons of Anarchy* and kissed at length. When I tried to go south, she froze me out, gathering her things, letting me know she had a boyfriend and that this was a mistake.

At first I was angry, figured the boyfriend line a fiction spun to avoid sex with me. She could've just said she wasn't into it. That's one part of a life among criminals I will forever respect. No one minces words. Amara, bloodless, backstabbing murderess that she was, would never make something up as an excuse to not screw you. She'd just laugh in your face and say something smart, probably teasingly employ the word "pussy" just to add insult to injury.

"Jon?" The woman in front of me had turned and said my name, probably twice, before I blinked my eyes to see Catherine Livingston, my longest-standing crush, standing before me in full country-girl regalia. Her handlebar hips barely fit into the tight black jeans she wore, the ends dipped inside red and white cowboy boots. When she grinned, I remembered the first time I met her offering to pour wine in her dimples. And those tumid lips, permanently puckered, suggested the kind of oral business that a lady of her stature was unlikely to encourage. Or maybe not. You never knew with women. Sometimes the dignified debutants hid horsewhips beneath their teddy bears. Sometimes those of ill repute only teased. They were as unpredictable as a tempest and, when my wits didn't fail me, I acted accordingly.

"If those lips could talk," I whispered of her once to Paul when we'd run into the cowgirl at some party.

"What does that even mean?" he'd asked.

"Jon Catlett." She took off her black cowboy hat identical to the style immortalized by Bobby Bare Senior, the brim curled, a red feather stuck in the band. She ran a hand through her thick black Irish hair, moving the strands from her eyes. "You're alive." She wrapped her fingers lightly around my wrist.

Now I am, I thought.

"I'm so sorry about Irina." She twirled her swizzle stick then stirred more Splenda into her Oolong tea. "When I heard, I didn't know if you guys were still together or not...but God, I should've called you right away."

The late Irina had been a close friend of Catherine's.

"It's fine." I waved away the thought of my late love as if Catherine were speaking of a party I'd thrown that she'd missed. "There's nothing anyone can say about something like that. It's horrible. She kept going back to it." *It* of course, meant drugs.

Irina had triumphantly achieved nine months of sobriety. She was clean the day they killed her.

I wasn't even allowing the girl her dignity in dying sober. I blamed Irina for her own death to save public face. I didn't just speak ill of the dead, I discredited their earthly victories and poisoned their memories with fictional shame.

Perhaps I was trying to coerce the devil into creating a new ring of hell, one for the all-encompassing sinner, for it seemed within me existed the drive to reach the lowest depths of depravity.

"She couldn't leave it alone," I kept on. "Started running with some real bad people."

"Have you talked to the police?"

"I did before I left town," I lied. "Then I called them again when I got back to see if there were any new breaks in the case. Since Irina was so secretive about her using, no one who would talk to the police knew much. And those who know anything, of course, aren't coming out."

"It's surreal. A few weeks after I read about it, I dropped by the store to see how you were doing. When Paul said you'd sold the place to him and left town..." She placed a hand just above her breast, where our hearts are supposed to be. "I was scared for you. I was sorry I hadn't kept up and spent more time at the store. I mean, God, I love that place."

"Well, it's still there. And if anyone can sustain the magic, it'll be Paul." I leaned closer and whispered, "Mum's the word on this, so keep it between the two of us, but I'm going to remain a sleeping partner. We got some big plans for Twice Told."

Then, I told her about the location in the West End and the Bookmobile and further emphasized my silent involvement with the expanding chain. She ate this up, placing a hand on my forearm as she stressed how staying involved, keeping busy, is what saved her when her older brother committed suicide four years ago.

What she'd never known was that both her brothers had

introduced me to heroin, and I'd gotten high with the eldest the afternoon of his death, approximately seven hours before he shot himself through the mouth with their late father's deer rifle.

She had to bring up Jamie right when we had almost successfully transitioned from the dismal subject of our dearly departed.

"Irina would be so proud," Catherine smiled wistfully. I was scared to death she'd start crying. I never know how to deal with weeping women. "I mean you two had always talked about turning Twice Told into a chain."

I abruptly changed the conversation's course. "You been playing?" Sometimes that was the only way to go about it, sudden and without apology. Luckily, it went over.

"You know I hate to talk about my music," she said.

"And deprive your biggest fan of the latest news? You'd do that? I thought you were that undyingly grateful sort of folk goddess that treated your followers with humility and respect." I'd been treating her like a rock star for years, as if she were the iconic equal to Loretta Lynn. She didn't try and sway our talk back to Irina and Jaime, thank God. That's what's great about grieving—people simply expect the unexpected out of you. That's why the cops couldn't read me. Mad Dog claims that homicide police rarely base their suspicions of spouses whose partners have been murdered on the widow's or widower's initial emotional reaction.

"I'm playing Chicago tonight," she told me.

Chicago was where Catherine had turned her honky-tonk hobby into gainful employment. She was one of the first songwriters to, with a bad attitude and more thoughtful lyricism than the usual protestant guilt and cheating confessions most of us associate with classic country, transform the genre into an act of insurgence. Her work influenced everyone from Wilco to My Morning Jacket. However, her gig profited her by only the smallest margin. Touring and cashing her monthly royalty checks barely kept up with the mortgage and bills that came tied to the house her father had left her.

She'd played a packed show at the bookstore the night before my first murder. Besides the attendant loin stirring and shortness of breath, looking at Catherine filled me with toxic, deathly shame. Over her brother and for what I'd become since we'd last spoken.

"Chicago," I said. "I mean, you do realize I've memorized most of your work so I sure hope those ingrate Yankees have fallen in love you like I have."

"Chicago is almost the definition of Midwestern," she corrected me.

"All I know is that it's above the Mason-Dixon."

"And 'love?' Really, Catlett? You've fallen in love with my songs?"

"I actually didn't say your songs. I said you. But your music...that's what I meant."

She blushed. "I thought you despised female singers, even if you can't keep yourself from leering at their busts."

Shit. I *had* been staring her tits, forgetting to leer with my peripheral vision the way my father had taught me in one of his hour-long rants about the assets and liabilities of the opposite sex. He was a man who knew how to gawk at any buxom brunette undetected.

Then I amended the statement, "I *do* love your music, I

mean. I am not a sexist. Sexists believe women are inferior. I just don't like most of them. Big difference."

"In that case, all is forgiven. Jesus, Jon."

"You must know you're one of the greats. I guess it never came up because I didn't want to insult you by stating the obvious."

Her dimples deepened and she looked away. I must have sounded at least half as earnest as I felt. I had her most recent album, at that very moment, in the CD player of my Crown Vic, awaiting the thousandth listen.

"You could come with me?" She curled back her lower lip and sucked her teeth into the pink puffy flesh.

"We're working on getting the van up and running." It killed me to turn her down this time. However, I wasn't about to let her leave without one of us inviting the other to a future social event of some kind. As bad as I was at parties, as alienating as my conversation would always turn in such circumstances, I had to see her again and I had to be certain it wouldn't be long from now. It worked best if the word "date" went unspoken until after the act of sex had been consummated, another trick my dear old dad taught me. "It's better for them to just wake up next to you," he'd said. "*Do not* under any circumstances allow them ample time for analysis. And once you get them talking, only speak about things you know they like. Like pizza." Sometimes he stupefied me. "For example, you can just keep reminding them, if they're a big pizza fan, that pizza still exists. That will keep them happy and on your side." He really didn't think much of the ladies. Though I'm loathe to admit it, most of the savage suggestions I took played out exactly as he'd predicted.

This same philosophy by which he lived, even while married, was what lost me my mother. I wasn't enough reason to stay around. And since mom was poor, she couldn't afford to bring me along when she left. One morning, she was gone. She didn't pack a thing. I imagine she stole enough money from my father's wallet to catch a Greyhound to parts unknown, leaving me to my inebriant patriarch and the Louisville streets.

"Damn." Catherine brought me back to Starbucks. "I was hoping you'd chauffer me." She let her simper fade, but her disappointment provided me some fuel.

"When's your next gig?" I struck while the flames still burned.

"Nashville," she said. "Next week."

"Let me drive you." That's another trick my old man taught me. Never say anything in the form of a question. Don't go around barking orders, but chose your words carefully. Allow them as few chances to say "no" as circumstance permits.

She said, "Come on. Jon Catlett playing chauffeur?"

"I'd love nothing more."

"It's a date."

She said it, not me. We stood and hugged.

"Maybe we can take your new ride," Catherine suggested. "It might look good to have a woman in the passenger seat so the cops don't think you're a diddler."

We shared a last laugh before parting and I bid her goodbye with, "You just saved me money on popsicles and candy corn. I thought I'd have to offer you some Kit-Kats to get in my creepy van with me."

5

I anxiously appraised the sovereign skyline of Chicago from where Mad Dog had parked facing the street on the sixth floor of the garage. He'd left the windows cracked to allow in the lonely wind the town's favorite poets had cursed in verse and prose. The cool did little to temper my fury. Of all people, Mad Dog couldn't wait just a few weeks for us to set up shop. He just *had* to bring more greedy and desperate men into our lives.

And importing from the Middle East?

Was he trying to catch us a treason charge?

Not to mention the possible executions we risked only using such an outfit one time then tossing them out like slovenly whores whose charms and skills had run their course. Who knew how those traumatized war vets would react to even the slightest hint of disrespect?

Lex, the new head of the Russian mafia's Chicago chapter, had my crew to thank for his esteemed title. I held onto this like a rosary, hoping that, since we'd helped him shotgun his way to the top, he might have mercy on us.

I also reminded myself that Lex had supplied me with the explosives that allowed our pasty drug cartel to effectively mount a siege on Luther's farm.

He'd chosen us over Longmire

But with all the bad press, the two dead women—one from an affluent family—and the loss of Luther's horse trailer distribution network, Lex might see our Louisville crew as too much of a liability. Perhaps Dog and I could convince the boss that our new business model would provide far better insulation from police scrutiny than Luther's old supply lines.

I checked my phone for the time. Mad Dog had only been gone ten minutes. He said he'd check out the scene, then call down to me, let me know I was safe to come up. With a hotel this size, it probably took at least ten minutes to take the elevator up to the penthouse floor and gain entrance. I glanced up from my phone and that old feeling returned, the sensation one endures when plummeting downward at mach speed on a roller coaster—with men it involved the testicles slightly inverting—something I hadn't experienced since I'd shot Amara.

A black van had circled up the winding concrete path that led from the parking garage entrance and stopped near the elevator on the third floor where Mad Dog had parked and left me waiting. The back doors swung open and two men jumped out, dressed like the heroes of that awful movie *SWAT*, one of many I'd watched when hiding out in Hazard, grievously comatose, laid up on my aunt's couch.

The mercenary-types all but blended into the dark. The lights from outside reflected off the flashlights and goggles strapped to the Kevlar vests worn over black thermals. I immediately thought of the Blackwater characters Mad Dog had colluded with to keep our dope game running.

The two who'd exited the hatch entered the elevator and the van slowly disappeared up the concrete slope toward the next floor, perhaps to drop off more men to surround their target.

I madly dialed Milligan's cell number and got his voice mail after two rings.

I texted him, I THINK WE GOT A PROBLEM.

6

I can most accurately describe my own actions while the conflict began to culminate twenty floors above, so that is how we shall begin my account of the shootout at the Hilton Hotel in downtown Chicago, now the subject of two documentaries and an HBO mini-series.

Not one of the versions I've watched contained a morsel of truth.

According to the writers in Hollywood and the reporters who milked the killings for fame and fortune, the Russian mafia shifted power that day, and the only culprits were of the Eastern European persuasion.

The Kentucky gun thugs who perpetrated the actual killings were never mentioned, nor the involvement of LMPD detectives, ex-mercenaries, or a bedraggled used book dealer.

Digging through the back seat of Mad Dog's rental Prius for some sort of disguise—I didn't want to be recognized on any hotel security cam footage, or easily described by an employee—all I could find was a broad brimmed Stetson cowboy hat strikingly similar to the one Luther used to wear. Later, I would discover these actions superfluous as the mercenary strike team had gagged, bound, and rendered unconscious the security guards in the basement and disabled all electronic monitoring.

However, I did the best I could with the information at hand and, after staring quizzically at the cowboy hat for a few moments, placed it atop my oversized helmet of straw colored hair.

"What the fuck, Milligan?" I checked my ridiculous disguise in the rearview. "I loved you in *Urban Cowboy*," I said to my reflection.

By the time I made it down to the front lobby, the first shot had already been fired upstairs. According to Mad Dog, he'd just been allowed a sweep of the suite, checking for any hidden assassins in closets or under beds. Milligan's phone buzzed again, my message that he ignored.

Lucky for him, he told me later, after a few amenities and suffering Lex's bad Russian humor, he looked at my text.

And he knew.

He checked the window to his right, scanned the top floor of the pay garage facing the hotel, and hit the deck.

The only sounds Dog heard were the sharp cracks of windows splintering. Then both of Lex's barrel-chested lieutenants crumpled to the floor. Another crack and Lex fell on his side, a single carmine teardrop descending from the pulpy mound of muscle where his right eye had been.

At this point, down in the lobby, I'd bullshitted the room number out of the cute little desk clerk, flashing her one of Mad Dog's narcotics placards he'd left in the glove box. I'd made sure to display the ID quickly. I told her I was with the FBI, the Chicago office. She suspiciously eyed the Stetson. The accent too probably baffled her. "I transferred from New Orleans. I'm originally from Fort Worth, but my family moved around a lot. That's why I got a little drawl when I talk. The department just went to shit after Katrina, darlin'." I didn't want anyone making any connection between Louisville and whatever horrors the Russians were perpetuating on the penthouse floor.

"I got reason to believe my partner might be in trouble."

The girl had a tiny wavy gold plated American flag pinned to her lapel. That'd be my in. "My man's undercover with some, I guess you'd call them Czechoslovakians...You know the former USSR—" I winked, "—whatever those commie degenerates are calling themselves these days. They might be discussing something nuclear."

She grasped and massaged her little pin.

"Now, sweetie—" I placed my hand on hers, "—the cavalry has arrived. Everything is gonna be just fine. I need you to stay calm, though. Can you do that for me? And tell no one that I was ever here. Do you understand? No matter what happens. Even if an incident, does, God forbid, occur. If you break our cover, it could mean this city becoming the next New York circa 9/11. You understand?"

She nodded frantically.

"And even if you're interviewed by other police, you never saw me here, you get it? We don't know who might be on the commie's payroll."

"You have my word."

She whispered the room number, vicariously aroused by her proximity to the clandestine.

"I appreciate it, hon," I said to the curvy little concierge with the hypnotizing bubble butt. "What's your name there?" I looked at her nametag. "Rhonda, huh? Well, thanks for helping me, Rhonda. Get it?" Then I started singing and snapping my fingers. "Help me, Rhonda. Get her out of my heart."

Her excitement faded and she said, "Like I've never heard that before."

"I'm sorry, that was profoundly stupid."

Her smile returned. I guess she liked me though, because, after everything that followed, she still bought my patriotic song and dance and kept her word. Our conversation never up and bit me in the ass. None of the news reports that followed ever mentioned the two Louisvillians who'd partaken in the famous Hilton firefight.

As I waited for the elevator, Mad Dog was crawling to cover, somewhere outside of the sniper's scope. He caught his breath and drew his drop gun, a blue steel .45. He remembered the two bodyguards Lex had posted outside. They would kill him on sight when they discovered their boss dead. There wouldn't be any negotiations, and even if they let him get a word out, they'd never believe he wasn't in on this.

He stood and edged along the wall toward the door, pressing the barrel under the peephole as he peered out into the hallway.

All he could see was that shitty portrait of some dandy colonial statesmen. For all he knew, the two guards he'd passed when entering now buttressed the other side of the door with their pieces out. They could be compromised, working for some third party that wanted to move up the criminal corporate ladder.

He considered this, but knew better. Those responsible for the killings he'd just witnessed were not Russians.

They were American heroes, at least some would believe.

He'd thought long and hard; the suppressors on the assault rifles had made so little noise and the cracks in the glass could have been something from the television Lex had been watching. For all the men outside knew, the meeting had been rolling along fine.

Perhaps the deaths were for the best. Lex had not guaranteed the survival of Mad Dog and his partners. And if it were the boys from Fort Knox looking to eliminate the competition and gain the bookstore's permanent patronage, Milligan would prefer dealing "the Taliban" from now on.

Too many angles to contemplate and not enough time to act.

He cowered back into the room's lifeless milieu and hid in the latrine.

I had considered none of this as I rode the elevator up to the suite. I just wanted a ride back to the Bluegrass state. If Mad Dog were dead, maybe I could sneak around the bloodbath and confiscate his car keys, slip out before anyone shot me.

Turns out, despite my literary background, Dog remained the more critical thinker.

* * *

Mad Dog considered the myriad of adversaries who may have ordered the hit. Was it a competing Russian faction? Lex's own men mounting a hollow-point mutiny? The crew who'd smuggled that high-grade dope from the Middle East? Enemies of Alexis that the dead mobster had never mentioned?

If Lex had caught wind that Milligan and Myron had kept business going behind Chicago's back, needing to make up for the losses the battle with Luther had caused, the Russian syndicate would have taken great offense.

All the outfits in Nashville, Memphis, and Atlanta had, at the very least, loose ties to the Chicago boys. And as far as Chicago knew, only one shipment, the dope taken off Luther's farm, had been made since the shootout outside of Louisville. But Myron and Mad Dog had no alternative. They weren't just unwilling; they were unable to go half a month without product to move, and had thus gone to another heroin source, knowing full well that Lex might deem necessary an appropriately gruesome Russian response. Mad Dog had banked on the Southern outfits needing their shipments bad enough to avoid curiosity, to ask not from where the better supply had come.

We rolled the dice, Mad Dog thought and smiled sadly, like a man remembering a joke absurd enough to amuse him through his last few steps toward the gallows.

We gambled and we lost.

He had only one hope. Whoever had started the shooting might take out the rest of the Russian bodyguards before they got to him. And he knew that if Lex had planned to kill him and the gangster's men didn't receive word soon that the Louisville cop was dead, the two outside and maybe half a dozen others would come in blasting. He had seven shots in the .45 and wouldn't have enough time to reload once the automatic weapons begun their chorus.

He couldn't believe he was admitting it to himself, but Jon and Paul had been right to be furious when they first heard what he and Myron had done. The brilliant Detective Milligan had screwed the pooch.

He pulled out his phone, texted me to drive away NOW. I should get what cash I'd saved, hit the road, and head as far away from Louisville as I could, preferably all the way to South America. He told me to advise Paul to do the same.

The despondent policeman crushed the burner with his bootheel and racked the Colt's slide.

"At least I get to skip Viagra and Alzheimer's," he said.

I got the message halfway up to the penthouse on the elevator.

I texted back, YOU HAVE THE FUCKING CAR KEYS, ASSHOLE, a response never received since he'd just destroyed his cell.

Then I closed the phone, putting my old friend's advice immediately out of mind.

7

While Mad Dog waited to discover what fate might befall him, I drew the gun he'd handed me in the car from the small holster I'd strapped around my right ankle. Despite my near-unreasonable hatred for cops and even their immediate families, I'd always loved *The French Connection* films and their hero, Popeye Doyle, played with a particularly Gaelic brand of madness by the raging and mercurial Gene Hackman. Maybe that's what allowed me to forgive Scott for becoming a traitor, the fact that, at his core, he was just a criminal with a hall pass, much like Doyle. The character, after accidentally shooting a fellow cop, a real asshole Popeye never cared for much, exhibits no remorse. I always loved that. He reminded me of Mad Dog in his unyielding and pugnacious resistance to bureaucratic and societal ennui.

Look at me, getting maudlin over Mad Dog's imminent demise.

I believed that dying to save a corrupt killer cop would be far more honorable than the overdose I was headed toward a year ago. The possible end I faced I also found preferable to withering away in some bed in the care of my born-again Christian children who rued my incessant tendency to go on breathing. I'd chosen a lifestyle that almost guaranteed I would not die of boredom and, with that, moments before everything went to hell on the penthouse floor, an eerie placidity becalmed my screaming nerves.

I ran my fingertip along the safety catch of the revolver, then the wheel. The six shots might be enough to get me out alive, but I doubted the round capacity would make for a remarkable body count. Those mercenaries had high-power artillery. They'd have to if they were going head on against the Russians, Mad Dog, or both.

"I should've kept that AR-14," I said aloud of the assault rifle I'd used to kill half a dozen of Luther Longmire's men on the psychobilly's dope farm.

If death had arrived then I'd just have to welcome him like an old friend, the way I'd invited Amara Longmire into my life, knowing she would undo me like scissors to a suture.

I held the .38 at my side, concealed behind my thigh.

I breathed deep through my nose to avoid panic like Mad Dog had taught me before we killed Luther.

The elevator doors slowly parted to an empty hallway.

I stepped out onto the burgundy carpet of the long corridor of penthouse entrances. Above each of the half-dozen walnut secretaries hung portraits of haughty and effeminate American statesmen from bygone eras. The men all looked like trannies in their George Washington wigs and liberally applied make-up. Another hallway opened to my right.

Mad Dog, I thought. You should've picked someone besides a loser junkie for backup. You should have kept better company, a pathetic epitaph, but nonetheless applicable.

The elevator adjacent to mine sounded its annoying jingle, catching me off guard. I looked over to see two husky men with coal black hair and Lex's same olive complexion. They had adhered to their master's unwaveringly predictable and drab dress code: Dockers, black leather overcoats, and off-brand loafers. They'd even sculpted their hair with gel into spiky tufts, again, like Lex. Russia was always ten years behind. The styles of the Chicago sect seemed to mimic NSYNC and other forgotten boy bands from the early aught years.

Neither of them had seen me yet.

One of the Russkie gun thugs lifted his wrist to his mouth and spoke into the tiny two-way radio, "Kick the fucking door down. No one answering cell or room phone. Don't make me tell you again. Only one man walk in, right?"

He then placed his wrist to his ear, listening for a moment and rolling his eyes. Then he huffed, stomping the floor.

"Let's go," he said to his compatriot. "Pussies afraid to go in by themselves. Afraid to piss off boss."

Then, as if choreographed in their timing, the two turned to see me standing there with my cowboy hat. *Kentuckian* might as well have been tattooed on my forehead.

"Just hold on, fellas." I couldn't help but imitate John Wayne, nearly greeting them instead with, "Howdy."

Then they noticed my hand was hiding something. I let them see the butt of the revolver but held up one palm. "I'm on your side, okay. I mean I think I am. I got as much of an idea what's going on as you two. No. Don't do that. We don't have to go down that road yet."

Both had unzipped their coats. Both went for the nines holstered in shoulder rigs.

"Goddamnit." I brought the revolver from behind my thigh and put down Lex's two men, one shot to the temple each.

The cost of doing business, I told myself, just as I had the last time our little crew caused a copious amount of death and mayhem in the Windy City to meet with Lex and discuss what used to be the future of our partnership.

Past the elevator to the right, a door with a placard reading *Staff Only* slowly opened. The gun shook in my trembling hand as I leveled the barrel where I'd seen movement.

Then I saw the barrels of the AK-47s edging out into the hallway. I needed cover. I lowered the gun and turned and ran the other way, but only made it to the closest desk with yet another portrait of some patriotic tranny hanging above.

Two avatars of the men I'd just killed stepped into the hallway.

But these guys weren't talking to the microphones hooked near their cufflinks in very angry Russian.

They were aiming their automatic weapons in my direction.

I dropped to my knees, grabbed the narrow table under the ugly portrait, turned it on its side, and breathlessly glanced over the useless cover I'd fashioned. I held the revolver with both hands and drew a bead on the goon who seemed closest to taking a shot. He had a confident grin and his right eye was pressed firmly to the rifle's scope.

Then, before I could take a shot, an arterial spray broke loose from his jugular and he collapsed. Behind the gunman who'd been left standing appeared the two ski-masked mercenaries I'd seen in the garage.

The other Russian glanced down at his dead friend then made a pathetic attempt to raise his piece when the two masked gunmen tore their surviving prey to shreds.

Since I still couldn't tell friend from foe, I'd taken advantage of the awkward pause before the fourth Russian guard's demise and made a break for the stairs. I wished things had turned out different, I said silently to the ghost of Mad Dog.

I kept glancing over my shoulder as I ran. I was somewhere halfway between the hallway's mouth near the elevators and the stairwell exit. I laughed out loud, a fit of mirth quickly suppressed by the sight of two more of those leather-clad commie bastards stepping out right in front of me from the door I'd thought might allow me exodus.

I backed away a few paces then turned around and there stood the mercs with their mini-arsenal.

Only one place to hide.

I fired a shot in each direction and dove into an empty doorway between the two parties of trigger-happy bed-lamites.

Then from the hallway, the machine guns began singing their atonal metallic verses.

8

The enfilade had all but ended. Every few moments a brief barrage of short rifle bursts would sound, followed by some screams and cursing and bickering from either side of the corridor amongst the confederates of both parties.

I couldn't afford to peek out. My crawl space was too small. By this time, both the Russians and the killers in combat boots had surely conjured their own makeshift covers. I imagined the killer elite lined up against a foyer wall near the elevators, arguing over their next move while, closer to the stairs, the two Lex look-alikes reminisced of better times replete with bottomless bowls of mother's borscht and human trafficking.

During the start of firefight, I'd heard Lex's men mutter a few American curse words. One had also said to the other, "No one said we'd be fighting a goddamn army today." But now that the noise had died down, the two Russians had dropped that broken English too easy to caricaturize. They'd switched to their native tongue.

To compound matters, the Americans were talking loudly and openly about strategies, none of which, to my relief, involved my ultimate demise. They kept speaking of saving Mad Dog too.

"Whisper low," I shouted. For now, the Americans were

more friends than foe, the enemies of my enemy.

After a moment, from my left, I heard one of the Americans say, "What?"

"They can speak English." I checked the load on my revolver and considered the two shots I had left and where best to fire them. "You're giving away your every move. Talk quietly for the love of all that's holy. Don't they teach you maniacs anything in boot camp? They're trying to throw you off by only speaking Russian. But trust me, they hablo Ingles."

"That's Spanish," a female voice sounded. "Not really applicable."

One of them was a woman. I should've known. They're the most vicious of killers from my experience. I clarified for the feline critic. "Who gives a shit? My point is, be careful what you say."

"Why?" The male American gunman asked.

"Why what?" I asked. "Don't you two want to be the ones alive at the end of this thing? Because the way I see it there's only one other option besides us coming out of this alive and I don't much care to die today, not after the shit I've survived this month."

"I guess we'll deal with the trust issues between us after we walk out of here," the female decided.

I screamed, "I feel so fucking validated. This would just be my luck. Shot to death while arguing with a goddamn woman. It's fitting, really. Thank you, you delicate little thing."

"Do you forget who has the bigger gun," she yelled back.

"Already cutting me down to size with phallic references," I said. "We're off to a nice start."

"You little shit. I'm considering saving your ass and you talk to me like a waitress at a truck stop."

"I take great umbrage to that. I've slept with more than my share of truck stop waitresses and aside from a few bad pennies, they were the finest women I've ever known."

The Russians must have thought we'd lost our minds.

"I'll deal with you soon enough," she said.

Her male counterpart in camouflage diverted Lady Death and I from our dispute. "The stairs," he said. "If you were mounting a siege, wouldn't you triangulate, attack from all entry points?"

There were more of them somewhere. We had back-up coming. All we had to do was wait.

"So, for now let's just hope these bastards don't try to charge us—" The American's second sentence was interrupted by two loud gunshots from a high caliber pistol.

"It's okay, boys, you can come out now."

Until today, I'd never have compared Mad Dog's growling to a choir of angels, but this hadn't been, even by Twice Told standards, a normal afternoon.

I stepped slowly into the hallway and stood beside Mad Dog where he admired his handiwork. The two dead guards had huddled for cover behind two upturned secretaries under the "Exit" sign hanging above the stairwell door.

"We got company besides the Russians," I told Mad Dog.

"I know. And worry not." Mad Dog thumbed the hammer down on his Colt and pointed the long barrel down the end of the hall. "They're not here to kill us."

"Would've been nice to have gotten that memo *before* we drove up here," I said. "How can you be so sure of that?"

"Because we'd be dead right now if that was their mission. Snyder, Rick, step out into the open please."

"You know these people?" I should've guessed that they were all thick as thieves. When you place no real value on human life, it's hard to find folks with similar interests.

The mercenaries stepped into dim light of the narrow passage, their guns lowered. They both curled their ski masks up along their hairlines. One had a mustache and the pale, pockmarked complexion of a young Ray Liotta. The woman had close-cropped black hair, shaven at the sides, a Mohawk without the gel. She had high cheekbones, and a revolver-brandishing cowgirl tattoo that ran beneath her chin, down her neck, and disappeared beneath her fatigues. She didn't look like any soldier I'd ever seen.

These were the Fort Knox suppliers Paul and I had been promised would accept a one-time deal and walk away.

"Where is he?" Mad Dog asked.

"Behind you," said the girl, Snyder I assumed.

The door to the stairwell stood open. A stout fellow with a flattop who'd allowed not a scratch to his bullet-proof vest nor a speck of blood to stain his cargo pants had joined the party. He had the barrel of a pump-action sawed-off dug into Milligan's temple.

"Thomas." Mad Dog kept his .45 trained on the girl and her partner. "I'll flat line both your people before you can pull that trigger. Quit fucking around"

Thomas with the sawed-off was maybe a decade younger than Mad Dog. He presented a proud and chiseled

Roman profile. He probably had to fight off the women with a bayonet when he hit the town in his dress blues.

"Idiot." The killer cadre's leader laughed. Then he lowered the scattergun and drew an arm around Milligan, saying, "You can thank me on our next payday, mother-fucker."

9

"Why are you here?" Mad Dog said to Thomas. "We had a deal, Thomas. I thought that might have counted for something with you, considering how far back we go."

"We just saved your lives. We can stand around here until the entire Chicago Police Department shows up or we can take this service elevator down to the first floor of the garage and get the hell out of town before the cops have any clue what might have happened here."

"You think we can walk away from this bloodbath without consequences. We just killed half a dozen Russian mafia lieutenants *and* their boss."

"You weren't walking out of this hotel alive, Milligan," Snyder said. Then she glared over at me. "Neither of you were."

"And how exactly is the A-Team here so sure about that?" I asked Thomas, ignoring G.I. Jane.

"We got it *all* covered, old man." Thomas ignored me, speaking only to Milligan. "I'll explain everything in the car."

I believed him on one thing. If these guys wanted us dead, we'd be dead.

"There's no point drawing more heat on us." I dropped the revolver in the pocket of my coat.

"What about our car, Thomas?" Mad Dog said. "What about the cameras, witnesses, et cetera?"

"Wouldn't worry about the car," Thomas said. "Or any of that other nonsense. You know me, Milligan. I don't leave loose ends."

I'd learn all about the man who left no loose ends untied and how seriously he practiced the principle. I'd learn more about Chad Thomas than anyone would ever want to know.

Like Mad Dog had said, Thomas was a cop and a veteran of the war on terror. He'd been the sole survivor of his squadron after an ambush in the middle of a routine supply run. He had fifteen confirmed kills and probably used cocaine as a sleep aid. I'd never met someone so desperately in need of prescription anti-psychotics and mood stabilizers.

"Let's go," Mad Dog said.

Thomas agreed and motioned for his crew to follow us.

When the mercenary leader turned away from us, had I known then what I know now, I would have shamelessly shot him in the back.

We entered the adjoining garage where the black van was waiting for us. Mad Dog and I sat in the very back. No one had asked for our guns, thank Christ.

Rick Bilotta, the portly driver who'd been partnered with Snyder upstairs for Mad Dog's rescue mission, made a U-turn and headed down the concrete slope. He slowed at the end of the row of cars where Mad Dog had parked the rental.

"You see this?" Thomas held up a multi-channel walkie-talkie.

I hadn't understood what he was doing when Thomas had leaned down before we entered the elevator and unclipped the device from the belt of one of the dead Russians Mad Dog had shot.

"You all saw me take this from that dead Russkie, right?" Thomas asked.

Confirming mumbles echoed through the van.

Thomas pressed the large round button on the side of the two-way.

The Honda went up in a ball of flames. Glass, plastic, and metal projected in all directions, denting neighboring minivans and sedans, shattering windshields. A rearview mirror even bounced lightly off of a Corvette's hood, setting off the convertible's annoying alarm, a robotic voice yelling at unreasonable decibels, "You are standing to close to me. Do not tamper with me."

Bilotta asked of the irritating car alarm, "Can we blow the Corvette up while we're at it?"

The cars to the left and right of the rented Honda, a Subaru Station wagon and a VW Jetta, had both caught fire as well and were moments from reigniting the explosion.

Thomas stared sternly at Mad Dog from the passenger bucket. "We weren't here to kill you, Milligan. We were here to stop Lex from cutting you loose as potential liabilities. Now, here's what happens. We're going to go to a safe place so I can explain further. I've allowed you and your partner to keep your guns. Are either of you going to make me regret that gesture of trust?"

"No," I said.

Mad Dog did not feel the need to echo me.

"Then let's get this fun-filled family vacation off to the right start." Thomas turned on the radio, AC/DC, fittingly, throwing down on a live rendition of "Dirty Deeds Done Dirt Cheap."

10

"What the hell is with the cowboy hat?" Bilotta asked while the rest of us exited the van at the switch point, an abandoned warehouse in Gary, Indiana, an industrial wasteland that had become one of the country's most dangerous cities with the closing of the Ford plant and the crumbling of the area's economy.

It was a perfect place to hide. Cops who patrolled such savage, gang-led war zones avoided unnecessary confrontations. Even the courthouse had bullet holes in it.

I removed the Stetson from my crown and offered it to Bilotta, now leaning against the concrete edge of the warehouse's loading dock. "I found it in the backseat of Milligan's rental."

Bilotta placed the cowboy hat on his head, drew his revolver and twirled the gun like a sharp shooter from the old west. He looked the part, with his thick moustache and bleary-eyed glare. The man smelled of over-applied aftershave and Listerine, a drunkard's dead giveaway.

Thomas had changed out of his fighting gear. He unfastened his Kevlar, which he threw along with his other fatigues in a duffel bag from where he retrieved a red polo that he draped over his undershirt.

"Lex had asked me to bring him a souvenir to remember

Luther by." Mad Dog leaned against the trunk of a black Cadillac El Dorado parked near the loading dock when we'd arrived, right next to a light green Humvee. These cars gave me the impression that there were men waiting for us behind those lowered warehouse doors. "When I went upstairs, I left it in the rental. Wasn't exactly my highest priority to provide entertainment for that son-of-a-bitch. So, Thomas, you *are* sure he was going to take us out?"

"I had proof, Milligan."

"Care to explain," Mad Dog said.

"You should have listened to me weeks ago," Thomas said. "What if we hadn't gotten to you in time today? We weren't sure we could stop them. But we tried anyway. I did that for you, whether you ever make me a dollar again or not."

Thomas had tried to convince Mad Dog to only import the Afghan dope since the drug smuggling A-Team had enough contacts in the Middle East willing to take the risks to keep the heroin flowing until the last American soldier was brought home. For the right price.

When Mad Dog had "declined to go American," Thomas had consulted with Corporal Donalds, the massive bald black guy we'd picked up at a stop light a few blocks from the Hyatt who'd been one of the snipers on the parking garage who picked off Lex in the penthouse. Donalds pulled a few favors with the FBI where he had worked for two years in the Boston field office before taking one in the line of duty during an undercover coke sting. Within a few hours, he had the mobster's entire file faxed to him.

"Lex was a piece of shit," Donalds said. "Zero loyalty."

Donalds explained how he had sent Snyder, the cadre's tech expert, up to Chicago three days prior to our meet with Lex. She had bugged Lex's apartment and the café the mobster did business in. She even wired Lex's Mercedes for sound.

"It became pretty clear that neither of you were leaving Chicago alive," Thomas said. "Lex sent some moles down south to see what kind of dope people were buying around the time your last shipment should've dried up.

Plagued with the true knowledge of what had just befallen our crew, I hung my head and renewed the discussion we'd let drift in the van earlier. "Milligan, you really thought those Russians wouldn't find out about you double dealing? You never ever get to call me an idiot again."

"When I told them Jon had hung back," Mad Dog shook his head, stunned at his own naiveté, "I told them it was just for security reasons. Then, Lex's bodyguard backed away, toward the veranda, so I couldn't hear what he'd said into his mic That must've been...those sons-of..."

"Yeah," I said, "That was probably around the time those two assholes I shot by the elevator rigged the rental with C-4," I said. "I wasn't in the car anymore and they knew it. They probably planted the bomb just in case one of us made it to the car without taking a bullet."

"No," Thomas said. "We've been following these Russians for three days. They had your car rigged at your motel out in the Illinois sticks. They weren't taking any chances one of you might make it back to Kentucky."

The thought hit me like a snowfall in August. "What about Paul?"

JONATHAN ASHLEY

"He's safe," Thomas said. "Snyder, the lovely lady Jon here can't stop visually molesting, noticed that two of the Russians who'd been sent down to check out your operation had gotten fairly comfortable at that Ramada on Hurstbourne Lane. Then we picked it up on the wiretap. Those two were ordered to take care of Paul and Myron around the same time Lex was laying out the tarpaulin for Mad Dog here. The shitbird was looking to get rid of your whole crew in one fell swoop. Time it like the ending of *The Godfather* when Corleone baptized his godson while all across town his enemies were taken out."

"I guess those wops didn't have Calamity Jane and the Dirty Half-Dozen backing him." Snyder lit a cigarette and winked at Mad Dog. "There wouldn't have been any sequels if the boys and I ran the Corleone muscle. Sonny was a pussy." I suppose they had a history, not of a romantic nature, but probably more paternal on Milligan's part. On the ride to Gary, he'd chastised her for the lowlife friends she refused to shirk, said she should be advising Bill Gates and designing robotic sniper rifles for the military rather than palling around with Thomas and the "fuck-around gang."

Snyder, now sporting an airy sleeveless flannel button-down, no bra—unfortunately she'd changed clothes on the other side of the warehouse—said to me, "I was the one that saved your partner in Louisville. Me, Catlett," she said.

I suppose she wanted to inspire some remorse over my earlier sexism.

"When he meets you, sugar, when he has to listen to

that mouth, I'm sure he'll be sorry you went to the trouble," I said.

"Prick," she said. "If it wasn't for me, you'd be crying your little cunt off right now over your butt-plug best friend.

"She can't help but brag," Milligan said. "Like she's talking about a beauty pageant she won."

Snyder ignored Milligan and went on with her tale. She'd taken great pains to hide her history, but the hint of Dixie cadence remained. She surely hailed from somewhere further south than my riverside Gomorrah home.

She mixed her best falsetto with that peculiar deployment of vowels heard most around places like Spanish Harlem and kindred Chicano neighborhoods throughout the country. "I said, *Hahskeeping*. One of them opened the door in nothing but his tighty-whities and a wife beater. Before he could say a word, I put one in his head, stepped into the hotel room, closed the door behind me. I could hear the shower running. I guess since I'd used a silencer and the first one had fallen on the bed, the second had no idea what was coming. I opened the shower curtain and pulled a Bates Motel on his ass. So, yeah, you're welcome. I saved your best friend and maybe his family too."

"A knife was used in Bates Motel. Not some massive hand cannon with a donkey-cock of a silencer," I said.

"I know." She looked at me coldly then said, "That's why I said Bates Motel, because I slit his throat. Slit, meaning I used a knife. Got any other corrections or complaints, asshole."

We were going to get along just fine. Most of the women who've had the more profound effects on my life hated me at first. And with her predilection for the irascible, that aquiline nose and, below her neckline, those lubricious arcs and bends, I eagerly welcomed the harshest of courtships.

"You're not careful, Catlett," Snyder said, "I'll paint you a much clearer picture of my talents with a blade."

"How does one paint a picture of 'talent?'" I asked her.

"Watch it, Jon," Milligan said.

Snyder stepped closer.

"Offended?" I said to her as she breached arm's length. "Well, I suppose you really are a delicate young thing."

She extended her arm and a blade projected from her shirtsleeve. The tip cut the skin of my throat and I backed away, blotting the wound with my palm, bending down to one knee to fake a more disabling pain. When she said, "How smart are you now, Hemingway?" I came up faster than she'd drawn her knife and dug the .38 barrel into the flesh of her chin.

Thomas howled at the hint bloodletting. "Children," he said, "potential lovers, show some etiquette. We have business to discuss."

The girl and I lowered our weapons and parted ways. She went to stand beside Thomas, and I sat on the loading dock and holstered my piece.

"As much as we'd all enjoy more gunplay," Thomas said, "we need to debrief and regroup."

I'll say this for the trigger-happy grunt: At least he didn't take everything so serious and develop anal papules whenever a plan didn't go exactly as expected like his old friend Mad Dog. I was already sold on making a few changes to the business model mapped out at the Chinese place on Broadway just yesterday. I wasn't sure how we'd handle the Russian blowback, once the rest of the mob found out what we'd done. I suppose Thomas had a plan for that too.

I just had one question before negotiations began.

"Who do these two cars belong to?" I asked Thomas, pointing at the luxury vehicles parked to the right of the van our mini-militia had used to save us from the clutches of Communist aggression.

"The Humvee's mine," the quietest of Thomas' crew spoke. He was skinny and pale and didn't appear cut out for military fieldwork. In fact, he looked more like those street junkies I used to call my friends. I'd seen little of him during the Chicago incident, so I assumed he was a sniper, maybe even the one who helped take out Lex's men from the roof of the parking garage. He must've driven himself because he hadn't been in the van. He relinquished his name faintly and I'd hear later that Jason Durham had been on more tours of duty than any of Thomas's other recruits. He was, in fact, the most dangerous addition to the team, a calculated stoic who betrayed neither fear nor hunger, the best shot, and the fastest draw.

"I stopped and switched out the plates at a rest stop between Chicago and here. It's what we're taking home while Thomas torches the van and heads back to Loserville to enjoy a little R and R with some sorority chick he met online," Durham explained.

Bilotta slapped Thomas on the back, a *you old dog* gesture between brothers.

"The other car," Thomas touched the hood of the Caddie, "I'll let the owner brag on it himself." Thomas cupped his hands around his mouth and shouted, "The coast is clear, comrade."

One of the warehouse doors rose slowly and with the rusty grinding of gears that sounded like they hadn't been spun since the town had gone dystopian. Once the door had lifted halfway, three men exited, the younger two adhering to the Russian dress code of black leather and hair gel liberally applied.

I leaned down from where I sat on the loading dock and furtively transferred the revolver from my ankle holster to my coat pocket.

"Calm down." Snyder had seen me readying my gun.

I really couldn't stop looking at her. When she placed a hand on my shoulder for assurance, my anxiety only worsened.

"These men are here to thank you, not to punish," Thomas said.

"THOMAS!" The shortest of the three, the elder, was as emaciated as a broken survivor of a third-world death camp. His hair was shoulder length and white as pure cocaine. He hobbled down off the loading dock and drew Thomas close to briefly kiss the mercenary's stubbly cheeks.

The skinny Russian was Joseph Barinov, perhaps the most famous Eastern European criminal to reside in North America, the Pakhan—Russian Godfather—who had begun his hostile takeover in New York City five years earlier.

Some clever crime reporter up north had fittingly applied the byname "The Butcher of Brighton Beach."

His involvement in today's coup made perfect sense. The man thrived off dissent among the ranks of smaller branches of his felonious family tree. He came and stood before me and Mad Dog, where we'd drew close by the van at the sight of more Russians. "These must be the Americans that helped us finally get rid of that cocksucker Alexis." He slapped both our cheeks affectionately. "Boys, I never wish to put down a fellow countryman. At first, I was glad to see Lex man helm. Then profits diminish. Alexis forget that he only brigadier."

"Brigadier?" I asked.

"You in habit of interrupting powerful men?" The Bucher of Brighton snapped.

"I'm sorry," I said, "Pakhan, sir." I'd learned enough about the Russian mob to know how to refer to their highest leader with respect.

"Lex was never boss. Lex never Pakhan. Is that how he ask you address him?"

I nodded regretfully and apologized again.

"He was brigadier. Underboss. Nothing more. Son-of-bitch. I allow him to take over Chicago because I wanted to replace that retarded fat fuck you helped kill. I let Lex take over Windy City and he goes round telling people he Pakhan. He nothing more than brigadier."

"Middle management," I muttered.

"Yes," Barinov said. "That's the American term. That's what we call underboss in Brighton. Brigadier. I Pakhan. I only Pakhan."

"My mistake," I said.

"Pakhan," he repeated.

More like jack-off, I thought but said nothing.

"Lex say unexpected expenditures," said the Butcher. "Cops and politicians on our payrolls getting greedy. He even blamed Luther for wanting a larger piece of the pie."

"Now, Joseph, you know how you told me you liked having good news delivered fast?" Thomas asked the frail gangster.

"And bad news quicker," Joseph agreed then took a cue from the killer and hurried his delivery. "I am running things in the Windy City from this day forth. I relocate. I have people in New York I trust—or should I say, they know what I will do if they fuck me. So, I move from Big Apple to Windy City. And you—" he ran his index finger along the line of us standing before him, Thomas, his militia, the two confused Kentuckians, "—are going to keep me fat off that Afghan heroin. It's the only way to undercut cartel prices and still push best quality product."

"You're telling me in three days you pulled all this off?" Mad Dog asked Thomas.

Thomas shook his head with a sheepish grin. "The siege on Lex. I'll take credit for that being a hastily planned operation. And I did track down Joseph after we unloaded our shipment to your crew."

"I almost shot the bastard on sight." For a cold-blooded Russian who would casually authorize the deaths of half-a-dozen of his former co-workers, Joseph Barinov smiled an alarming amount. "This G.I. Joe looking bastard flies to New York, takes the train to Yonkers, walks into my uncle's café off McMicken Street, and comes right up to my table, sits down and tells me he understands I'm none too happy with Alexis." Joseph, talking too loud, had to take a moment to catch his breath. Then he pointed at Donalds who returned the Russian a nod and a friendly smile. "Then I saw this sheep-fucker who used to tail me everywhere I went when I ran my crew in Boston. He tailed me, that is, until I put him on my payroll. Then he just started making shit up to boss while I live my life as I pleased."

"I figure this is America," Donalds said. "Last thing this poor immigrant needs is more oppression from the government."

"I see what's happening here." I looked at Thomas, the perfect specimen of American manhood; I trusted the proud patriot as much as a vampire offering a blowjob. "And I'm fairly impressed. You went to the Russians and offered them an alternative to Lex and his network. You've set it up so the whole operation, the export, the import, the re-supply, the pick-ups, we're responsible for all of it. What about the people Lex was buying from? How happy are they gonna be when you start dealing strictly in this Afghan H?"

"The Greeks?" Barinov grinned. "You know what we were paying them? Just to smuggle in a few kilos of shitty dope that they stepped on further. I talked to Lex's numbers man. Our arrangement with the Greeks is finished. As a matter of fact—" Barinov glanced at his golden Rolex, "—Chicago Greeks out of business now."

I was briefly silenced by a mental montage much like that which Lex had in mind for me and mine. Snapshots flashed across the black screen of my inner eyelids, throat slitting, poisonings, machine gun attacks, car bombings. And there'd be men and women bound and gagged, husbands and wives, lovers forced to their knees so their killers could stand behind their quarry and make them wait in the worst kind of anticipation on this earth, for that sharp crack and the big darkness that would follow. The most violent day in recent Chicago history. I just hope Barinov had left the children of his competitors out of his master-plan.

"So, we're your sole suppliers now?" Panic set in like a flu-season fever once I realized that standing before me was, hands down, the most ruthless business partner with whom I'd ever considered making deal. "You severed your other ties without even consulting us?"

Barinov cleared his throat and smirked sourly. Not a fan of the word "no," I gathered. "I did not anticipate such resistance and ingratitude, Mr. Catlett."

"You mean us doing all the work and you taking a huge cut?"

"It's not that simple." Thomas tried to mediate. "Joseph will connect us with well-paid, high-ranking police in every city that will help prevent the interception of your deliveries by DEA or local city narcotics bureaus. And from Memphis to Meridian, his customers are now yours. You communicate with them. You handle details. Is this not worth a percentage?

"I continue to manage distribution in Chicago and its suburbs," Barinov said. "It's tradition, the king run his own kingdom. But south of Cincinnati, you are hereby in charge, Mr. Catlett."

"That's a fair deal if I've ever heard one," I told the Butcher. "I bet we get what, three percent of the profits and hourly pay commensurate to that of janitors."

Thomas guffawed. "You think I'd engineer a deal like that? You think I'd mount a siege on one of the largest cities in America for pennies?"

"I wasn't talking to you," I said to Thomas, my gaze

still fixed on the Butcher. "I'm the one who'll be taking the risk."

"We," Thomas said. "I think you meant to say, 'We.'"

I looked at Mad Dog and nodded toward Thomas. "Who's the language Nazi now?" Then I turned back to Thomas. "I meant me and my crew will be putting our asses on the line."

"You meant," Thomas said, "that since you'll be pushing the dope I bring in, we are joining forces, Catlett. We're sharing a life raft now, get it?"

"Says fucking who?" I asked.

Mad Dog mouthed the words *Shut up*. I pretended not to notice. "We're taking the lion's share of the risk. I want to know how the profit will be divided. That's the million dollar question, comrades and comradettes."

Snyder shook her head perplexedly, probably asking herself how I'd cultivated the cojones to stand up and speak so recklessly to a man like Barinov five minutes after meeting the savage. "And Thomas, you need to listen to me carefully," I said to the mercenary commander and gangster who still found time to moonlight as a police officer, "Dog and I have agreed to absolutely nothing, not yet. So, watch your tone when you're speaking to me. In fact, if you could avoid eye contact for the duration of our time together—" I indicated my eyes with my middle and index fingers then drew them together and pointed toward the overcast sky of industrial Indiana, "—could you avert your gaze, please. That'd be great for me, thanks."

Thomas didn't so much as twitch. Most men, especially the all-American alpha male types, would have at least squared up. This guy relished every word of my uncensored invective. This I considered more distressing than a swift kick to the testicles.

"What is our take?" I asked again. "If we agree."

"If you agree?" Joseph shrugged and gauged the two Louisville boys as if studying a pair of starving animals refusing their feeding. "As far as profits, I believe that supplier and distributor always take biggest piece of pie."

This even inspired Mad Dog to speak out of turn. "We'd take the biggest cut?" he asked.

"I never knew of any kind of organized crime operation, Russian or otherwise, to let the lackeys take the largest cut," I said.

"Lackeys?" The butcher laughed. "You think I'd call my best earners lackeys? I know what people call me, 'The Butcher.' And, perhaps, I've done a few things in my life that might have earned nickname. But you men will find, I'm fair and reasonable fellow. Think of how long it took me to decide to kill cocksucking Alexis."

"May we have a moment?" Mad Dog asked the Butcher.

"Of course," Barinov said demurely. "I told you. Fair and reasonable.

Milligan hurriedly nudged me away from the Pakhan and Thomas and the Mercenaries who'd all aligned in a unified front before the loading bay. We faced the rail yards to our north and Mad Dog whispered, "Jon, just because you've been in a few shootouts and got to talk tough to some black kids in the West End don't make you John Gotti. You still got a lot to learn about organized crime economics. For heroin, yes, we will be taking the biggest cut of the pie. I've heard of it done with other crews and it's not unheard of. Happy worker bees hustle harder and Barinov is smart enough to see that. With the kind of money we made Lex and Luther, the Pakhan knows it's best to keep us satisfied. He'd rather have a constant cut than kill us and have to create his own sources and distribution networks. See, the Butcher has his hands in every black market known to man. He even owns some considerably profitable legitimate business concerns. I been around a while and I know enough to assure you, you pig-headed little shit, that he most certainly would tell us if he planned to keep most of money. He's the Butcher of Brighton for Christ's sake. He doesn't need to lie. He'd just tell us to accept his terms or make peace with our creator. He will not mind allowing those with their asses on the line the biggest cut. He's going to be making a fortune just through his connections and by not murdering us and everyone we love. He knows he's getting his cut, basically, for a series of phone calls and some regular follow-ups with his paid-off cop contacts. Unlike Lex, he won't even have to spend a fortune on the product, not as cheap as Thomas gets it for in the Middle East. Barinov is taking less of a percentage, yes. But he knows we'll be making more money and he'll have less work to do. Lex's profits will pale in comparison to Joseph's percentage, as long that Afghan H keeps flowing."

He made sense. I'd been blinded by panic and fear and resentment over Thomas making so many decisions with-out consulting me or Mad Dog. The man *had* seized his opportunity at the cost of my fragile intellectual pride and several lives.

"It's a good deal, isn't it?" I finally agreed.

"Yes, you fucking dunce."

"I'm sorry."

"Just shut up and let's try to not piss the man off anymore."

We shifted our heels back toward Barinov and company.

"Perhaps we can reach an amicable arrangement," I said.

"Wonderful." Barinov graced us with a patronizing golfer clap.

"When's the next batch arriving?" Mad Dog asked Thomas.

11

Since Mad Dog's rental had been burned to bare cinder—
he complained bitterly of the deductible he'd have to pay
under his assumed identity—Thomas ordered two of his
"best people" to escort us back to Kentucky.

Bilotta stopped on 75 for gas, food, and lodging. The
hour had grown late and as I'd been set on a hotel experience, Mad Dog finally agreed that we could pull off, wash
up, burn our criminally soiled clothes in some hobo jungle's fire pit, and rest a few hours to restore our sanity
before we completed our journey south.

I'd nearly fallen asleep on the queen mattress, the cover
layered in the dried and cracked evidence of ten thousand
lascivious couplings between partners chained to loveless
marriages or affairs in varying stages of commitment and
decay. Hank Williams sang "Lovesick Blues" on a radio
channel that I didn't altogether despise.

The doorbell rang an annoying chime that sounded
eerily similar to the theme of *The Andy Griffith Show*. The
half-dead steel town we'd chosen for our furlough was no
Mayberry and the jingle came off as freakish as a lullaby
sung in a funeral parlor.

The door flung open. I'd passed out forgetting the lock
and bolt.

Snyder entered. She wore a leather jacket over a short red dress and Doc Marten shit kickers. She appeared less than amused and, to my great relief, unarmed. She let her shoulders slump and the jacket fell to the carpet. She staggered as she stepped toward the mattress. I could smell the whiskey piercing her pores from across the room.

It looked like *someone* had stopped by the Turtle Inn Bar and Grill across the thoroughfare from our motel to enjoy a few libations.

"One," she stood at the foot of the bed and extended an index finger, "why would anyone in your line of work leave their door unlocked? And two, don't ever look at me like you did in Gary."

"Then make it easier on the men folk," I said, "and go get a breast reduction surgery and splash some acid on that beautiful face. Otherwise, I'm gonna look and so is every other swinging dick that crosses paths with you. Now, if you don't mind, I was planning on masturbating. I don't get a lot of opportunities these days and this place has pay-per-view porn. If you'd be so kind as to put your coat back on and get the hell out of my room. I've been avoiding your gaze for hours and I'm tired of having to fight a hard on. It's been a while." I rolled over on my side.

"I heard your ex died a few weeks ago."

"We hadn't made love in months." I didn't bring up Amara. "And that's the longest I've gone without pussy since high school. So, for me, it's been a while."

"Pussy?" she laughed. "Hell of a way to talk in front of a lady."

"The lady that stabs naked men to death in hotel showers."

"Good thing for you, you already bathed."

"I was actually having a pleasant dream when you burst in. The first time I've slept without nightmares in a month."

"I'll alert Dr. Phil."

"While you're at it, give him the four-one-one on your daddy issues. Maybe he can help you wade through 'em and save a few lives."

Drunk or not, the woman was fast as a Jack Russell treeing a squirrel. Before I knew she'd taken a single step, Snyder had pulled me from the bed by my hair, stood me upright as if I weighed no more than an inflatable doll, and braced me against the closet door.

"Do you realize how lucky you are to be alive?" she asked.

"Lucky?" I laughed. "Yeah, now I get to deal with more assholes like you until the next firefight when maybe the Good Lord will finally bless me with a quick death. It'd be a merciful ending to a life of incessant trauma and obscurity."

She stepped back and examined me like a coroner would a dead man at an autopsy. "I'm so used to macho douche bags, most of whom, by the way, are scared of me, and for good goddamn reason. I'm at a loss when a man is at all in touch with his emotions. And I have to admit, you wear that well."

"You like that song."

"I worship early Rod Stewart."

"Finally, we share a few sentences that don't involve threats or merciless character assassination. We've made a real breakthrough here...You know, I'm sorry, but I don't even know your first name."

"Jonette."

"You're shitting me. Jon and Jonette."

"Shut up."

I couldn't believe it. The tough girl could blush.

"Come on?" I laughed. "Don't you love alliteration? We're a sit-com waiting to be made."

"Or a tabloid murder/suicide story."

"Same difference."

I was now making no attempt to hide my leering. And, this time, she didn't seem offended. She even arched her back and stuck out her rump, which, with its perfect plumpness, gave her bust a run for its money.

"I suppose," she said, "that I'm also not accustomed to someone fearlessly back sassing me. Or unapologetically eye-fucking me like I was some coked-up whore who worked at Hooters and had a Dirty South tattoo above her navel."

"In my defense, the hooker thing...that was not the sentiment I meant to convey."

"The Dirty South tattoo could also be stitched into the small of her back." Her drunkenness was showing again. She was getting sillier. "I didn't think of that. That would intimate anal, obviously. Either way, I'm not used to men looking at me *that way*."

"Looking at you like you're *not* a murderous lesbian."

"I wouldn't choose those exact words, but yes."

"Like you aren't the biggest Liz Phair fan ever to purchase a double-headed vibrator."

I stepped out closer. Even though she'd sweated out

some booze, I could tell she'd showered and thrown on some kind of perfume designed to leave a man light-headed and vulnerable. It wasn't necessary. "Let's not get all emo here, okay, kitten?"

She pimp-slapped me twice then pulled me to her by the scruff of my neck.

"That's more like it," I said.

She whispered my name.

"Oh, Jonette." Our lips finally met.

"I can't believe this...I hate my name." She took over the kiss, long and wet and breathless. "But I like the way you say it."

She strengthened her grip, nearly choking me out, then, with her free hand, reached inside my unbuttoned jeans and began extending and retracting. "Good God." She looked down at what she'd done. "You really aren't gay, are you?"

"What?" I nearly went flaccid with embarrassment.

"Me and the guys had a bet." Then, before I could ask more questions or declare any righteous indignation, she pulled me toward the bed by my prick as she sat on the side of the mattress, licking her lips like a famished cannibal.

12

Our drug front on wheels would from henceforth be referred to as The Bookmobile, a christening that had the originality of a new age Christian bumper sticker. Despite these reservations, I voted for the name, as I understand that Americans trend toward the most simplistic and obvious.

"It sounds a little like Meals on Wheels," Paul said.

"It's boring," I said. "Clunky and boring."

"Who cares?" Mad Dog asked from where he sat on the sill, his back to the display window.

The store was closed for, as the sandwich board read, *Renovations*, and Dog had, quicker than I could've predicted, somehow sufficiently calmed Paul's nerves after he'd learned about Chicago. At least we hadn't had to call the EMTs to address a heart attack on store property. But I knew I'd yet to hear the last of it from my former manager. Before I retired to the office to try and get some sleep, I counted on a predictably dramatic morality lecture. The head case wouldn't move on from it until he'd spread his panic like an airborne STD. He'd allowed us to move on with business, but I figured only because he feared our narco bureau partner enough to shut up when told sternly.

"Besides," Dog continued, "we want it to sound boring

135

and sterile. We don't want a city cop, a sheriff, or a state trooper looking twice at this thing for any reason."

"It sounds like Batmobile," Paul said. "Bookmobile. Batmobile. People love that Batman bullshit. That could work in our favor. Except our Bookmobile will be used to perpetuate crimes, not prevent or avenge them. I never did understand the appeal of a rich kid beating up poor people. That's basically the plot of Batman. Rich little shit ignores civil rights and clobbers anyone who dares to break the law to climb out of poverty. The son-of-a-dead-rich-bitch is a glorified fascist. I'm sorry, Bruce Wayne, but none of us at Twice Told Books had filthy rich daddies and people like you don't read, so our penniless customer base has forced us to come up with some goddamn hustle just to keep the lights turned on. Call Alfred and come on after us, mother-fucker."

Paul had his moments.

"My father watched that stupid Adam West Batman show when I was growing up," I said. "Did you see the outfits they wore? Especially Robin. Green briefs. That's it. He looks like a male stripper with an untreated mental illness. And my dad watched every re-run. For an alleged alpha male, that old asshole sure did love the most homo-erotic program on television at the time."

"Do I look like your fuckin' therapist?" Mad Dog said. "Do I care about your gay dad? No."

"My dad was not gay." My face went red. "My father got more pussy than a rapper with a reputation for domes-tic violence."

"My son's gay," Mad Dog said. "Is there something wrong with that?"

"Your son's gay?" Paul asked.

If I'm being honest, I was just as shocked.

"So?" Mad Dog eyed Paul grimly.

"Is he adopted?" Paul asked.

"No, he's not adopted. Are you purposely trying to antagonize me here?

"No," Paul said. "It's just—"

"You've actually had sex before, Milligan?" I said. "That's the part I'm most shocked about."

"I'm giving you both one chance to help one another refocus." Mad Dog tapped the butt of the gun he'd chosen for the day from his vast arsenal, a Walther PPK hanging from a shoulder rig beneath his Western suit coat.

"Back to the Batmobile, then," Paul said. "So, we've decided on a name. It's final? Going once. Going twice. And we never bring up Mad Dog's gay son again." He pounded the desk, his gavel the Ross MacDonald paperback he'd been reading when we arrived.

"Where are we on Bookmobile Two?" I asked. "We're not going to be able to keep our delivery schedule with one vehicle. Not after the game changer that me and Dog just survived."

"One of Myron's corner boys knows a guy works third shift at Ford," Paul said. "The guy is hooked bad and needs cash ASAP. They're gonna meet, along with the artist Myron knows, tomorrow early at the seller's house near Shelby Park. If it's drivable and they come to a decent agreement on price, Myron's Van Gogh will do the labeling right in the owner's driveway."

Paul started pacing now, lighting a cigarette and cursing to himself. He always submitted to debilitating anxiety whenever he attempted to repress anything.

"Just let it out already," Mad Dog said to Paul. "You're scared. We're in the big leagues now. Why's that a problem? These Russians have half the police in the Midwest on their payroll. We've bought ourselves immunity from prosecution by throwing in with Barinov."

"You mean the guy people call Butcher," Paul said. "Yeah. Just his name alone makes me feel all warm and safe inside. That's not to mention the black ops killer who got us in bed with the Brighton Beach terror."

"And if anyone can help us survive this game, it's Chad Thomas," Milligan said. "He's one of the most fearless and loyal men I've ever worked with. He's also smarter than he looks. You boys have been working with me long enough to know I try to stay a few moves ahead on the chessboard. Thomas has already won the tournament and he's plotting his strategy for the next game." Mad Dog looked at me. "You saw what he pulled off in Chicago."

"And we all saw what you and Luther pulled off in Cincinnati," Paul said to Milligan, "when our former employer decided it was cheaper to cut out the middle man and kill Jon's old connect so that we'd have a direct line to Chicago. We turned Over-the-Rhine into Bagdad."

"And now we have Chicago endorsing us," I said, "not some gangbanger taxing the shit out of us every time we want to re-up. You seem to forget that, Paul."

"You seem to forget that," Paul said, "after all the blood we shed for that bastard, Luther was going to kill us just as a precaution against the possibility of future betrayal."

"Thomas ain't Luther." Mad Dog said. "Luther was

insane, out of control. He had periods of clarity and brilliant business sense, but he'd get so neurotic so often that I almost quit him more times than I can recall. The only thing that kept me around was the money. Why do you think I jumped at the opportunity to bring you two assholes into the fold? You might be a couple of goofy fucks, but you don't go on kill crazy rampages for no reason. I hate to say it, but I had kind of hoped from the beginning that it would all end with us still moving weight and Luther either dead or retired to South America."

"Oh, he retired alright," Paul said. "My concern is this: are we going to have to, one day in the near future, offer this Thomas character the same retirement plan?"

"Thomas is more solid than most honest cops. He served the military and headed top secret security details for Blackwater. Well, they called them 'security details.' More likely, he coordinated assassinations our government didn't wish to officially authorize. I know this: he and Snyder and Bilotta got their hands pretty goddamn dirty working the private sector. None of them will talk about it, as they shouldn't. Thomas also served two major metropolitan police departments before relocating to the River City, and he's been screwing the system the entire time in one form or another, either smuggling Marijuana from his first tour in Afghanistan or running every gang in Cincinnati. When he was Lieutenant of an infamous elite narcotics unit in that city, the murder rate was cut in half for two whole years. You know why? He had an understanding with the main players. No bodies—at least no bodies discovered. No taxpayers get hurt. And you only deal in the abandoned districts Thomas designated. And, of course, Thomas got a cut. He allowed the gangs a few blocks of condemned walk-ups the city had unofficially disclaimed. He pulled this off for two years until the day some weak-kneed patrolman ratted, probably in hopes of a promotion. The constant collusion and shifting loyalties and daily betrayals of the street ain't nothing compared to what goes on within a big city police department. Luckily, there wasn't a lot of evidence that Lieutenant Thomas had made any deal with the Cincinnati kingpins. Only a few sergeants knew the details. Patrolmen were told simply to avoid certain streets because of orders from on high. Thomas' response to the accusation was, 'Why was my officer somewhere I told him not to be?' Then he shut his mouth and lawyered up while IAD spun their wheels trying to find a witness willing to testify or wear a wire on the lieutenant. While it was mainly rumor and conjecture, the experiment was over. The chief started patrolling the areas where the alleged free zones had been set up and within months the violence began again. They dropped the investigation but knocked Thomas down to sergeant. He only stayed on another year before taking on another tour in the desert then signing on with the LMPD. Thomas used to run the gang squad here in town. The only unit in the department that accomplished a goddamn thing, if you ask me."

"Yeah." I remembered what should've been a front-page scandal a few years back that reaped only a paragraph on the third page of the Metro section. I always followed city government cluster-fucks. They only reinforced my inherent distrust in our system and its engineers, Godless, spineless politicians and the upper one percent they so faithfully served.

I hated all of them. I would trust a trembling junkie seven days a week before I believed one word that came out of the mayor's mouth.

"The mayor—" I began.

"Former mayor," Mad Dog interrupted me.

"Whatever. They're interchangeable. Anyway, the ever-incompetent Mayor Abramson and the chief of police held a press conference and claimed that the gang squad was unnecessary."

"Because after all," Mad Dog winked, "Louisville has no gang problem."

"Then that reporter wrote that cover story for *Kentucky Weekly*," Paul said. Politics always brought Paul and I back to common ground. We both believed an armed uprising in our country was long overdue. "He cited statistics that ranked us in the top ten cities plagued by gang violence."

"I'd call that a gang problem," I said.

"So, would the taxpayers of Possibility City," Mad Dog said, citing the town's nickname the old mayor and his marketing advisors had conjured up. "It's a miracle that story made it to the front page of any local periodical. Google that reporter. He writes in Bumfuck, Indiana, now. You know why? *Kentucky Weekly* is owned by Senator John Yardale who is also buxom buddies with our mayor."

The incestuous splendor of Kentucky politics never ceased to amaze me.

"You can ruin yourself quick in this town," I said. "Makes me kind of proud to be in this business."

"At least we're not responsible for institutional neglect that has resulted in the deaths of countless innocents."

"The gang squad made a difference," Mad Dog said. "Believe it or not. They tried to intervene before kids were too deep in the dope game to escape. They coordinated with social workers and halfway houses and community organizers. But they were bad press for the city. And at the time, Fourth Street Live was opening downtown. The mayor and the investors couldn't have the Hard Rock Café or Coyote Ugly pulling out and leaving that stretch of commercial property empty. It could have bankrupted every big wig in the city."

"So, Thomas lost his unit because the city fathers were scared they'd lose their investment?"

"What about blowback?" I asked. "What happened when the CEOs of places like Hard Rock found out?"

"Found out what?" Milligan said. "The violence is contained. West of Roy Wilkens. The moment some massive shooting occurs close to the big business districts, you'll see a flurry of press releases and task forces organizing."

"No wonder Thomas turned to dope dealing," Paul said.

"I bet that reporter got a hundred fan letters from Louisville cops. Because we all knew the fix. The KFC stadium was being built." Mad Dog referred to the YUM Center, a giant fax-machine of a sports coliseum, that welcomed tourists coming in from the Second Street Bridge. "The last thing anyone wants to hear about a possible franchise location is that there's a bunch of black kids running around downtown every night playing tag with sub-machine guns. No one cares if a bunch of ghetto kids blow each other away, not even if it's by the hundreds. As long as it doesn't affect business."

"We can all relate to that," I said.

"The chief of police, the mayor, they're no different than us."

"They might be worse, Milligan," I said. "We admit, at least to ourselves, that we're criminals."

"We're in the wrong business." Paul forced another breathy series of stifled giggles. He sounded like Woody the Woodpecker when he discovered something truly hilarious. I found the laugh endearing, but it unnerved most customers and betrayed the old punk's numerous neurotic disorders. I'd encouraged the weirdo to seek professional help, but like a good paranoiac, he nurtured a blind and imperishable distrust for physicians.

"Maybe after we make a few million," Paul said, "we could enter politics." He outstretched his hands, forming Ls with his thumbs and forefingers to frame an invisible billboard. "Jon Catlett for mayor. Vote Paul Frank, city council."

"You're getting all the political practice you need," Mad Dog said. "But count me out. I prefer to make my money honestly."

13

Paul had asked for a moment with me as Mad Dog threw on his blazer and made his exit.

"Before you even start in on me," I told Paul after the door shut, "I'm gonna keep crashing here at the store." I drew an invisible line on the ground between us with my hand flat. "That's non-negotiable. You never even use the office."

"You've been crashing here for a week. May as well get comfortable. I mean why move into a new place when you probably won't be alive long enough to enjoy it."

"My sentiments exactly," I said. "Could you tell me, please, how exactly the smart TV thing works? I understand that one of the controllers is for the cable and the other is for Netflix and Amazon, but what I don't get is—"

Paul interrupted me, shouting, "You and Mad Dog McNutjob, once again, left a bloodbath in Chicago. Do you even *know* how many people you killed today?"

"I suppose you'd rather it had been us that died?" I said. "Or you. If Thomas hadn't been so vigilant, those two hitters at the Ramada would have come for you. And wasn't Adam with you yesterday?"

Mention of his son robbed him of his indignance and the crimson faded from his sallow cheeks. He said, in a tremolo, "Come on, man. I just think…"

"Where's my dog?" I asked.

"Mad Dog just left."

"Not Mad Dog. *My* dog."

"What?"

"My dog. The light of my life. That beautiful little furry bundle of fucking joy I brought back from Eastern Kentucky."

"She's at the vet. She had an appointment. Your erstwhile roommates back east had neglected to de-worm her or keep her vaccinations updated. You can pick her up tomorrow."

Thank God. I thought for a moment Paul might had sold her to a Chinese restaurant. Then I'd have to kill him and I'd be out one of the only two friends I had left in the world.

"I'm sorry," I said.

"So, I guess that ends our little discussion over the body count we're remounting." Paul resumed his seat at the store laptop and cleared his throat a few times, signaling me to apologize as soon as possible and to thank the misunderstood literary martyr for his altruism and dignity.

"Thanks for taking care of Irina." I really should have reconsidered the dog's name. But the little beauty had begun to answer to it and I didn't feel like confusing the poor thing.

"Speaking of your copious dead," Paul said, "again, how many people do you think you two killed today?"

"Is she okay?" Another attempt to avoid the subject of mass-murder. My dad always told me, "Son, if you're not cheating, you're not trying."

"She's doing better than the females who came before." Paul couldn't eschew such revilement for long. He remained focused on some coed crossing Highland Avenue, staring at her from behind our window like a post-punk Boo Radley. "You're never gonna learn," he said, heavy on the solemnity.

I finally admitted, "I try not to count my dead. I don't see the point."

"I think that's part of the problem, Jon."

I smiled. "I get what you're doing there." I pinched Paul's ear. "You're adorable."

Paul backed away, cocking his head over his shoulder as if straightening a crick in his neck.

"Oh, goddamn." He put his hands on his hips like a dissatisfied housewife and shook his head hysterically. "Goddamn. Your sense of humor is going to be the end of us all. We were talking about Batman. Well, the goddamn Joker has nothing on a sociopath like you."

"That's a little much, don't you think? I mean he blew up hospitals and shit, although to come to think of it, that does sound like a real fun Thursday night."

Paul squinted at me as if studying a rabid animal in a cage. "You don't remember the old man in front of the bar we blew up in Chicago last year? He had a dog too."

"Why do you have to bring that up?" I yelled, then pointed, as Paul had, to the walls around us, reminding him that the bookstore might be wired, the same possibility I'd discredited earlier when it didn't suit me. "Plus, that was an accident."

"Accident or not," Paul said, "the result was the same. Dead innocents. And concerning..." He indicated the invisible and likely fictional wires hidden somewhere in our store. "Mad Dog swept the place today just like I sweep it every morning."

"So now you trust him."

"Same as trusting you."

"What did I fucking do?"

"What about today? Do you know how many lives you ended today? That'd be a start at least."

"Two. I killed two people today. Fuck. Same as Milligan" I bit my tongue. "I hope this place isn't wired. I don't think we've hit the radar that hard yet, do you?"

"You kill two human beings and think it's a joke." At least he was whispering now.

"I didn't see your tear ducts turn Niagara when you shot-gunned that West End gang-banger by the banks of the Ohio," I whispered back.

I hoped *he* wasn't wearing a wire.

"What's your point? Just because I'm a killer doesn't mean I can't be ashamed of my actions, and terrified of yours."

"Some people, they just need to go."

"I am very, very concerned about your attitude." Paul drew the curtains, closing time duties. "And while, no, I don't believe we're on anyone's radar or enough of a concern to the DEA or LMPD for any judge to authorize a wiretap, our names are associated with a mass murder out in the boonies, two dead women, and a drive-by in the middle of a quiet suburb. So, I don't think now is the best time for you, Mad Dog, and his maniacal black-ops buddies to coordinate a siege on a four-star hotel in a major metropolitan area, killing Lex, who, if he hasn't already, will soon be associated with Luther Longmire."

"So?" I shrugged.

"So?" Paul repeated.

"Is there an echo in here?"

Paul launched forward and grabbed the lapels of my coat. "I don't want to go to prison."

"No one's going to prison."

"And we're too deep in this thing to quit." Paul took a deep breath. I could see it, his eyes refocusing on the big picture, the money and his son's future, neither of us having to live hand to mouth ever again. "I just wish there'd been a discussion. And we don't know these people. Thomas and his band of killers."

"We didn't know Luther."

"And look how that turned out."

"I don't believe in much, Paul. However, I'm fairly convinced that it's nothing short of a miracle that we're both still alive. Can you trust that at least?"

We would meet the next morning, Thomas and the Twice Told crew, to look at the possible locations Myron had found for our West End store.

Paul stumbled down Highland Avenue on his bedraggled walk to Irish Hill where, despite the hundreds of thousands of dollars he'd earned over the last six months, he maintained a humble studio apartment.

I retired upstairs and disrobed, eager to begin my battle with insomnia in hopes of a few merciful hours of unconsciousness.

The sun had set beyond the gabled rooftop and I was almost asleep when the doorbell downstairs jingled and I looked out the bow window onto the street below.

Scott Morgan stood before his state police cruiser waving a half-pint of Kentucky Gentleman and cursing at me to open up.

Alcohol had robbed me of sleep again and I didn't even drink.

He looked like a J. Crew model past his prime but who had not robbed himself of the arrogant charm and beguiling wizardry he'd practiced when we were younger that had wooed him many a dissatisfied housewife. In a lot of ways, Morgan resembled Chad Thomas, the Roman profile and high chiseled cheekbones. Unlike Thomas, he smiled little. And he hadn't shaved his head like half the storm troopers that patrolled the Louisville alleys and back streets, allowing instead his flaxen hair to grow into a nest of unwieldy curls.

His ring finger was now bare.

I'd been right. Linda had left him.

"I warned you not to film your extra-marital affairs with your cell phone," I said. He'd dragged me out to The Phoenix Inn around the corner from my shop. The bar had been a Bardstown Road staple for two decades and had showcased the best Louisville punk rock bands in their prime opening for acts like Fugazi and The Red Hot Chili Peppers before they were famous. From our table near the back, I spotted three low-level heroin dealers doing business out in the open. All of them probably peddled the Taliban and didn't even know who imported it.

"This place is gonna get fuckin' raided soon." Scott ignored what I'd said about his infidelities and scanned the poolroom and its pin-eyed fawners. He kept reaching beneath his parka, pretending to scratch his lower back, but I knew he was really massaging the grip of his off-duty piece, itching to "nail one of these scumbags" as he'd said earlier. He could drink. He could pop Percocets. He could cheat on his wife and talk bad to all of his friends. But let some Bardstown Road skell try the pettiest of drug deals and God have mercy on the little bastard's soul.

He enjoyed judging the junkies for a few more moments then turned his attention back to the one who'd been his best friend for a decade once upon some forgotten adolescence.

"You usin'?" He finished his bourbon straight and switched it out for the bottle of Miller he'd been waiting to sip on. "You don't look like you're using but, you know, I gotta ask."

"I haven't in a long, long time."

"What's a long, long time?"

"A year," I lied. It had been a few months. Longer than I'd been able to put together since I first got strung out.

"You aren't using, yet your junkie girlfriend gets shot by a drug lord who died in a massacre last month out in the county."

I knew if he hadn't known when he first reached out, he'd have probably found out by the time he came calling. I'd prepared.

"Is that any of your business?"

"I'm a police officer and my best friend—"

"Your best friend who you disowned half a decade ago."

"My best friend..." His brow lost its deep ruts when he

met eyes with me and, for the first time in five years, it felt like no bad blood had been shed between us. "My best friend is a recovering heroin addict. I mean, I *hope* you're recovering and not active and I'm trying to believe you, but your name gets brought up alongside murderers and heroin importers and I'm not supposed to do shit?"

"I didn't know it was a concern of yours," I said. Then I fed him the same story I'd concocted for Neil and Bob.

He stared at the bottom of the empty glass while he finished his beer. I couldn't tell if he bought it or not.

"You know you helped save my life," Scott said.

I could not have been taken further aback had he proposed marriage or confessed to pedophilia. Jesus.

"How's that?" I laughed.

"My brother..." Scott took another drink. "That coke-head degenerate who Mom and Dad always let run the roost but if I got caught smoking a cigarette...shit, man...the least I could expect was a good tossing down the basement steps."

He wasn't lying. I'd seen the bruises.

"It's like you had to walk all over my folks to keep them from doing you dirty."

And eventually, Scott did just that. Got himself thrown into a psych unit his freshman year of college. Became a true embarrassment, destroying himself just to hurt Daddy.

"You stood up to my brother when he was about to kill me in a drug-induced rage."

His brother had thrown him through the glass door onto the patio of their St. Matthews childhood home. Scott's ear had been half-severed from his head. I'd gone into his father's man cave basement, gotten a .45 automatic, and held it on the speed freak while Scott got to his feet and we made our escape. When we got to the hospital, Scott fabricated some story that did not involve family. "Then," he said, "in college, when I freaked out and flunked out, you took me in and cleaned me up when I didn't have a friend in the fucking world. And now, I'm praying, I mean, I'm fucking praying your only connection to Luther Longmire is some skirt. I can't believe that you'd be capable of pissing in the same latrine as a mass murderer."

I don't know how, but I concealed the shame that must've been growling from my stomach like an ulcerated intestine. "I'm clean." Then I mixed the truth with fiction, the best kind of lie. "I met Irina at an AA meeting. Didn't know she was that deep into the madness. Then I hired that cooze Amara." I added a new twist to the story Paul and I had ad-libbed. "I was sleeping with both of them. Then they hit it off. Started running with Jimmy—"

"Jimmy," Scott said. "Fuck." Jimmy and Scott had both lived in a rented house with me off Frankfort Avenue years ago, when we were all young and unsoiled by a dirty river of dope water and Kentucky bourbon. "I couldn't make it to the funeral." Scott hadn't even called when Jimmy died. We'd never spoken of it. "I wish I could've been around. I would have killed Longmire myself."

I took care of it for us, I thought.

"But it ain't your fault," Scott said. "We tried to straighten Jimmy up years ago."

"I know. I didn't go to the services either. His mother probably wishes I was being tortured at Guantanamo Bay."

"Why would she blame you?"

"She knows he was spending a lot of time at the store. The lady ain't stupid. If she even suspects I used dope, which I did for so long, she would blame me. Shit, I blame me."

"But you didn't have anything to do with the drug dealing. The killings. The venal sins these sick fucks committed daily."

"It was a big mess," I said. "But I was only tangentially involved. Like I said, all I did was sleep with the wrong women."

"Amen to that," Scott said.

"I guess if that's a capital crime, then I'll see your sorry-ass on death row, Morgan."

Scott changed the subject again. I wondered when we would ever get around to discussing his divorce. "Did you use with them?" Scott asked. "Tell me the truth."

I figured I'd give him this one. It'd make for a more convincing tale of woe.

"Yeah. And when I got clean again, they abandoned me."

He nodded like he'd figured as much.

"I'm gonna get another drink," Scott said. He stood and took a step toward the bar then stopped, looked down, and placed his hand on my shoulder.

"I miss Jimmy." Finally, I told the truth.

"Me too, Jon."

While he ordered another bourbon with a beer back, I finished my diet coke and went to take a piss.

When I entered the bathroom, I nearly gagged on the stench of vomit and urine. It'd been lifetime since I'd patronized The Phoenix. They only cleaned the toilets every leap year. A homeless black guy I always saw outside had sunken into the corner, slurring, "Change puhlease. Missur. Can you…"

I ignored him, stepped to the pisser, and unzipped.

I was almost done when Scott stumbled into the latrine, sat his drinks atop the paper towel dispenser and sidled up beside me. "I want to buy into the bookstore."

Oh shit, I thought.

"My career is going nowhere," Scott said as he groaned and made room in his bladder for another visit to the booze buffet. I washed my hands and tried to think of a way to talk him out of this very silly idea.

He complained again of his wife leaving him and the loss of his sergeant stripes and his reassignment to the Richmond barracks after the mishandling of a cartel case. Then the pan handler stepped beside him and began mumbling again, although now a bit more coherently.

"Mang," he said. "Buy me a drink, mang."

"*Fuck* off," Scott shouted. "Fuck directly off. I've got to deal with you monkeys nine hours a day. Not on my watch. Not on my off-time, cocksucker."

"Fuck you, mang. I know you can spare *one* drank."

Scott started yelling again and letting loose more fluidly with the racial epithets of which he'd grown so fond since becoming a cop.

Then he calmed down and began nodding like perhaps he was lightening up on the poor street urchin.

"What you got, mang?" the bum kept on. "Come on, come on, brother."

"I'm not your fucking brother." Scott drew his revolver from the small of his back and let it rest on the shelf above the urinal for the panhandler to see.

The bum looked at the gun, not too afraid, but convinced Scott was a dead end for a quick touch. "So...it's like that, eh?"

Scott zipped his fly with one hand and twirled the pistol. "Yeah. It's like that."

"Are you fucking serious?" Scott nearly stepped into traffic when I told him that buying into the business was a bad idea.

"Watch where you're walking," I said.

We passed The Athenian Grill, an upscale Greek restaurant that charged ten dollars for a gyro. I preferred the place a few doors down from the bookstore, Gyro Central. What it lacked in ambiance, the foul-mouth chef proprietor compensated for in price and culinary prowess.

"It's complicated, Scott."

I was beginning to explain why a career policeman might not want to buy into Twice Told Books without mentioning my association with the Russian mafia and corrupt city cops when Wiley Cobble in all his perspiring and corpulent effulgence ambled out of the Athenian Grill, blocking our path.

"Mr. Catlett." Wiley laughed. "Good to see you, fellow bookman."

His breath reeked of curry and lamb and he'd obviously been drinking a fair amount of craft beer.

"Cobble," I said. "I'm not in the mood—"

"Who is this asshole?" Scott asked, nodding toward the bespectacled tub of lard.

"Asshole?" Wiley stopped laughing and looked at Scott. "You can't talk to me like that."

"He *can't?*" I said. "Well, I guess my friend just violated some fundamental law of physics, because somehow he just did talk to you like that, dickspit. And I don't have time for you tonight, Wiley. In fact, from here on out, stay out of my bookstore and cross the street when you see me coming."

"Who do you think—"

He didn't finish his sentence. I punched him so hard in his stomach I could have sworn my knuckle bypassed all the fatty tissue and briefly nicked his spine.

He collapsed, his boxes of rice and lamb exploding across the sidewalk.

"I'll have you arrested," he wheezed.

Scott flashed his badge, bent to his haunches, and told the tubby literary fanatic, "The way I saw it, asshole, you drunkenly attacked a police officer and this concerned citizen intervened."

"Oh, shit," Wiley said.

"Shit's right, fat ass." I leaned next to Scott. "You keep my name out of your mouth unless you want more problems like this in your life."

"Let's go," Scott whispered.

"Nod that you understand," I said to Wiley.

Wiley nodded.

We'd just rounded the corner toward the store from Bardstown Road.

"You are one vicious bastard." Scott laughed. "You

didn't even tremble back there. You been fucking people up lately? Getting in a lot of barfights?"

"This is the first time I've been to a bar in over a year," I said. "I barely leave the store. I told you I've been living upstairs. All I do is go to meetings and sell books."

"You do look sober. But goddamn, I know cops who can't maintain that kind of cool when violence breaks out."

"The perks of clean living."

"Well, fuck that guy anyway, right? Who was he?"

"A competitor. Spreads bullshit about my business. Loves it when we're struggling."

"I doubt you'll be hearing from him again."

"If he's smart."

"Look, I wouldn't quit the department immediately," Scott said. "I'd wait until we were really turning a profit. I'd put in enough money to expand. I've been saving, man. I didn't lose much in the divorce. She just wanted free. Rich bitches, right? I got lucky I didn't marry a peasant. I'd be shelling out half my shit-pay. Instead I played it smart. I live cheap and I got my 401(k) I can draw from."

"Scott, stop," I said.

"Why can't I buy in? See what just happened? There's perks to having a cop in your pocket."

If you only knew, I thought. Images of a bloody-faced, Kevlar-clad Mad Dog Milligan danced across the neon skyline ahead.

"We hardly make enough profit to eat," I said. "And it's boring. We stock books. List books. And try to Jew down retirees and drug addicts so that we can make a few bucks. And Paul? My manager? Five minutes with him and you'd catch a murder case yourself. You'd hate him as much as you hated the work."

"Not any more than I hate ghetto crime and solving predictable homicides."

"You get to carry a gun."

"I can still do that."

Having an extra gunman would help a little, I thought. What I said was, "Scott. It's not for you."

"Look," Scott said. "I know I freaked out when I found out you were on junk."

"You came to my apartment and tossed a dude through a glass table."

"He was negatively influencing you! I—"

"I influence *me*, Scott."

"That's what I'm saying. I know I freaked. I know things have been shaky between us. But truth be told, I talk about you all the time. I tell all my fuckin' cop friends how smart my friend Jon is, how he's built his life from fuckin' nothing. I mean your parents may as well have shot you in the face. They gave you like *no* chance in life, man."

"Gee. Thanks?"

"I'm serious. I had more of a chance than you and look what little I've done with it."

I stopped in front of the store and made no move to unlock the door. I didn't want him coming in tonight. As much as I loved the degenerate, I needed a reprieve from drunks and madmen. It was three a.m. and I had less than four hours until I had to see Paul and Mad Dog and the rest of the fuckaround gang. "You're truly generous," I said of Scott's offer to hand me thirty thousand dollars, work alongside me to learn the trade, and consider himself a shareholder. "If you really are burning out, man, you might need that money to live on while you look for something else. That'd be the smarter bet."

"You make bank, man." Scott laughed. "With the on-line sales. I remember you told me how your mentor made a killing at the old store, buying books for fifty cents, sellin' 'em for a hundred, and that you were learning the con yourself. That was five years ago. You must have it mastered by now, right? Buy low, sell high, right?"

"There's a lot of overhead and wasted time."

"I need this. Jon, you've got it made. No bosses. No women except the ones you want for the evening, unless of course you fuck up and fall in love like you've done a few times. And you get to be around the boys. I bet you got a whole crew of savage social deviants who all worship you and call this place home."

They don't exactly worship me, I thought, but as far as the rest goes, you're not far off.

"Just think about it, man." Scott turned toward his cruiser. I would've told him not to drive but I'd known him long enough to predict the futility of attempted intervention. He turned and looked at me over the hood. "Jimmy would love it, man. He'd love it if we were partners again."

I couldn't believe it. Yesterday I watched half a dozen people meet their ends and didn't shed a single tear. Now, thanks to Scott Morgan and these precious memories he couldn't let die, my eyelids burned like knife wounds and I struggled to see through the buildup.

"Remember," Scott said. "You used to say that when you died, you'd have them carve the word *PALS* into your tombstone and me and Jimmy would know you were talking about us."

"I got that reading about Billy the Kid."

"I know."

"I'm sorry about Jimmy, Scott."

Scott nodded and rattled the keys on their chain. "Think about it, alright?"

"Pals," I said.

Then I turned around and let myself into the bookstore so my friend wouldn't see me sob.

14

Mad Dog stepped off the sidewalk, back pedaling for a broader view of the empty retail space in the West Broadway Mall. "We have a winner," he declared, clapping his hands together and beaming like a freshly laid high-school sophomore.

"Look at the size of those display windows," Paul said.

"It's perfect," said Thomas, who'd replaced his ski mask and cargo pants with torn jeans, Doc Martens, and a black Ramones T-shirt that featured a disproportionate and faded cartoon drawing of the band. Perhaps I'm shallow, but the shirt, and the mercenary cop's resemblance to so many militant and maniacal punk rockers of my generation worked to soften me a bit to our new heroin connect.

"This is it," Thomas said, as if his vote were the only one worth counting.

We all mumbled assents.

"My people will be thrilled," Thomas added.

I wanted to ask which people—the dope importers or his small army of relentless murderers.

"Why didn't you bring us here first?" Mad Dog said to Myron.

Despite a cacophony of protests, the narcotics sergeant had insisted on riding shotgun for our tour, the rest of us in

161

the spacey backseat of Myron's brand new Cadillac, Darth Vader black, boxy and angular. Paul rode bitch, of course, between me and Thomas. So far, Paul and Thomas hadn't spoken much, aside from Paul's brief but awkward introduction as we'd entered the car: "Great to finally put a face to the name." He'd shaken Thomas' hand with the superficial hero worship of a used car salesman shooting a commercial for a Fourth of July sale. "I just can't tell you how refreshing it is to finally have those commie bastards under *our* thumb for a change."

Thomas, to placate Paul, then forced the fakest grin I'd seen since George Bush had, upon leaving office, forced out a few kind words about his Nubian replacement, an informal tradition the vengeful Texan drunkard was forced to honor.

Myron's sense of geography and direction left much to be desired. The first place he took us had formerly served as a liquor store in Old Louisville, not the West End as we'd specified. Back before busing and white flight, Old Louisville had once been the neighborhood that all the commonwealth's movers and shakers aspired to call home. The red maples and Ohio Buckeyes formed a canopy over the streets. Tiny city parks beautified every block.

The district's days of Dixie gentility had now gone the way of the eight-track and LaserDisc, thanks to the construction and various expansions of the University of Louisville on the neighborhood's southern periphery. When blacks began moving in, students sharing apartments or the few families that could afford the rent or mortgage, wealthy whites moved out in droves.

Old Louisville soon filled with students, radicals, bums,

junkies, and larcenous punk rockers. One's safety walking through the neighborhood depended on many factors: the day of the week, the season, the block in question, whether U of L had won their most recent home game, and, of course, if it was a dry time for the year's drug of choice.

"This place got history," Myron had smilingly declared after we'd stepped out of the car in front of the liquor place.

"The precinct two streets over has more cops assigned to it than any other in the city," Mad Dog said.

Made sense. Old Louisville marked the boundary between the ghetto and bohemia. It's fall would leave the rest of the town vulnerable to what we'd allowed for the West End.

"Get a fucking compass," Thomas said to Myron before resuming his window seat in the back of the Caddy.

The next location was on a block of 23rd Street so drenched in the corner drug trade that we didn't bother to stop.

The final spot, where we now stood, should have been the first on our three-hour tour.

"I figured y'all at least wouldn't bitch 'bout this one." Myron showed us the back entrance that opened into a loading dock—ideal access to storage for our local corner boys and out-of-town buyers purchasing in bulk.

Of course, the product would never be warehoused on the property for longer than twenty-four hours preceding the re-up or re-supply.

"We still need an official vote," Paul said to Mad Dog. "We also need the place clean and, from now on, we need everyone a bit more focused. By next Monday I want a location. I want shelves. Jon and I can get the books. Easy."

"Fuckin' A," Thomas said. "You're starting to talk like an honest-to-God businessman and not a special-needs extra from *Wayne's World.*"

"I genuinely appreciate that, Thomas," Paul said. "I sense the sincerity."

Thomas did Paul one better, hanging an arm around my former manager's shoulders, the two together beholding the skeleton of our most ambitious venture. As if preparing to pose for a family photograph, Mad Dog and Myron buttressed the pair from either side.

I remained the only one out of the picture.

"Just when I hoped we might enjoy the luxury of boredom." Mad Dog offered his embrace to the others and joined closer in the malevolent huddle.

It was a short vote with unanimous results. A hard rain fell upon West Louisville, the dark clouds that had been gathering for the better part of the morning pissing down on us like a frustrated archangel awaiting the green light to unleash his full wrath on this Southern Sodom.

"I don't even know why we're doing this," Mad Dog responded when I asked how many were in favor of renting the retail space in the West Broadway Mall.

We'd run for cover when the first bolt of lightning crashed, cowering against the display windows. The flagstone awning covered us from the storm's downpour, but the wind tossed rain our way and rendered our shelter superfluous. Thomas had pointed out that above us ten probation officers served the commonwealth out of an office that spanned half the second floor of the strip mall.

"Why are we doing this?" I said. "Why vote? Oh, I don't know. Two reasons that just immediately pop into mind: you're not Hitler and we're not Goebbels and Goering, waiting in line to slob on your fascist, vitamin-B deficient knob."

"I'm not sure," Mad Dog said, "but that sounds a little homophobic to me."

I didn't want to incite the psychopath's wrath and get him on some kick defending his gay son again. I fought the urge to press his buttons and continued, "Secondly, as Thomas pointed out, what about the probation and parole office?"

"I think it's great." Mad Dog shrugged.

"Great?" I asked. "Having more dickheads with badges and guns hovering above our heroin front five days a week is 'great?' Am I missing something here or are you just a closet masochist, Milligan?"

"Keep your enemies close and all that. They're probation officers, you moron. They don't get paid to investigate possible drug fronts. If they did that, in this neighborhood, they'd never make it home from the office."

"They're not even real cops," Thomas said. "It doesn't concern me."

I had that feeling you get when a patrol car pulls behind you and you know in your gut that you're going to get pulled over. Even if you've kept to the speed limit and the car's tags are up to date and all your lights are working. You just know sometimes.

The vote passed, despite probation and parole, "glorified rent-a-cops," according to Thomas and Milligan.

Thomas motioned for each of us to draw closer lest some parole officer upstairs step on the ledge for a smoke break and overhear us. "The next delivery is less than a week from today. We need this place open. And legitimate enough in appearance that a soldier on leave wouldn't think twice about stepping in and checking it out, maybe offering a free used book or two for your inventory."

"Damn, we got work to do." Myron seemed on the verge of a panic attack.

"There ain't a cop I know who'd be quick to harass a soldier in uniform," Mad Dog said.

"And POs?" Thomas said. "Those pencil pushers wouldn't dare harass an American hero."

"Nice to know you two think so highly of your brothers and sisters in law enforcement," I said.

"We kick down doors and crush fucking skulls," Thomas said. "We take the real risks while the officious probation automaton administers Tyrone's weekly piss test in hopes that he'll fail and the judge can revoke him. Petty bastards."

"Tyrone?" Myron said. "That's some racist bullshit, mang."

"Jesus," Thomas said. "I suppose I'm behind on my sensitivity training."

"Pigs always gotta be talking slick." Myron shook his head somberly. "Even when we on the same side."

"Look...dawg," Thomas said. "I'm playin'. We be copasetic." Thomas grinned and offered his fist for Myron to bump.

Myron asked me, "Is this motherfucker for real?"

"He's got the plug," I said. "Without him, we got no Afghan fire to spread. You best make friends, Myron."

The West End kingpin hesitantly touched Thomas' knuckles with his own.

"You're the one that's gonna be running this place, right?" Thomas said to Myron. "I'm expecting big things from you, P-Diddy. My guy, the fellow dropping off the books, he's skittish." The heroin would be brought directly from Fort Knox to the store, right through the front door, stashed in the crevices carved in the pages of a dozen hardback encyclopedias. To a passerby, he was simply a soldier donating a box of his old books to a business bold enough to hang its shingle in a district decimated by poverty, ignorance, and institutional neglect. "He's the one taking the biggest risk."

"That's arguable," Paul said.

"Even so," Thomas said, "we don't want him in an overheated interrogation room being questioned by the DEA. He knows too much about my crew for me to allow that."

"He doesn't know us," Paul said.

"Thomas does, though," I told Paul. "And if they get to Thomas..."

"Then you fellows are in a really bad spot," Thomas said. "You either gotta kill me or trust me. That's a hard decision."

He had a point. I wouldn't want Thomas for an adversary. I also wasn't ready to depend on the happy bastard not to cut a deal to save himself a thirty-year prison sentence among men he'd himself arrested and helped convict.

"I'd rather avoid putting you in that position," Paul said to Thomas

Myron backed away from our little criminal sewing circle to more pompously address us. "Whatever we do, we ain't got much time. While y'all working behind the scenes my people out there making excuses for why we can't sell no tenths, only half-grams and better, not until we get good again. We about dry out there. Hungry junkies gonna be turning elsewhere."

"I'm not oblivious to this, Myron," I said.

"And what if their tolerance goes down then they bang that fire?" Myron asked. "We'll have half our customers falling out. A whole fucking wave of ODs. We don't need that kind of heat."

"You mean when the big bad Taliban returns there might be casualties?" Paul sneered.

"What?" At the word 'Taliban,' a bulky vein at the side of Thomas' temple inflated and he yelled, "What the fuck did you just say about the Taliban?"

"Don't worry about it," Mad Dog said. "Myron's simply indicating the last thing we want is to have to woo our local customers back from rival vendors. We don't need a goddamn street war."

"I hadn't thought of that," Thomas said. "We don't want a war. Bad for business. I should know that better than anyone."

"War," I said. "The Taliban. You know. Myron was just using street code."

Mad Dog stayed behind to seal the lease. I agreed to head back east to open the store late while Thomas and the others went to work securing the second van.

We parted ways. I declined a ride from my iniquitous confreres in favor of a taxi. I needed a break from my business partners and perhaps I could sleep on the long cab ride back to civilization.

I started to dial, in my estimate, the most reliable of the local taxi services. Most drivers, those born in this country, were proud members of the felon class, my kind of guys. Vietnam vets, alcoholics, three-time losers. But this cab company did better background checks than most, so I at least wound up with a somewhat law-abiding reprobate as my temporary chauffeur.

When I recognized the men standing before me in the middle of the rainy lot, I clicked my phone shut, stared down at the pavement dejectedly and laughed. "I was just thinking of you two yesterday, and wondering," I said to the two homicide detectives blocking whatever tenuous escape route I may have chosen, "how is your timing so horrible? I don't need this shit right now."

Like typecast actors playing to the detective cliché, their fedoras matched the shabby black raincoats that kept them dry from the downpour. They looked sleep-deprived and sexually frustrated. Poor Kneel and Bob, I thought. If only they'd grow a pair of balls and could summon the nerve to knock some poor bastard around with a telephone book occasionally.

I wondered, had they seen me with Mad Dog?

I couldn't exactly ask, so instead, I ridiculed them further. "Aren't you worried that your spouses are going unsatisfied? I mean take some 'me' time guys. It's not healthy to put *everything* into your work."

"I have a feeling the joking is going to come to a sudden

stop once you shut up and let my partner talk."

Well, fuck me, I thought. I had treated them as if they'd arrived today for the specific purpose of entertaining me. Bob had finally hit puberty though.

"Believe it or not, we weren't following you. Well," Neil said, "Not at first. We dropped by the ever-depressing West Broadway Mall to check on a parolee."

"Could you please try to propel your story forward? I'm kind of in the middle of important business. We're opening a second location."

"Here?" Bob laughed.

"Are you insinuating that the patrons of the West Broadway Mall are all illiterate?"

"We don't have time for this," Neil murmured.

"And I don't remember sending you an invitation to interrupt my business commitments."

"A few years back," Neil said, "We arrested this junkie skell for killing his stepson in a drug-induced stupor. He got a light sentence and parole. We were pulling in, hoping the bastard missed his meeting with his P.O. so we could lock him up again. No such luck. Me and my partner were about to leave when I spotted you, two fellow officers of the law, and some black kid. Your little motley crew were having some kind of tête-à-tête. I found it funny that one of the officers was the same one hanging around your bookstore the other day."

I laughed openly, letting Neil know how silly and paranoid I considered him. "That Milligan asshole and whatever fascist pig he brought with him were shaking me down too. Making fun of me like I was their personal court jester. Did you see how happy they looked?" I knew the two dicks would wonder why we all seemed so friendly so I answered their question before they could ask. "And I guess it's two for Tuesday, right. Dutch door action. First, they fuck me, then I get to bend over for you two. And the black kid's an employee. He's helping us get the place off the ground." Then I lied, "He's brilliant and ambitious. He'll make a perfect manager." I pointed to the space I'd just rented. "Our online sales are crazy. I mean it's sick how much we make off eBay and Amazon. We could go a year without an in-store sale and still enjoy a steak dinner three nights a week. The actual stores are merely labors of love, shelter from the storm of mendacity that began around the time Kurt Cobain committed suicide—a case you should look into. I personally think he was murdered."

"This ghetto kid likes books?" Bob asked one of those questions to which his own cynical tone served as the answer.

"Again, with the race shit," I said. Then I started speaking louder to quiet both detectives who had opened their mouths in unison to espouse procedural protest against such allegations. "So what? My new manager is black. What of it? You mad you can't find something to arrest him for? Is it driving you nuts to see a black man get ahead honestly in the world? What do you even know about these people other than what you learn through police brutality and intimidation? As far as I can tell the only claim either of you could make to a positive personal connection with the African-American community prob-ably involves memberships to *The Fresh Prince of Bel Air* fan club and maybe unhealthy fixations on Beyoncé. Now please move away from me so I can proceed with my business plans."

"Or what?" Bob took a step toward me intended to intimidate.

"You're trying to trick me into threatening a cop," I said. "How about this? You want to hear me make a threat? Well, use your imagination and, as I'm sure you already know, remember that I have severe mental problems and have spent more time inside psych wards than you have in your wife."

Bob did that thing angry men do when they're prohibited by fear of unemployment or a massive lawsuit from enacting their rage physically. He stomped around like a disappointed pre-pubescent and cursed quietly to himself.

Neil refocused the questioning. "In regards to your loyal, well-read employee, Myron..." Bob grinned when he saw my mirth dissolve into a stifled frown. "Yes, we know his name, Jon. Called it in and had dispatch read off his record. One of the parolees we stopped to ask about the rental space recognized him, gave us enough intelligence to narrow him down. Not much of a record but some interesting known associates. Many of them recently deceased."

"Unlike most employers, I don't hold those kinds of things against young men trying to get ahead in this world."

"Well, at least he doesn't have any felonies." Bob gave Myron that much.

"A white man with a felony in this country can get a job easier than a black kid with a negligible record of misdemeanors and traffic tickets." I rattled off the young man's fictional talents. "Myron reads two books a week. He knows more about jazz, early R and B, rockabilly, rock 'n' roll, and New York punk from the seventies than any hipster could memorize in a lifetime." None of this was true but it sounded good and I felt vaguely righteous defending a friend to these totalitarian white-devils. "Myron deserves a break. He's a good kid." Then I lied again. "Never lifted a finger against nobody."

"Speaking of innocents," Neil said as I began to walk past him, my cell cupped to my ear. "You seen Adam Frank lately?"

I froze in my tracks.

"I've been dropping in to check on him every so often," Neil said mournfully. "The kid looked alright our first meeting. But ever since, I've noticed him losing weight, acting a little frantic, gesturing like an un-medicated manic depressive when he's talking to his buddies, I've had a bad feeling. So, I went back through my phone to look at the pics from a week or so ago on a day, one of those clear days when you can see forever, a day Adam was wearing short sleeves."

I hadn't talked to God recently save the few times I held my little dog close and thought to myself, something this beautiful doesn't happen by accident, a freak result of mere chance.

So now I silently prayed that either the cop was bluffing about Adam, that I'd been dreaming, or that the detective, despite his proclaimed evidence, had been somehow mistaken.

"I focused on his arms. I borrowed one of those state-of-the-art cameras from our boys at narcotics. I didn't bother asking Mad Dog since he obviously, for some reason or another, believes you and your butt buddy Paul are exemplary white men. But Milligan ain't the only narco brass with pull in the department."

Stupid Neil, cocky, his chest puffed like a horny rooster, had grown so full of himself, relishing my anxiety, dragging out the anticipation. "Our boy over at the Portland precinct gladly supplies us with not only a camera with the lens the size of a damn horse cock. But a van too. Hard to observe these junkies in a Crown Vic."

My eyes fluttered. He'd spoken of Adam and now he was throwing around the word "junkie."

Paul would lose his goddamn mind over this.

And then our body count that he decried a few days ago would double at his hands.

The pig continued: "And what do you think I saw, plain as a meth-head's rotting teeth."

"Bullshit." No conviction or authority in my voice. This wasn't a bluff or a play because Neil knew all I had to do was go visit Adam to see if this cop had lied about my best friend's son.

"Tragic." Neil was now the one walking away. Bob followed him. The elder seemed to take little pleasure hearing his partner deliver the bad news. I guess the senior detective retained some sense of shame in his investigative misadventures.

"What drugs have done to you and your loved ones," Neil said over his shoulder. Then he stopped and turned to face me. "But who could have predicted a fifteen-year-old skateboarder from St. Matthews with a four-point-oh GPA would ever turn to the needle? I bet you wish heroin had been a little more prejudiced, don't you, Jon? Stuck to the blacks and hillbillies in Germantown. But no, sir. Dope is all about equal rights. It don't see skin color. It don't care about financial statements. And innocence is but a hurtle, my tortured literary friend."

I had spoken two words to the taxi driver: "Bardstown Road."

I needed to get to Adam before Paul had a chance to even suspect that his son had started shooting the same heroin we'd been moving.

I did not know for a fact Adam had fallen prey to the Taliban or Al Qaeda or whatever heinously offensive term the lower echelons of my organization had allowed customers to call our blitzkrieg product. For all I knew, Adam did what so many junkies in Louisville had turned into a daily routine before the influx of heroin after the pill crackdown: He either drove to Cincinnati once a week and stocked up on dope three times less expensive than anything a fiend could find in town, or he paid double to some Germantown hustler who so severely cut the product, a user had to shoot fifty thick CCs just to achieve the mildest of buzzes.

Not that I'd wish a bad high on anyone—forgive me, but as a once very active drug addict, I will always empathize with those poor bastards that lie, beg, cheat, and steal all day only to get sold a baggie four-fifths Coffeemate—but it would make my job, forcing Adam to kick, a lot easier if the kid weren't hooked on the pure. And, if Paul somehow got wise, he couldn't blame me or Mad Dog or Myron for getting the boy started.

Blame would surely fall, though. It was inevitable given the high emotions certain to run once Paul learned what Neil and Bob had told me.

My taxi passed the down-and-out denizens of the Bardstown strip where a Highland low life of any persuasion could discover romantic catastrophe and truth. Here lived my extended families of alleged free-thinkers and alkies, the homeless, the artists who didn't own canvases or paint brushes and thought Chagall a foreign brand of clove cigarette, and my favorites, the poets and writers (most of whom had never completed so much as a haiku and spent their waking hours discussing big plans and projects with fellow ne'er-do-wells at one of the hundreds of coffee shops and wine bars that plagued our city like a medieval disease).

At the sight of these lost souls, these smug and unjustly confident dreamers who believed a walk on the wild side consisted of a Jaegerbomb and quickly forgotten, shallow conversations inspired by shitty cocaine, the guilt over what had befallen my godson rapidly worsened. The pride morphed into homicidal shame. And the identification with my old neighborhood ceased altogether.

I wasn't like these people anymore.

I didn't care about philosophies. Peace, especially in the dope game, was a gift for the dead. And the only art that mattered to me anymore were Playboy centerfolds circa-1973 and the craftsmanship of my favorite sidearm, the Walther P7. Mad Dog purchased two for me upon our return from Chicago and I currently wore one in a shoulder rig under my denim coat. I had no problem using it if I discovered Adam in a bad way and any of his enablers tried to impede his rescue. I may shoot a few people anyway if I suspected some other crew trying to sabotage the Twice Told boys through narcotic subterfuge, messing with our families, getting a teenage kid with a bright outlook and a heart as big as Kentucky hooked on the Ron.

"Yeah," I said aloud to myself, then, lowering my voice, "No one gets diplomatic immunity on this one." Then, realizing I'd just quoted Danny Glover in *Lethal Weapon 2*, I pro-claimed under my breath, "God, I'm such a stupid ass-hole."

"What?" the Middle Eastern cabbie snapped rudely. The prick did little to hide his irritation. I'd interrupted him as he tried to maintain a ritualistic reverence to the monotonous, maddeningly repetitive desert dirge blaring from the radio that had entranced him for the better part of five minutes. I guess I should have known better than to disturb his mechanical nodding at the thunderous tribal beat blaring from the taxi's shitty speakers.

I wanted to point at the meter and remind the bastard who he worked for and who was paying the fare, that is, if I felt like it, then perhaps disfigure his gruesome mug with an exit wound the size of a baseball, courtesy of the illegal hollow-points with which I kept the clips of my HKs loaded. Mad Dog had fast tracked a concealed carry permit for me. He had blackmail on everyone even marginally involved in the criminal underworld, it seemed, and as a result I now legally carried a gun.

But I thought better of inciting any unnecessary con-frontations, not yet at least. We'd yet to reach my desti-nation, and saving Adam was more important to me than relieving my annoyance over a taxi driver who'd be less than a memory soon enough.

"Just drive," I said. "I was thinking aloud." I had granted myself carte blanche when it came to Adam, a license to maim or kill anyone complicit in the boy's downward spiral, either for profit or to get to his father.

I quietly considered my dilating cruelty and cursed aloud, my obstreperous delirium alerting the irritable Paki who glanced at me incredulously in the rearview. He was deciding if I were just a little looney like all his fares or a dangerous psychopath in need of immediate ejection. "I'm fine." I tipped my mesh cap at my rearview reflection. "Just mentally preparing for a little business meeting. Thinking of jokes to break the ice."

"Everyone love joke." The guy forced a belly laugh. He was big-boned, his dark hair slicked back with gel so thick I wondered if he'd misread the labels and applied axel grease. He turned the volume knob on his ancient radio to the left and finally the torturous sounds faded to silence. "Try joke," the cabbie said. "Better be good since I must turn my music off to hear. Good jokes make laughter. Laughter bring everyone together. Wanna try joke on me?"

The joke was this: I'd carefully contemplated Adam's possible current whereabouts and the gun tucked beneath my arm. It might be good for the kid, I thought, if I have to shoot whoever's feeding him this shit or one of his half-wit friends. Maybe the sight of a dead body, the bowels evacuated, brains looking like bloody hamburger meat all over the floors and walls, perhaps, after such a traumatic experience, instead of remembering the dope rush, the next time he considers using, the macabre imagery will substitute for any euphoric recall.

"The joke's not that funny," I said to the cab driver.

"Come on." He slapped the empty seat beside him.

"Forget it."

"Try me."

"No," I said coldly. "Just trust me."

No one else does, I thought. But I'm paying you to drive, so shut the fuck up.

I said as much when he requested to hear the joke again.

15

The bitch, as I often referred to Paul's ex—I also was fond of *whore, cunt, strumpet*, and even the British favorite, *slag*—lived in her new husband's riverside mansion off Rose Island Road. The bus Adam would take dropped him three blocks from his school on Lucia Avenue to where he'd skateboard the rest of the way. He'd pass by the old bookstore where his father and I had worked together for half a decade. The route was also home to a dozen other counter-culture snares that attracted any teen cursed with the capacity for abstract thought.

Bardstown Road had simultaneously saved and ruined my life. I could only hope to spare Adam the more painful portion of such a bargain. I felt sorry for kids like Adam, outsiders who missed the era of Bad Brains and the Clash. What were the modern means to survive the viciousness of youth and western culture's derelict rites of passage (losing one's virginity at all costs, peer pressure and abuse, the merciless competition over the most mundane rewards, et cetera)? Often these practices were most encouraged among adolescents by their shameless and spineless caretakers, prom queens and jocks who'd peaked at eighteen and continued to pathetically lament their past glories. So many of these loveless, mostly divorced couples fully intended, upon the initial breaths of their firstborn, to relive these lost years vicariously through their poor children.

If I hadn't had punk rock, I don't believe I would've made it through my teens without turning to schedule—three narcotics. And I likely would have at the very least *planned* a school shooting or two.

I had my reluctant and resentful driver cruise by every cafe, skate shop, and comic bookstore in the Highlands. I had him stop at the fast food chains so I could check the bathrooms. That's where I always went to shoot up when I could find privacy nowhere else. The rear of most of these establishments fed into the infamous Punk Rock Alley as the ruffian survivors of the eighties and nineties hardcore scene had nicknamed the narrow cobblestone back street that ran between Bardstown and Cherokee, where all the bars kept their trash and where drunks made their long treks home after closing time, where junkies like my godson often scored.

After searching for an hour, the meter running every minute, I had the driver drop me off at my car in front of the store.

I found him at the shop. Home. The sight of your earliest scars. Always the last place you wish to look.

Sickly and disheveled, an obvious street urchin lounging comfortably—if you call twitching and obsessively scratching his track marks comfort—Adam sat on the front stoop of my store.

"I need to talk to you." Adam's voice cracked. "I mean…" He stuttered and nervously twiddled his thumbs.

"I mean, we need, I mean *need* to talk."

"No shit." I'd never so harshly spoken to my dear godson. "We're gonna go find something to help with those shakes. Something over-the-counter, at least until you spill your guts."

"I can't." Adam glanced in the direction of Punk Rock Alley. "I'm meeting someone in a minute."

"Goddamn, kid."

Adam wasn't here for my help. It was a safe place to score. He'd scoped out the storefront and, when he noticed the place was closed, posted up.

"How'd you know your father wouldn't pull up and find you like this?"

"I called him. Felt it out. He told me he was downtown shopping for new inventory. I asked when he'd be back, said I wanted to stop by after class. He said he'd be out all day."

"So, you're skipping school now?"

"They don't have truant officers in this city."

"Municipal negligence working in your favor."

"Are you gonna give me a bunch of shit? Uncle Jon with his wild exploits. All the stories I've heard…"

"What's the dope called?"

"What?"

"The street name, the fuckin' brand name, man."

"I don't know. I've been doing regular Cinci dope for a few weeks now. I was getting it from a dude who stock-piled. Now this new guy…I've only dealt with him a few times. He's pushing the Taliban and its fucking fire, man."

It had to be our stuff, didn't it?

But what got him started?

182

"My old connect, Texas, he's so fucking stupid he never knows what he's buying and what he's selling. Couldn't tell me if it was dry wall in the bag—"

"What the hell is the Taliban?" I feigned ignorance over the poorly chosen street name of the product that was about to make me and my business associates richer than the corrupt mayor and overpaid police chief to whom we'd so disdainfully compared ourselves. "Have you gone so far off the deep end you're mailing fan letters to Bin Laden's extended family?"

"It's what you asked, the street name."

The kid had changed so much since the last time I saw him. Physically, a vague likeness remained. There all resemblance ended.

Adam began to cry. "I came here for your help. I just needed one more fix. I was looking out for my dad. I didn't want him to see me like this. I was hoping you were the one that showed up."

What was I supposed to say to that? Employ tough love? Tell him to kick rocks?

"Go inside." I threw him the store keys.

"Wait."

"Don't worry. You'll get your fix. Then we'll talk."

"Really?" His face it up at the mention of a fresh shot.

"One other thing...what kind of car does your new plug drive?"

While Adam languished in the upstairs office, cradling his cramping stomach, dry heaving, suffering the torture of heroin withdrawal inexplicable to those who've never suffered it, outside, I stood near the alley mouth, waiting.

Concerning this new downtown connect, I only knew what Adam had told me, that the guy called himself Blacksican, a street moniker that honored his heritage, half-black, half-beaner—"his words, not mine," Adam assured me—and that he drove a brown low-rider Oldsmobile from the late nineties.

"Last night," Adam had told me, "the asshole said to be at the Kroger parking lot on Second Street at six p.m. Didn't show up till close to seven. I will say that the wait was worth it for the Taliban."

I'd immediately checked my phone. Adam was supposed to meet this skell at five and it had just turned quarter past. We had plenty of time. I ran over to Walgreens, bought Adam a forty-ounce of Milwaukee's Best, some Imodium AD, some capsules of Nyquil, and a bottle of Ibuprofen, the perfect cocktail to fight withdrawal without a prescript-tion.

The only thing left to do was meet up with Blacksican, procure Adam's promised shot, and teach the street dealer a lesson about selling to teenagers in neighborhoods east of Roy Wilkens Boulevard.

The man obviously didn't know shit about business.

I decided to phone Thomas, the only one of our crew who, for some reason, I trusted to keep this secret.

"Where are you?" I asked after he picked up.

"We're working on these vans over in Portland." Thomas laughed at something someone said on his end of the line. "Myron happened upon this white van on cedar blocks. Can you believe that shit? I mean I've seen old Lincolns and El Caminos on blocks, but a Ram Promaster?

You know what I'm talking about. Thing looks like it could haul the Rolling Stones *and* all their groupies. Only in River Park. All the thing needed was tires. Runs like a dream."

"That's great," I said. "Now, Thomas…"

"Catlett, this whole thing, it's all so fuckin' *brilliant.*" He was in a mood all right, taking care of business with the enthusiasm of a true American lunatic. "You should come by, man."

"Why are you even there?" I didn't remember requesting Thomas' counsel regarding any of the operation's superficial details.

"You know, lending a helping hand." Thomas spoke like a damn Eagle Scout accepting his badge. "You need something, Jon. We're blood brothers. Literally. The other day, side by side, together we drew a copious amount of Russian blood."

I loudly coughed and reminded Thomas that we were speaking on a telephone.

"My point is that, if you need to talk or whatever, we're almost done here," Thomas said. "Then Paul is heading back to the West End store to start nailing some shelves together using some of that extra lumber from the basement. I don't think I'm needed anymore. I know it sounds bad. But to be honest, I just assumed all these ghetto gang-banger kids were only good at pimping their rides and slapping their wives. And while this Myron idiot is close to useless, his two buddies decking out the vans are true artistic savants."

"Thomas, shut up."

"Excuse me? Who the hell do you think you're—"

"I'm serious, shut up a second. We have a situation on our hands and I need you to take a Valium or massage your balls for a second or whatever you have to do to calm down and listen."

"Go ahead," he said after a deep breath and a pause.

"I need you at the store on Highland right now. I need you to ask no questions. Get in your car and speed. Use your police lights if you fucking have to. I don't care. Just trust me when I tell you we have a situation that, if not dealt with immediately, could go nuclear and threaten everything we've been working for. Also, get on your phone on the way over and send Paul on some menial errand. I know you can think of something and he's scared of you so he won't ask any questions. Get rid of him for a few hours. Keep him away from the Broadway store. You have enough distance, emotionally you know, since we all just met you, to be of service here while Paul and Mad Dog might make things worse. So, under no circumstances, tell either of them anything. Just say you're done for the night and headed home."

He assured me that he'd be at the store in ten minutes.

"You had a good idea." He spoke with the innocence and enthusiasm of that little demented Aryan from *A Christmas Story* when he finally receives the BB gun he wants for Christmas. "Sometimes I forget I'm the *po-muthafuckin'-lice.* I'll hit the lights and use the siren."

The Pontiac pulled into the alley behind the Taco Bell parking lot a half a block east of the store. He began to slow and parked right where Adam told me he would, behind an empty garage that extended backward from a condemned frame house, the paint peeling, the windows spray painted black, ideal real estate for squatters of which the Highlands produced no shortage ever since the new governor took office and gutted half the state's social services.

I quickly traipsed over the cobblestones. I released the HK's safety catch and threaded the suppressor to the pipe.

"The silencer will show these pieces of shit we mean business." Thomas had explained after he picked me up in his police unit, a turquoise Cavalier with a rhino guard obscuring the grill. We'd cased the alley for about ten minutes. I informed him that someone *might have* bought a boatload of the Afghan shit off Myron, upped the street price, and expanded the drug's market into the Highlands.

"This could ruin us," Thomas said. "We can't have too many wealthy white kids overdosing on our product."

We discussed the imminent investigation that would follow if some rich teenager wasting his daddy's money pursuing a career as an interpretive dancer or microbrewer up and fell out, and the heat our little clandestine business concern would suffer.

"I guess we better not leave a dead body in the Highlands tonight," Thomas said. "This guy, the one that was gonna get Paul's son high tonight, was he the one peddling the Taliban?"

"Thomas," I said, "I'm sorry that the street name of our product was so unfairly—"

"The kind of business we're in, we'll never have the luxury of controlling every aspect of the marketing process. I can't hold you accountable for street slang." Thomas paused and violently cleared his throat. "But we really do need to somehow break the habit of calling it that. Look, we don't *know* that it's our product flowing into the Highlands."

"Adam said—"

"Drug dealers lie about their product. Every last one of them claims they got the best skag in town. You think it would profit this half-wetback to tell Adam, 'Hey, what I got is total shit. It won't even relieve the pain the prick of the syringe causes. However, if you did some digging you could easily get your hands on the purest heroin known to man. But buy from me anyway. You can afford to piss away fifty bucks on non-dairy powder creamer with a grain of dope thrown in, right? Throw me the business for old time's sake, Adam, you know, because we're such loyal pals and money grows on stop signs.' If you believe every word a corner boy ever shouted, you'd also believe that there's no such thing as an unfair deal in this shit city. So, we need to find out *for sure*. The Taliban. Jesus Christ."

"I thought we were gonna try to stop calling it—"

"You know how many of those motherfuckers I killed?"

Thomas went on, ignoring, of course, any of the observations I made. I hate to diagnose neuroses, but the flask he'd offered, which I'd declined after getting a good whiff of the top-shelf whiskey within, concerned me. In my experience, if one goes to the trouble to purchase a flask, they have an unhealthy relationship with alcohol.

"I've shot children." Thomas took another pull from his rusty flask. "Those Al Qaeda fucks. I've torched their homes and helped detonate bombs under school buses full of teenagers because one of them just *might* be strapped with C-4 they *might* set off as the bus passed through town and by the barracks. So, if any of us have earned the right to call our product anything terrorist or durka durka related, it's me." Then he screamed in a primal baritone, "I'll call it fucking Saddam Hussein if I want. I was dodging IADs while you were masturbating to Stephen King."

I laughed. "I'd never masturbate to King. Exley, maybe."

"Shut up, shut up, *shut up.*"

I assumed, at this point, he was experiencing a vivid post-traumatic stress-induced flashback. At any moment, he could ghost me with that AK I spied in the backseat, mistaking me in his derangement for an Islamic insurgent.

"Of course. Of course, man. I didn't mean you couldn't call it that. When I said 'us' I meant me and the other guys. We don't have the right. And I was thinking, maybe, just maybe, it'll draw too much attention from the wrong parties." I winced at the last statement, half expecting a beating.

Thomas pursed his lips hungrily. "You're thinking Homeland, I hate those bastards. They should've let us turn the Middle East into a shopping mall with a giant parking lot. Don't they know the best defense is a good offense? Instead, I get to watch half my friends die in a goddamn desert so that we as Americans can continue to download Lady Gaga and shoot heroin and so I can strip in front of some fat fuck, probably an illegal himself, whenever I want to get on a plane."

I pointed out the time and Thomas mapped out our plan of attack, all orders, no suggestions. Before we parted ways and he went to hide in the weeds near the meeting spot, he'd asked me, "Did you play it cool when Neil dropped the news on you?"

I nodded proudly, feeling a sudden rush of affection for Thomas and a strange desire to gain his approval. Maybe this was what drew so many men into the military and police work, the comfort of kinship and the righteous indignation that accompanied a blind sense of duty.

I drew nearer the dealer's Pontiac. The tinted driver's side window slowly descended. I edged along the car, checked the rearview mirror and caught a glance of Blacksican, perhaps one of the most physically grotesque human beings I've ever observed. He lit a spliff and enjoyed a long drag. The skunk scent of kind bud wafted out into the alley.

Now was my chance.

I rose, took a large step toward the driver's door and maneuvered the suppressor through the half-open windowsill until the tip dimpled Blacksican's pockmarked jowls.

"Breathe," I said. "You know how the cops are supposed to read you your rights? Your only fucking right is breathing, one which I can revoke at any moment."

The passenger's window shattered and tinted shards of jagged glass rained down on the pusher like hail. Blacksican instinctively spat the spliff onto the pavement at my feet and covered his face, perhaps anticipating the rupture of his windshield next. He removed his cupped palms and looked to either side of him. He was book-ended by armed white men, neither of whom seemed inhibited by civil rights or due process.

"Don't shoot me," he moaned. "Please. Take what you want. I only got a half-gram and about six hundred dollars but—"

"Shut the fuck up," I said. "We don't give a shit about your money."

While Blacksican wiped the glass from his face and picked out the few fragments poking out from the flesh of his neck, Thomas reached through, unlocked the car and entered. He dug the barrel of the AK-47, the stock of which he'd used to bust out the window, into Blacksican's bulging beer gut.

"Listen, my friend here's gonna hold cover on you while I slip in the backseat of this two-door piece of shit." Thomas appraised the interior with a look of nausea. "I'll give you this. And take it with the tiniest grain of fucking salt you can imagine. At least you buy American. Listen to me now, very carefully. Once I'm comfortable and have my little friend here," Thomas patted the stock of the assault rifle, "keeping watch, my associate will calmly cross the hood and plant himself into the passenger seat. As a matter of fact, Black Asshole or whatever you call yourself, why don't you go ahead and get all that debris out of my friend's way before he sits down there. What? Were you raised in a barn, or, no wait, with your name and all, I guess it was the entrance of a Home Depot."

Later, Thomas would explain to me that he was not, in fact, a racist, but wasn't above speaking like one to intimidate or confuse a suspect.

After I entered, Thomas told Blacksican to drive.

* * *

191

We didn't have far to go. Blacksican was ordered to take a left onto Bardstown once we'd reached the end of the Punk Rock Alley and hit Highland Avenue.

Thomas said, "Right here."

Our detainee turned onto Lucia Avenue.

The collegiate duplexes and shotgun shacks gave way to two empty retail spots, office spaces with rent signs nailed into littered, abandoned lots. Thomas told our hostage to park at the end of the street.

Thomas then pointed to the abandoned gas station on the corner of Lucia and Baxter. "That's where we're going, Mexi-pad. I want you to walk like you just got laid and don't got a care in the world, just enjoying a night out with your homeboys."

Blacksican nodded and asked permission to exit the vehicle.

"Jon goes first." Thomas leaned in, placed a hand on my shoulder and whispered, "Stay alert, ready to rock. Keep that piece kind of tight against your side as you walk."

"Got it." I gave a half serious thumbs up.

Thomas punched the back of my seat. "This ain't fuckin' around time man. It's 'let's play the Grim Reaper' time, and guess who the reaper's guest is for the night." Thomas tapped Blacksican on the temple with the AK's barrel. "Now let's move. When we hit the station's lot, head past the pumps and to the left. There's a bathroom the previous owners left unlocked. Me and the gang squad boys used to meet our snitches there."

You mean savagely beat information out of accomplices or recalcitrant witnesses.

I was sickened at the thought that Thomas had used this exact spot for similar purposes in the past.

"What the fuck we need with a bathroom, man?" Blacksican asked.

"All will be revealed," Thomas said.

The moon hovered like a disembodied skull over the rooftops and cast sparse light on the darkened lot.

As Blacksican and I walked briskly across Lucia toward the abandoned BP, Thomas opened the duffel bag he'd brought along and retrieved a large tin thermos.

"Fuck is that?" Blacksican asked me.

I knew what it was for. And for the first time since I'd drawn down on him, a piece of my heart went out to Blacksican.

16

Thomas stationed me outside the bathroom to play lookout. I scanned the corner and the streets for cops or passersby. The awful sounds from the filthy restroom grew louder. Last I checked, Thomas had Blacksican zip-tied at the ankles and wrists, the back of his head resting on the edge of one of the urinals. Between lengthy pours from the thermos, Thomas flushed the latrine, a waterfall of toilet water descending on that atrocious face masked by a thin bandanna.

Ever witness a waterboarding? It's a real stressor. After another ten minutes of screaming, Thomas exited the bath-room, wiping his hands off with a paper towel, his AK strapped tight against his back.

"What'd you do with…" I began to ask.

"I left him crying in a pile of his own shit dampened by the pool of urine I'd scared out of him."

"Did he spill?" I asked frantically. "Did he give up his supplier?"

Thomas nodded.

"And?"

"Go get him, will you?" Thomas started the car while I wearily ambled to the bathroom door to retrieve our broken prisoner.

We entered the vandalized Pontiac. Blacksican sobbed in the back seat. He'd left the giant boxers he'd soiled in the gas station commode and washed off as best he could, but when he lumbered in with us, the car instantly filled with the feculent stench of freshly emptied bowels. I sighed and made a few suggestions where we could ditch the stolen car.

"Okay," I'd figured it out. "I drop you off at the store. I'll take Blacksican's low-rider somewhere inconspicuous. Then you come pick me up." I glanced over at Thomas, hoping that he'd been listening—a long-shot considering the post-orgasmic swagger he'd walked with since the torture, and the beating he'd been giving the dashboard, imitating Joey Ramone singing "Time Has Come Today," a sound which inspired a wistful sentimentality that battled briefly my breathless panic.

Thomas responded, "Your head's in the right place on a few matters. Yes, we're going back to the store." Thomas produced two small tinfoil pouches. "Kid needs his fix, especially before we take him with us for the rest of the evening's adventures. But it's better neither of our vehicles are seen while we're on Mr. Toad's Wild Ride."

"What are you talking about?"

"Is Adam locked inside the bookstore?"

"I told you he was."

"I'm debating whether we should leave him locked up and high or bring him with us."

"With us where? You've yet to tell me where we're going after we stop to get Adam well."

"Adam's coming." Thomas decided, just like that, as if we were reading from dialogue he'd scripted. "Shit-ass back there told me everything. And guess what?" Thomas stared until I realized he expected an answer to what most would assume a rhetorical question.

"What?" My voice contained about as much enthusiasm as a pre-coital victim of female circumcision.

"Blacksican's supplier? The man he got our product from, he's a white dude as well. I'm beginning to blame the blacks of this city less and less for the drug problem."

"You do remember how we met, right, Thomas?"

Thomas had just escaped the bumper-to-bumper traffic of Bardstown and taken the right onto Highland. "'Course I remember how we met. And I see where you're going with all of this. I'm no hypocrite. I never signed on to deal with anyone who'd poison high school kids with this shit. As a matter of fact, as soon as we handle Adam's drama, I call a band meeting."

"Band meeting?" I repeated. "Is that what we're calling them?"

"And from now on there's gonna be some order. These aren't group therapy sessions. Now go in there, hand the kid this." Thomas slipped me one of the packs. "Let him do his thing and then bring him out here."

As I exited I heard Thomas tell Blacksican, "This is what you get for dealing to white kids, esé."

If you're looking to reach the lowest of rock bottoms, short of diddling an altar boy or murdering a nun, try standing outside your bathroom while the son of your best friend shoots heroin.

"Where the hell are we going?" Adam had trouble keep-

ing upright. He'd let his flaccid noggin sag in the direction
of every sharp turn, until he slid across the backseat and
collided with our prisoner, the kid yawning and resting the
dead weight of his flagging head on Blacksican's shoulder.
The kid looked like he'd aged five years since I last saw
him. In bad need of a haircut, his unshapely strands matted
to his brow nearly hid his eyes. The white lettering on his
black T-shirt advertising some local metal trio had cracked
and faded and his jeans were caked in dirt and bloodspots.

"Get the fuck up off me." Blacksican nudged Adam
away.

"If he needs a shoulder, you give him one," I screamed.
"It's on you that he's in this condition."

"But the niggah smells," Blacksican whined.

"You're the one who just shat yourself," Thomas said.
"That's what I'm smelling. You got no room to criticize
hygiene."

"You know you can't smell yo' own stank. This mother-
fuckah here ain't showered in—"

I loudly chambered a round and Blacksican quieted.

Broadway had cleared of rush hour traffic. We hadn't
passed any cops, but if we'd been so unlucky, Thomas did
have a badge. The mercenary leader was distracted by some
text conversation he couldn't seem to make himself
postpone. He turned from Broadway without so much as a
glance, then we headed south on Seventh and slowed to
park in front of Playa's Urban Men's Club. I felt the place
had been awkwardly and inappropriately titled. True
players, men irresistible to anything with a clitoris, what
use would they have for a nudie bar? The whitewash
façade had been painted bright pink, the front and side

windows tinted black to assuage the puritanical city council and dissuade passing perverts seeking a free show.

Outside the Pontiac, I asked Thomas what he planned to do without the automatic weapon he'd just locked in Blacksican's trunk.

"I can't exactly walk into a place like this with an AK strapped to my chest." Thomas lifted his black T-shirt to show me the grip of the gracelessly bulky revolver he'd tucked into the waistband of his faded, knee-torn Levi's. "Don't worry, I'm not rollin' into Playa's naked."

"If there were any establishment in the city in which carrying a machine gun might go unnoticed, it'd be here."

"Naah, man," said Blacksican, standing beside Adam. "The Green Room about a mile south way worse, dawg."

"While I don't appreciate the interruption, Blax," I said, "my second question is something you'd probably know a little more about, seeing as you're tight with the owner. Why is there an apostrophe between the 'a' and the 's' of Playa's? I mean one would think this was a place for all quote Playas. But the apostrophe implies otherwise. It implies possession, ownership. Is there a man named 'Playa' that owns this gaudy post-natal abortion clinic?"

"All due respect, professor," Thomas answered for his prisoner, "I'm afraid, for the sake of punctuality, I'm going to go ahead and interrupt your English lecture."

"Punctuality?" I asked. "I didn't realize we had an appointment. Is someone expecting us?"

Thomas ignored the question and drew the hand cannon from his belt. He jabbed it repeatedly into the base of the weeping heroin peddler's skull. He said to Blax, "Let's go," then to me, "Catlett, you've been running the West End and enduring its dirty children for long enough to know it's nothing short of an urban miracle that the adult crack babies who opened this place could spell at all. Let's give them a pass on the grammar error." He pushed Blacksican while dragging Adam toward the Seventh Street exit.

Thomas' phone sounded a slightly muffled sample of Jimi Hendrix's live Woodstock interpretation of "The Star Spangled Banner." For a man proclaiming consummate professionalism, he had been more fixated on his cell phone than a nympho-maniacal sorority sister. He glanced at the screen, faintly smirked, then flipped the burner shut and asked Adam if he'd ever seen what a Colt Python could do to a human face.

When I reached the entrance, I turned to see Thomas studying his phone's screen again, scratching at his temple with the long barrel of the Python. He finished reading the text and rushed over to join the rest of us. Before Thomas could say anything, the hip hop music within the gentleman's club grew louder with the tinted glass door's abrupt opening, and who walked out but Mad Dog Milligan in all his mustached, bolo-tied corruption. He dragged behind him the unconscious body of a brawny bouncer, which he tossed out onto the sidewalk at our feet. The back of the man's blue nylon jacket read in bright pink letters PLAYA'S SECURITY.

"So, is that Mr. Playa's security guard?" I laughed.

"Not now, Catlett," Thomas said.

"And thanks, Thomas, BTW," I spoke churlishly in the fashionable initialing of texts and social media instant messaging. "Cute. Calling Mad Dog after you'd sworn not to. LOL, FML, FTP."

"What's FTP?" Adam asked.

"Fuck the police."

"That's awesome," Adam said.

"It's yours," I told the kid, glaring at Thomas grievously. "I hope every skater in town is texting it by the end of the week."

"How many more security douche bags?" Thomas asked Milligan.

"Just him downstairs," Mad Dog said. "Not sure about the second floor. I was waiting for you two to head up. From what I overheard at the bar, though, this one is supposed to be head bouncer. I got a feeling he's gonna need to hit the unemployment office when he regains consciousness."

"Why are you here?" I asked Mad Dog.

"You two," he ignored my requisition and delivered his own orders, "Drag this giant pile of ignorance and cholesterol down to that alley. I'll make sure your guests don't decide to leave the party early." Milligan popped his knuckles.

"Does Paul know?" I whispered to Mad Dog so Adam wouldn't hear. "Please tell me you didn't hit detonate on our entire goddamn business by telling Paul Frank that he was unknowingly complicit in addicting his son to fucking heroin."

"How long you think I've been at this, Catlett?" Milligan said. "If Paul knew anything we'd already be standing in the middle of the very bloody crime scene and, at best, Paul, in the manic state of unceasing paranoia that the crazy bastard has fallen into, may well have shot me or you. Think about it? He'll blame himself. Then he'll blame the rest of the crew. Also, LMFAO—" he winked in homage to my earlier chastisement of modern smart phone vernacular, "—Frank has grown by leaps and bounds as a sharp shooter. After Luther, he started frequenting that indoor gun range on Algonquin. He's got himself a few choice pieces too."

"Which, drum roll, you provided him, right?"

"I support the NRA," Milligan said. "How am I to deny my business partner his legal rights?"

"Of course."

"We leave Paul out of this. We're all in agreement, Jon. Now dump this fat fuck in the alley and let's do what we came here for."

After we tossed the head bouncer onto a pile of trash bags, I took a moment to examine the body. I felt his pulse; still alive. Mad Dog had either used the butt of his sidearm or a black jack. There was a small rouge indentation from where a thin line of blood ran along his temple, beginning above his right eyebrow. The kind of head blow that, if not administered by a veteran of street violence and hand-to-hand combat, could leave a man mentally disabled.

Milligan waited for us at the side door, stuffing his hands into thick black leather gloves. He reached in the pocket of his blazer and handed out two identical pairs.

"Put these on," he said. "Then meet us inside. We don't look right standing out here. Too many square-looking Caucasians. We don't want anyone giving our boy upstairs a heads up." Milligan opened the side door and prodded Adam and Blacksican along as they entered Playa's.

I pulled my pair on quickly and, while Thomas was otherwise engaged with his hands, grabbed him by the shoulders and whispered, "Why is Milligan here?"

"Calm down," he said.

"You swore that no one else had to know about this."

"Now you're just being redundant, man."

"Why did you have to involve him?"

"When that bitch boy dope peddler told me the name of his boss's place, something rang a bell. So, before saying anything about you or Adam, I texted Mad Dog and asked why that name meant something. Just the fact that I asked had Mad Dog blowing up my cell, which I ignored considering I wanted you to remain calm till we got here. But I discovered that this big time 'Playa' Blacksican slings for, he's a fucking DEA agent."

I stepped back a few paces and stared burdensomely at the tinted windows of the strip club. "You mean—"

"I mean the man filling the Highlands with *our* heroin is a federal agent."

"My old unit," Thomas said, "the gang squad, we busted Sexton. Had him on a wire-tap selling two kilos of cocaine to one of our snitches. The charges disappeared the moment his ASAC arrived to bust him out of custody. His superiors swore he was simply doing his job, working undercover. Tell me this. Even in the movies, you ever hear of a cop *putting* drugs back on the street? Undercover men look to buy dope and place it into evidence, not sell it. Plus, I swear, Catlett, we never once observed him reporting any

202

of his business back to any kind of handler or fellow agent."

"And you never thought, before tonight, that this guy might be a concern," I said.

"I hadn't heard his name in years. I figured he'd been reassigned to another office."

"How did he get a hold of our product?" I asked.

"He probably had some junkie buy in bulk. Fucking Myron. He should, from now on, notify us when *anyone* buys more than two grams. That's classic sting procedure. The cops want to catch dealers selling real weight. Thank God the cop that bought this batch is dirty."

"How would he profit?" I asked.

"Stepped on it," Thomas said. "I took a look at the point we took off of Blax and it's not nearly as pure as what my people smuggled in. Asshole's gonna get rich by giving our dope a bad name."

Now I was pissed.

"Is he all caught up?" Mad Dog asked Thomas as we entered Playa's.

He and Adam and our hostage stood just inside the club, lined against a pink wall beside the bathroom door. Men of all colors and creeds tossed dollar bills to some of the most beautiful black women I'd ever seen.

"I'll give Sexton this," I said to Thomas, "he's got great taste."

"Yeah," Thomas said. "I always heard he preferred dark meat."

"Wow," I said. "You just can't help yourself, can you?"

"You kind of walked right into that one."

The ladies contorted lithely and ascended their dirty golden poles on the two overlapping oval stages.

"I would think the DEA would frown upon such prurience," I said.

"Sexton's a silent partner," Mad Dog said. "I asked some of my C.I.s when I got word from Thomas. Everyone on the street seems to know about him."

"He's a silent partner, but he has an office upstairs." I said. "How exactly does that work out?"

"He's a very loud silent partner," Mad Dog said. "My point is his name is not on any of the articles of corporation or liquor licenses. Now, are we gonna talk all day or are we gonna put the fear of God into this asshole?" Mad Dog nodded toward the balustrades of black carpet and golden rails. He unzipped his trench coat and removed a double-barrel Remington scattergun, cut down to almost pistol-size.

Adam looked at the gun with bulging eyes, as if the sight of a mechanism that only had one purpose, the extinguishing of human life, had snapped him out of his nod. "Holy shit."

"That's right, kid." Thomas had to yell over the bass heavy beats dictating the rhythm of the women writhing on the two stages. The bottom of the stairwell began in the darkest corner and so far, it seemed, our odd quintet had gone unnoticed.

"Do I need to explain certain obvious sentiments to the fruit of Paul's loins?" Mad Dog asked as he cracked the breech of the shotgun to confirm its load.

Thomas opened his eyes as widely as the sockets would

stretch and said to Adam, "We were never here tonight. You saw nothing. You heard nothing."

"You were out skateboarding," I added.

"Or even masturbating in a public park."

Adam gazed quizzically at the madly chortling Thomas. "That's an awkward ass alibi, mister."

"Yeah." I drew my P7, ready to sprint up the steps to Sexton's office and teach the bastard a lesson right in front of my godson who'd learn that this is what happens to people who help poison children. And these are the kind of people with which you'll eventually be involved if you survive a few more years of the junk life. "Why does the kid have to be masturbating, again? Seems to defeat the purpose of a safe alibi."

Mad Dog shared my taut expression of concern.

"Trust me," Thomas said. "If he admits to jerking off in public, it'll throw everyone off. They'll be like 'why would anyone make something like *that* up?' They won't ask shit about dope." Then Thomas waved a finger at Adam. "You may however be court-ordered to a shrink for a while."

"That's his office." Mad Dog pointed to the closed door at the end, camouflaged in its black paint by the hallway dark.

"Where are the other guards?" Thomas asked.

"I told you," Milligan said, "I only saw the one. And I took care of him."

"*We* took care of him," I whispered. "I didn't see you throwing out your hip dragging that fat fuck down the block."

"I'm taking into account that you're under a fair amount of duress, Catlett." Mad Dog raised the sawed-off;

one hand on the cut-down grip, the other beneath the two barrels. "But you talk to me like that again and I'll make this whole thing look like a murder suicide. Guess who the suicide is gonna be." Milligan inhaled. "Now please, shoot that knob, Jon. You're the only one of us with a suppressor."

I followed the sergeant's orders without question, moving back to avoid flying shards of wood and steel. The gun made a sound like air let out of a tire and the knob popped out of place, hitting the wall to our right then ricocheting through one of the openings between the golden bars of the railings.

"Shit." I hoped that metal globe hadn't hit anyone below.

Mad Dog pressed the door open and the rest of us followed him inside.

The first figure we faced could've been twins with the unconscious rent-a-cop we'd left atop the garbage pile in the alley downstairs. He'd been standing in the far corner of the garish office. He began to rush Mad Dog when Thomas stepped between the two and pressed the long barrel of his wheel gun into the bearish black man's forehead.

"Close the door," I whispered to Adam who did as he was told.

"Turn that music up." Mad Dog waved the shotgun at the man behind the desk.

"Thomas?" Sexton said. "What in God's name do you think you're doing? Haven't we been over this? You know you can't touch me." He dressed like a third-rate private investigator in chinos you could buy for a buck at St.

Vincent de Paul, a dark tropical button-down T-shirt—the kind cool dads and salt-less plainclothes men tried to pull off—and a poor, pitch-black toupee drastically opposed to his gray sideburns and the brown hair that ran along his temples.

"We're not here in an official capacity," Thomas said to Sexton.

"Then why didn't you just knock?" Sexton asked.

"We know you well enough, Sexton," Mad Dog said. "If this is your office, there's a control device for everything that goes on downstairs. Hell, you could probably unsnap the bra strap of your favorite pole dancer from up here. So, as I requested before…" Mad Dog thumbed down the two hammers near the shotgun's breach. "Turn that shitty bass-driven sludge up as loud as it can go."

Sexton nodded, opened a drawer. Thomas ran over to Sexton's side to make sure our second hostage wasn't going for a piece. "It's just a control board," Sexton said.

The hip-hop downstairs turned into a sonic thunder-storm of bass so loud the floors began to quake. I glanced out the window across from Sexton's desk. The patrons and dancers had all ceased their routine, struck dumb by the sudden sound breach.

"This'll only take a moment," Mad Dog yelled.

Then he turned his gun on the second guard, the one who'd met us at the door, and released both barrels.

Everyone in the room stepped back a few paces.

Sexton nearly fell out of his chair as it rolled toward the window behind him.

"You can turn that shit back down now," Mad Dog yelled at the retching federal agent.

17

The rent-a-cop rolled around on the carpet and crossed his arms over his man-boobs where the blast had spread.

"Everyone calm down." Mad Dog had cracked open the sawed-off and popped two black shells from the breach.

"Oh shit." Adam had sunk to his knees, his hands on his cheeks. "He just shot him. He just fuckin' shot that guy. Oh, Jesus. This is all my fault."

While keeping my gun trained on Sexton, I moved toward Adam, bending down on one knee. I reached beneath his damp, pasty armpit, helping him to his feet.

Mad Dog was busy reloading while Thomas leaned over the wounded guard, examined him head to toe then, after a moment, erupted in psychotic giggling. "Rubber bullets."

"That's right." Mad Dog waved the scattergun at Sexton. "Good old riot ammo. Your boy will live. Probably got a few broken ribs. I'd call the paramedics soon though, in case something pierced one of his lungs." Mad Dog slammed the breach shut then pressed the two barrels under Sexton's chin.

Thomas placed the folded cut of tin foil on the dirty drug fed's desk.

"That piece of shit works for you." Mad Dog tilted his

head briefly toward Blacksican, now cowering in the corner.

"No." Sexton's voice broke like a hormonal adolescent's. "I've seen him around. I don't deal. I'm a distributor. I don't have corner boys and lieutenants. I have associates."

"Well, he knew about this place," I said.

"He might have purchased a few grams from me here and there. What he did with them is none of my business."

"It is now," I said.

"Were you aware that he's selling heroin in the Highlands?" Mad Dog shook his head like a nurse catching an invalid in the act of making Barbie dolls out of his own feces. "And to white kids? Teenagers? Kind of a no-no. An unwritten rule among those who want to stay in this business long enough to maybe someday retire with all their limbs. The fact that you did not make this clear to him when you unloaded your product is deeply concerning to me."

"Milligan." The fearsome tremolo had gone from Sexton's voice. The man had readjusted. He probably would've snapped out of his panicked catatonia anyway considering he'd likely developed the skills of a Shakespearean actor while he cultivated the triple-life of a corrupted undercover man. "Milligan, we can work this out."

He'd probably authorized and partaken in many an execution himself.

"How are we going to work this out, Sexton?" Mad Dog asked. "You know what's going to happen when white kids from the East End start overdosing by the dozens?"

"I'm sorry if someone I do business with sold a tenth to a white kid," Sexton said. "You want me to promise you it won't happen again? I have no way of controlling these cretins. Look at it this way, if it wasn't Blacksican, it would've been some other skell. This town is going to shit faster than Rome. And when in Rome, do as the Vandals do."

Mad Dog gestured toward Adam, still battling shock and leaning heavily against my side.

"That kid is the son of a friend of mine." Mad Dog pressed the barrel deeper into the fat between Sexton's chin and collarbone. "If I'd just heard on the street what you were up to, I wouldn't be here right now. I might spit in your direction if you walked by, but nothing more than that. I'd let you walk. This one's personal"

"I get it. The kid's off limits." Sexton's tone left a bit to be desired.

Mad Dog's face beamed with a manic iridescence. "They don't know," the detective whispered as he waved his shotgun back and forth between Blacksican and the prostrate guard.

Sexton's people had no idea that he worked for the federal government.

We had him by the balls.

"No more selling to Adam here." Mad Dog nodded toward the kid. "Make sure of it. Send out an email, a memo, whatever. And I'd prefer you keep your business west of Fourth Street."

Sexton kept nodding.

"And you only buy from Cincinnati. Or Atlanta. Or Detroit. Shit that's already stepped on by the time you get your filthy hands on it. This pure shit—"

"The Taliban?" Sexton asked.

Thomas cocked his revolver and leveled it on Sexton. "Don't call it that."

"What? It's—"

"Just don't," Mad Dog hissed. "And don't buy from anyone local. Stop being lazy. Get off your ass and do some leg work if you're gonna push."

"Now you're dictating my import and export policies?" Sexton said. "That's rich."

"Trust me. We find you selling that shit that's flooded our streets—" Mad Dog paused at his mention of the Taliban, "—or one of your associates sells to another Highlands teenager, then we forget about your day job. We find a way to kill you. All the way out, motherfucker. Maybe we tell everyone the truth about you..." Mad Dog winked then whispered, "*Agent* Sexton."

"I can make adjustments to the business model," Sexton said, then took a long look at the emaciated Adam, the track marks on his wrists and inner elbows, his sunken, jaundiced cheeks. "How long you been using, kid?"

"Maybe a month." Adam shrugged.

"If I may." Sexton said. "I've got something that will help him." He kept the one hand extended toward the armed men looking for a reason to blow him out of his seat. With the other, Sexton slowly reached to open the drawer opposite that which contained the mini-sound censor.

"Easy," Mad Dog said.

Sexton came out with a prescription bottle and relinquished it to Mad Dog who read aloud, "Suboxone."

"That shit really work?" Thomas asked.

"It'll help Adam kick," Sexton said glibly. I'd begun to detect the faintest trace of a northern accent, maybe Jersey. Sexton wasn't a native. He'd probably been reassigned to the Louisville command post as a punishment for prior clandestine chicanery. No wonder he didn't mind turning my hometown into the next Detroit. He could always request reassignment to a new office from where he could collude with new kingpins and assist in the decay of yet another dying American city. "Suboxone is a miraculous decoction. It's turned heroin into more of a recreational drug."

Heroin a recreational drug? Yeah. And Stalin was a humanitarian. I hoped Adam wasn't retaining any of this nonsense. Sexton exaggerated like a serial date-rapist with an endless Rufinol supply describing himself to some unsuspecting Match.com divorcee. Suboxone did not cure heroin addiction. It severely tempered withdrawal symptoms. But it did not relieve the mental obsession nor serve to battle the post-acute phase of detoxification, the insomnia, the chronic fatigue, not unless the addict in question simply substituted the medication for his opiate of choice, surrendering to a lifetime dependence on prescription narcotics. With a Suboxone script, a dope fiend could legitimize a habit that, without that piece of paper, could easily lead to a five-year stretch in a state penitentiary for possession charges. The only reason I had yet to relapse: I didn't have the time nor could I afford watering down my already tenuous judgment and vigilance.

Then it occurred to me that Sexton, on top of disgracing his office by profiting from the very crimes he'd been charged with preventing, had gotten himself a habit. The glassy eyes, the slow gesticulations, his voice's droning cadence all led me to conclude that he'd been getting high on his own supply.

"Trust me," he said, then confirmed my suspicion with, "the subs work, kid. I know from experience. I enjoy a little binge myself every so often. Then I gotta clean up to take care of business. Without those orange little treats, I'd never be able to take a break from the H."

I wanted to slap him, but further violence would detract from the calm that had descended mercifully over the room and its high-strung inhabitants.

I grabbed the bottle from Mad Dog. "I know how to use them. They got me clean. I'll explain when and how to dose to the kid." I turned to the double agent who we couldn't kill, at least not tonight. "Don't ever call him 'son' again or I'll kick your dick in the dirt so hard you'll have to squat to piss like a woman."

"I didn't catch your name," Sexton said to me.

"That's because I didn't offer it."

"You're not the kid's father." Sexton extended a thumb, counting off the possibilities that might explain my attendance. "You're too young, unless you knocked his mama up when you were twelve, and you two look nothing alike. And you're not a cop. These two," Sexton nodded to Mad Dog then Thomas, "they're the bentest of the bent. But anyone can tell from a mile away that they're police. How do you fit into this picture?"

Sexton grinned, as if he'd just enjoyed some vengeful epiphany, some foresight that he now knew would allow him a small fraction of comeuppance for the embarrassment, damages, pain, and suffering we'd caused.

The agent didn't break our stare as he addressed Mad Dog. "What exactly have you been doing for side work lately, Milligan?"

"Shut up," Mad Dog barked, gritting his teeth and clenching his weapon.

"Is this *just* about the kid?" Sexton asked. "Or are you boys making sure that when the Taliban returns there's an understanding, a peace between organizations. Let the customer decide. That's always my philosophy. We live in a free-market economy. And maybe you don't trust me to vend *your* imported product."

"You rat fuck." I brushed past Mad Dog. Before Sexton could turn, I slapped the swarthy fed across his face with the P7's suppressor. His swivel chair swung ninety degrees and the side of his head bounced off the windowsill. When he turned back to the desk, I pressed the suppressor to his temple, where blood had already begun to flow from a large knot. His nose was broken, bent to the left, blood and snot blocking each nostril. "I'm this boy's godfather and now you know what will happen if he gets back on that shit."

"I also know that you're a fucking dead man." Sexton laughed. "You just committed suicide. In the know or not, involved or not, doesn't matter. I don't care if your golf buddies with the governor. I'm gonna kill you and everyone you ever loved. Massacre them like Mai Lai. And I'll get away with it too. I've got dirt on every DEA ASAC from here to Tucson. No one wants me on a witness stand and if any of them had as much as half a testicle between them, they'd have done me like I'm gonna do you, son."

Mad Dog dismissed Sexton's threats with a yawn as he moved toward the office door I'd destroyed. "Please, Sexton. You're not stupid enough to kill a white man, especially a pillar to the community. That could bring enough heat to slow down your cash flow."

"And cash is one thing I think you're gonna be in dire need of now, bro." Thomas observed the damage we'd done, from the door to the wounded bouncer coughing in the corner. "I have a feeling you're gonna need to hire some better help too."

I was the last to exit. Before I did, I said to Sexton, "And change the sign outside. That apostrophe makes you look like a moron."

18

I didn't know it at the time, but the contract was out on me within minutes of our departure from the nudie bar.

Sexton identified his third assailant with the help of Google and, with a single call to the command secretary who he'd caught screwing a fellow agent, a married man, he was emailed my entire criminal record, all misdemeanors. Loitering in a drug area. Sexton had never even heard of that charge. I had also been cited for, on the same day, possession of paraphernalia.

"A junkie's junkie." Sexton grinned.

Both charges had been dismissed—the cop who'd written the citation didn't show up to the court date.

"Jon Catlett," he said to the laptop screen. "So, you're what happened to Luther Longmire. You and those sanctimonious hillbilly LMPD detectives."

You've fucked the wrong bull, Sexton thought.

He placed a phone call to a man he knew from his days infiltrating cartel factions in southern California.

"I got a job for you." Sexton's voice continued to quiver. "I need you on a plane now. Yesterday. Last week."

Sexton listened.

"Fly into Cincinnati. Tonight, if you can. I'll have a car

waiting for you at the airport. When you get to town, come to my place and we'll talk."

The man on the other end of the line had traveled to Louisville with his partner just three months prior to silence four witnesses in a high-profile trafficking indictment that, had it gone to trial, could have caused Sexton a lot of trouble.

"No," Sexton said. "This time, it's just one. And no women or kids are involved, so please don't try to haggle with me on the price. A single, Caucasian male. Early thirties He should be easy to get alone."

Sexton listened again.

"I know white people are more of a liability, but it is what it is. Trust me, if I could make him black I would. Goddamnit, listen to me. I called *you* because I need a professional. I'm not gonna entrust some illiterate gang banger who doesn't know how to aim a pistol properly. I need this done right. But I want him found. You don't have to worry about disposal. I want everyone to know what happened to him. Speaking of which, do I get a better rate since you get to skip the clean-up this time?"

I told Adam that I would blow the kid's cover if he didn't drop by the store right after school and look me in the eye so I could tell he hadn't had anything that could adversely interact with the day's dose of buprenorphine, which I'd personally administer.

"If you shoot dope and then take the sub," I'd told him the night before, "you will get sicker than you've ever been. You'll literally feel like you're dying."

"It can't be worse than I felt this morning." Baring witness to gunplay and bloodshed had killed the kid's buzz.

"You get a fix then drop that sub any less than twelve hours later, what you will experience will make this morning seem like a massage parlor hand job in comparison. Do not, under any circumstances, try to sneak in a shot before you come see me."

He told his mom he was spending the night at a friend's—in my day, kids didn't have sleepovers two nights a row in the middle of the week, but then again, Paul's ex-wife, as I've said before, was a horrible person even by drug-dealer standards. He crashed in the recliner five feet from my inflatable mattress. We laughed ourselves to sleep watching episode after episode of *It's Always Sunny in Philadelphia* on Netflix. I liked having him around, despite my prejudice against young people and parenthood.

The next morning, I awoke to an empty office.

"Shit," I murmured. I assumed that the kid had run off to cop the moment I drifted off. "Little bastard," I said to myself. "That little shit."

I began to fall back asleep where I sat upright at the edge of the mattress.

"Wake up, Uncle Asshole," Adam shouted as he entered the office.

"Where the hell did you go?"

"I ran over to Starbucks for you."

He placed a steaming cup of fresh coffee under my nose.

"What'd you think of the redhead?" I asked him.

"She must not have been working."

"You'd have noticed her. I almost—" Then I remembered the example I had failed to ever set for the kid. "Never mind."

"Sugar," I slurred my words after one sip.

"Here." Adam's voice contained an alarming urgency. "Drink up. We need to talk."

Great, I thought. The kid's brain has been further poisoned by some newly acquired counter-cultural knowledge courtesy of Myron, his new hero.

Last night, after we left Playa's, I took the bus to meet Paul at the West Broadway Mall. From there we drove the second van to Paul's place, where I dropped him. Bookmobile One would remain parked in front of the Highlands store until we got word from Thomas that the new batch had arrived. While Paul and I were en route, Mad Dog and Thomas took Adam out for a drink at Freddie's on Second and Broadway—the place hadn't carded since I was in high-school—and, when they got my text, dropped the kid off at the new location for Myron to babysit until I had Paul out of the way.

While Paul and I navigated the naked city, Myron had probably plagued the kid with all sorts of hip hop trivia and pop culture garbage as the West End kingpin had begun surprisingly disciplined research on the history of jazz, the civil rights movement, Malcolm X, all things men with his painful background should've been taught by their parents, had the elders of the community not been poisoned by the same system that had claimed to do them so many favors at end of the free-love era. While a note of annoyance might malign these verses regarding my old friend Myron, I was impressed by the younger man, and grateful that, for a little while at least, he found something to believe in.

"Please don't tell me Myron got you converted from punk rock to hip hop," I said. "The last thing we need in this neighborhood is another slacks-sagging, Caucasian urban enthusiast who willingly covets token admission into black culture."

"It's not that," Adam said.

"Jesus," I said after downing half the cup. "Okay, I understand. You're still going through it. I'll get you your dose."

"I already took it. For a criminal, you're a real shit hider. You left them in your shoes."

I spat out my next gulp. "How much did you take?"

"Calm down." Adam had regained some confidence now that he wasn't blitzed past the borders of Jupiter. He didn't resemble the walking dead anymore. Color had returned to his face. He still smelled since he hadn't brought a change of clothes. But the uncontrollable perspiration and random twitches had ceased. "I Googled it and took a fourth."

"Thank God." I breathed after what seemed like the length of my affair with Amara, Lord rest her Godless soul. "Look. If this is about last night, those guys are friends of mine. They're cops. We're not in any trouble. Those people, Sexton and his lackeys, won't come anywhere near you now. I know Milligan and Thomas came across rough. But sometimes, when your friends are in trouble, people have to get hurt."

Paul was right. It was a good thing I wasn't a father. Listen to the life lessons I imparted on my godson.

"It's not about that," Adam said.

"Well then what the hell is it, kid?" I said. "I could still be sleeping. And why aren't you getting ready for school. I thought we had a deal."

"I can't go home, Jon." Adam sat on the floor. Little Irina slowly trotted over to the boy, nuzzling her snout beneath his hand, demanding affection. Adam glowed like the child I remembered and leaned back for the dog to seat herself in his lap. He began caressing her as she'd requested. Then he started crying.

"Excuse me?" Now I had real issues. A teenage boy spending one night looked bad enough. An indefinite stay?

"I'm sorry." Adam wiped the tears from his eyelids.

"I know your mom's a bitch and everything but it can't be that bad."

I, to this day, commend the kid for having the nerve, especially after watching my gun-toting comrades and I do our thing, to calmly lift Irina from his lap, place her on the floor, rise, step forward, and backhand me like an insouciant housewife from the 1930s.

"Don't ever talk about my mom like that again."

I stood slowly.

"What?" Adam yelled. "Are you gonna hit me now too?"

Stop the press. "Too?" I asked.

"That's what I've been trying to tell you," Adam said.

After a long beat, I said, "Is it some kid at school?"

Almost right before my eyes, he turned back into the scared, sunken little boy I'd held and watched sob and babied to bed the night before. "It's the doctor. It's Sullay." Doctor Sullay, AKA Sulliaman Nevoka, was the drunken

Bosnian plastic surgeon Paul's ex-wife had married.

Turned out the marks on Adam's arms weren't all from needles.

19

Women enter our lives at the most inconvenient of times. As if expecting a new love interest to cloud my judgment and cause me to act imprudently and self-destructive, I spent most of my off days working on the Bookmobiles and avoiding irking any of the unpredictable homicidal maniacs in my life. Adam split his time between home and the office, when his father was busy elsewhere committing crimes of which the boy would have never believed his solemn patriarch capable. I'd fattened my unofficial retirement plan purchasing thirty acres of fallow fields and bluegrass pastures in Oldham County, far away from Bardstown Road and all the other shakedown streets that circled downtown concentrically.

But one can't seek the simple, semi-monastic farm life and continue in a line of work in which a big part of the job included semi-regular executions. Seems like a no brainer, but I had trouble accepting any further abuse of Adam, seeing him waving his hand into the breeze as we drove back to town after the farm purchase had gone through. Maybe he could spend some time working on the grounds with me, I thought. Perhaps he may come to consider the place a second home, a sacrament to ward off the demons I'd helped introduce into his life.

I dropped Adam at his grandmother's and met Paul at the Starbucks down the street from the bookstore. The granny had a volunteer commitment she would never cancel that evening—the woman was a saint and perhaps the only reason Paul hadn't turned out as bad as me—and I knew that somewhere around six o' clock tonight, the boy's step-father would come home, get drunk, and put hands on either Adam or his mother, making sure not to leave any obvious marks. Lucky for the abusive bastard, Adam had taken to only wearing long-sleeve shirts for other reasons equally tragic.

I sat outside, nursing a cappuccino, chain smoking, and waiting for Paul to arrive with the newly painted Twice Told Books delivery van when Catherine called reminding me of our date in Nashville this coming weekend.

The same day I was to deliver several kilos of heroin in Music City, USA. The cowgirl's timing could not have been better.

While I'd been busy investigating Adam's heroin sources, our new branch had opened for business. Shipments had been delivered to Lexington, Memphis, and Huntington, Virginia, Paul at the wheel on every run.

Nashville was my turn, the second Bookmobile's virgin voyage.

Jimmy Dale Gibson, a new ward boss had taken over the Central Tennessee sect of the Dixie mafia and we had yet to break felonious bread with the man. Paul, Mad Dog, and Myron had decided it best that I be there in person for the first transaction.

"There's a few old friends I'd like to drop by and see anyway," I told Catherine after she'd admitted to fearing I might back out. "Maybe while you're setting up and the first act goes on I can drop in on them."

Was I about to execute a major heroin deal while on a first date?

She hung up before I could change my mind.

At this moment, Myron was waiting for Thomas' soldier boy to arrive to sell another batch of extremely rare used books, kilos of pure Afghanistan heroin molded to fit the holes carved into the middle of the pages. Only Thomas and his mules knew the location of the full supply.

"It's hidden on government property where no one will look," Thomas had convinced me of the product's security, "and where all employees are too inept for civilian life."

During all this, I had to somehow figure out a way for us to murder Adam's step-dad.

Paul wouldn't have it any other way.

Once Paul had entered the coffee shop, gotten his tea, fixed it to his liking and returned outside to meet me on the patio, I'd decided it best to come clean about the date I'd scheduled with Catherine. Perhaps our new Dixie contact could meet me close to the Sweetwater, the classic country music club near the Parthenon in Downtown Nashville where my evening escort had been invited to lead an all-star set, warming up for Jim Lauderdale who'd written a series of hits for George Strait. The top seller, "She Used to Say That to Me," was a favorite of mine which, ever since Dog Hill, never failed to remind me of Amara.

As Paul exited the coffee shop, our old regular Albert passed him, a thick volume under his arm. Paul grabbed Albert by the wrist and pulled him back out onto the side-walk. He jerked the book from beneath Albert's armpit and took a long look at the dust jacket.

I could see the spine: *The Fifties* by Edmund Wilson, a history classic we always kept in stock.

"You took this from the store, you old bastard," Paul said to Albert.

"I was just borrowing it," Albert whined. "I didn't mean nothin'...I mean you boys know I'm in there every day."

"Not since I banned your dusty old ass," Paul said.

"Paul, I didn't—"

"When did you take this? You must've had it for weeks. Were you ever planning on bringing it back? We're not a goddamned library. We have to actually sell our books to keep the lights on. How many items of ours did you steal all those years we put up with your incessant jibberish and your refusal to make a single purchase?"

"I never stole nothin'. I love that store, Paul. If you'd just—"

Paul said, loud enough for all our fellow patrons to hear, "You come into my business again, you try to steal from me, I'll have your whole fucking family killed."

"Shit," I said to myself.

Albert scampered away, scurrying across the street, horns blaring when two cars almost rear-ended as the drivers avoided the sprinting senior citizen.

Paul glared at the horrified Highlanders. "Problem?" he asked, dusting off the book cover.

They all hurriedly resumed their conversations.

* * *

"The place will be packed." I explained my scheduling conflict to him after he'd taken a few deep breaths and a long pull off his tea. I wanted to remain in his good graces, so I didn't bring up the gruesome spectacle he'd just made.

Threatening to murder a retiree's children over a book we'd purchased for fifty cents at a yard sale. Christ, Paul had turned into one mean son-of-a-bitch over the last few months.

"I'll meet our guy on some side street close by, make the switch, then slip back into the show," I said.

Paul choked with disgust, nearly spitting out his tea. "You and that hard-on of yours are going to be the end of us."

"Can you work with me here? Can you call Chicago?" Since I'd been babysitting the kid, I'd encouraged Paul to take over communication with the big dogs up north, a decision that served to distract the bastard while also assuaging his ego and relieving me of the annoyance that accompanied regular check-ins with the vociferous Joseph Barinov. "Have them change it up. The Parthenon should be our dead reckoning. We meet somewhere in the vicinity."

Paul glanced at his watch. "As if you'd take 'no' for an answer. I'll make it happen. I'll use the ice cream truck while you're gone to ravage all the Goodwills and Salvation Army stores."

"We're on track."

"Sounds like it."

"Except we're not. It's Wednesday. I have to leave town in two days. But we have something very serious I think we have no choice but to deal with before I go." Then I went silent a moment, closing my eyes, dreading what was coming.

"I'm dying with anticipation." Paul removed his Ray Bans. "What is it?"

"I want you to take a deep breath, Paul. And once I'm finished talking, I want you to understand, this is your play."

Then I told him about the marks on Adam's arms minus those left by the syringes, their clear plastic chambers saturated with the same heroin his father had gotten rich importing.

20

The bartender at Molly Malone's, when asked by police the following morning, would admit that the murder victim who'd been drinking there the night before had been cut off around ten thirty. Apparently, the Bosnian doctor had made a habit of turning predictably verbally abusive once in his cups. He would gleefully employ various racial epithets when addressing the wait staff. *Slope, dink, darkie,* to mention only a few, slurs that, while egregiously offensive to the politically correct Highlands clientele, applied to not a one of the bar backs or bus boys to whom the doctor had directed his nonsensical invective. When asked to leave and threatened with police intervention, Sullay, on his way out the door, assured the bartender that he would "keep getting his drink on somehow" despite the "nigger attempts" to thwart the night of debauchery a man enduring the pressures of a medical practice had rightly earned.

The doctor then stopped by Captain Liquors on Lower Brownsboro Road for a pint of Kentucky Gentleman he could finish on his way home to the East End.

Somewhere near his estate off River Road, Sullay lost control of his Mercedes, weaved through a field of witch grass, and flipped his luxury sedan into the river, drowning and dying the way he'd spent most of his existence—drunk, lost, and confused.

Paul and I both had alibis.

We'd spent the night working the Highlands branch. There had been enough customers who'd provide testimony to our whereabouts, regulars, weirdoes who could not bear the thought of losing their subversive haven.

Strangely enough, despite all the mayhem associated with our names as of late, detectives never questioned us about the doctor's death. Most still consider the official police version—a drunk driving accident—to be the truth to this day.

Chad Thomas, vocal anti-narcotics crusader and decorated LMPD detective, who relished the opportunity to dispatch a child beater, didn't need an alibi. No one questioned could link him with the late physician.

"Last year when I paid for Adam to go visit her parents," Paul said of the former missus, "I didn't even try to protect her. Didn't give her a heads up or nothing. Just told her that Adam deserved a vacation, that it was important Adam get to know where he came from, and that her mom and dad might not be around much longer. She bought it too. Luther was ready to go after anyone related to me and I left her out in the open. She's lucky we got to him before he got to her."

"So, you're saying you have a good relationship with women," I said. "I always pegged you for a feminist."

We were on our way to his ex-wife's mansion on the banks of the Ohio.

"How do you think he'll take it?" Paul chewed at a hangnail. I felt like I was driving him to homecoming. Except, as far as I know, teenage Paul didn't have his date's significant other killed the night before the big dance. "I mean, Adam."

"Adam?" I slapped the steering wheel. "Adam? That was the confusion. Here this whole time I thought we were discussing our esteemed colleague, Mr. Chad Thomas. Makes sense now. I was wondering how logically one could fit words like 'grief' or 'mourning' or 'human' into a sentence with his name."

"I thought you and Thomas were getting pretty tight."

"I don't mind him. He's quite a conversationalist. He likes the Ramones. He tells great racial jokes, which, of course, everyone loves. But he does have a nasty habit of rather drastically devaluing human life when deciding on business matters."

"I'm thankful for the man," Paul said. "Because of him, the piece of shit who hurt my son won't ever eat a steak or enjoy an orgasm again."

"You're becoming so goddamn..." I couldn't think of an appropriate term.

"Morally flexible?" Paul laughed. 'Those were the same words I used to describe you when we committed our first murder so many heroin deals ago."

"I was high," I said.

"When you came down," Paul looked at me, "did you feel bad about killing that little worthless shit?"

I kept my eyes on the road and forewent further discussion of the life we'd chosen and the possible karmic consequences.

"Adam will be fine." I lightened up on the worried father. "He hated that bastard. Said he had nightmares from the stories Sullay would tell at the dinner table of the torturous shit the drunkard had done during the Bosnian Civil War. The doctor would tell these heinous tales then intimate how, if the rules of his house weren't followed with religious precision, he was not beyond enacting the same war crimes on Renee and Adam if they did not 'respect his household.'"

"Why did he come to you?" Paul asked me.

I knew this subject would arise and, as usual, had rehearsed a credible response.

"I think he was afraid what you'd do," I said after a moment.

We shared the kind of glance only men who'd spilt blood together can understand. Then we laughed like permanent residents of the maddest looney bin south of Cincinnati.

He hadn't said it. But I knew Paul hoped that with Dr. Arm Bender out of the picture, this new life Adam and Renee were to build might include him. I watched from the book van as Paul ran to the front door, Despite how I'd taunted him, the red-haired widow Sullay still had that figure that had made me vicious with jealousy when Paul was married to her. Renee stood at the door with Adam, the widow weeping. Adam appeared next to her and opened his arms for her to fall into, massaging her shoulders and whispering into her ear.

The kid grinned briefly as he waved me goodbye and his

blood parents embraced for the first time in half a decade.

I wondered if Adam had already figured out that Paul and I had arranged for his step-father's death.

The things we do for love.

21

"I'm so lonesome, I could cry," Catherine sang from the passenger side, plucking the strings of her Gibson with metal picks affixed to each finger. With that woebegone Appalachian warble, she sounded like a young Maybelle Carter. For the first time since Irina last kissed me, the back of my neck tingled as it always did when I felt myself falling. It was a feeling best captured by the crooners who'd sung Catherine's life back to her in the doddering frame house on Rutherford Avenue where she'd grown up, voices tangled in the wire circuitry of half-broken radios and record players.

She let the last chord echo.

Like an idiot, and as per her request, I'd agreed to wear her Bobby Bare Stetson with the red feather rising from beneath the beaded hatband. I looked like a gunslinger gone native, or so Catherine had said.

Catherine peaked back at the vacant chamber behind us, the mostly empty shelves Paul had nailed up after he'd purchased Bookmobile 2, the Dodge van on cinderblocks that Thomas had furnished with four new tires after removing all the seats behind the cab. The singer appraised the storage space a little too long for my liking, so I drew her attention back to the guitar in her lap. "Play something else."

"This thing..." she said. "I love it. Great idea, Jon. You'll make some trophy blonde a nice sugar daddy someday."

She rested her boots on the dash, the heels worn to stubs. She was thick in the legs, like Bettie Page, and wore her hair similar for the evening's performance, black Elvira bangs and shining roan strands detaining down her shoulders over her brown denim coat. "Why don't you sing something with me. I know you still got a voice. You probably sound just like you did when you were nineteen. Just name something. I'll play, you sing. It'll make the trip go faster."

We were on 75, far from any exit, rolling fields of broken horses leering from behind crooked fences. "Why would I want to speed up our time together?"

"You're good." She rested the guitar's neck against her breasts and mimed two gunshots, forming pistols with her hands. "You're a fast draw. But I'm not letting you off that easy."

"I probably don't even remember how."

"It's like riding a bike." Catherine picked the notes of the G-run slowly, turning the simple progression into a waltz and, miraculously, she made the hillbilly breakdown sound sexy.

Maybe the sensuality had nothing to do with the music.

Then she twisted the knife, leaning closer, canting her head. "It's like riding a bike or making love. Ain't something you forget."

"I haven't owned a guitar in five years."

"You don't forget that either. Also, no one's asking you to play. I just want to hear that pretty voice."

"I probably sound like Big Bird imitating Tom Waits at my age."

"You're ten years younger than me. That what I sound like? Or worse?"

"You've been touring that whole time. Practicing."

"I'll sit here all night. Let the show go on without me. Get in debt with the club."

"Enough." I dispensed an asininely clamorous burst of nervous laughter. Under any other circumstances, I'd allow her to remain in the van as opposed to ever singing in front of her again. "Just let me think of something we both know."

"I know all the good ones."

"Let me think of one that's easy to sing." I bought some more time before the imminent embarrassment.

The truth was that I had hated music and resented most musicians ever since I'd pawned my guitars and broken up the last band I'd formed. I had a choice, finish my education or tour with a honky-tonk group. At my father's urging I picked the former. I trusted that dear old dad was telling me the truth when, despite his own talents—the senior Catlett could play piano, dobro, guitar, banjo, and would randomly break into song without leaving a dry eye in the house—he warned me to avoid show business like a plague. He claimed I'd wind up a bum digging ditches if I further pursued such nonsense.

So, I gave it up, worked part-time at my favorite used bookstore, and graduated from Indiana University Southeast with a degree in Humanities, a piece of paper that I have never needed and that has not, despite my father's prophecy, earned me a cent.

I fell into selling books online and before I even earned my degree, had forty grand in the bank. My former boss, Hank Maier, who ran Second Story Books until 2009 when he closed shop to sell strictly online, had provided me with more of an education than any high school teacher or college professor I'd ever studied under. He also told me I was a talented singer and songwriter and never to give up on my craft. The old curmudgeon not only schooled me in the tools of the book dealing trade, he also introduced me to James Ellroy and Frederick Exley, to Pete Dexter and William Kennedy. These authors have since become like home to me, like Hank and his store.

The old man was the one who turned me onto the great American songwriter Mickey Newbury who, while never achieving commercial success with his own recordings, composed some of the most beautiful songs and arrangements I'll ever hear. He made his living writing hits for everyone from Waylon Jennings to Jerry Lee Lewis. He produced his own records as a labor of blind love.

Before I'd even finished saying the title, Catherine kick-started the rollicking number, strumming slightly off-rhythm just as Newbury did on his largely unknown cut of sonic brilliance, "Sunshine."

By the second verse, we were singing together, and I had to admit, we didn't sound half bad:

Sunshine, you may find my window
But you won't find me

And sunshine, I've got my friend of darkness here
Tonight to hide me.

I'd sung another Newbury song, "Heaven Help the
Child" at the old man's funeral the year before I started on
heroin. The ballad was fitting for our farewell to such a
literary figure who'd so influenced the town's underground
community, me crying over the casket and crowing our
magisterial Mickey's musical homage to the great authors
of the twenties and thirties, from Hemingway to Fante to
Fitzgerald.

As Catherine and I neared the end of our duet, I was
suddenly besieged by a nauseating hybrid of gratitude and
remorse, gratitude for Hank never seeing me strung out,
remorse over failing to properly honor his memory and
allowing the bookstore he'd inspired me to open to fall into
the hands of dirty cops and drug dealers. A torrent broke
the levees of my tear ducts. I had to pull the van over.
Catherine let the guitar fall to the floor and shot across the
panel between our seats to embrace me.

I told her everything.

Hank. The junk. My drunk of a father. My suicidal
mother. The habit I'd almost died kicking.

Everything but what lay hidden in the etched spaces of
the first editions shelved in the hatch behind us.

I pulled onto the residential cul-de-sac two streets parallel
to the Parthenon's rear column. I could hear the music
from the Sweetwater and, just for a moment, considered
going back and skipping the shipment.

Catherine had promised a Tom T. Hall cover. I could hear her high-lonesome vibrato somewhere between my ears, belting the lyrics to "Old Dogs, Children, and Watermelon Wine," or perhaps "I Miss a Lot of Trains." I would have stayed to watch her prepare, flex her vocal chords, maybe howl at the moon a few times, but sadly, for survival's sake, business took precedence.

Paul had told me enough about the Dixie mafia to scare me. Mad Dog provided us with extensive criminal profiles, the longest on the Nashville tribe's leader, Jimmy Dale Gibson. He'd come from Knoxville and graduated three federal prisons. Unlike so many pompous leaders, he didn't fear dirty hands. From executions to torture, he played an active role in the mob's local proceedings. He favored castration for the worst trespasses, for rats and turncoats, employing only the dullest steak knives while the victim lay bound to a gynecologist's awkward slab, stirrups and all.

That's why I decided not to pull a no-show.

Gibson had promised to make a personal appearance tonight along with a few armed flunkies for our first exchange as new business partners.

I did not look forward to meeting him.

Headlights reflected through the side and rearview mirrors. I adjusted the fixtures and blinked to escape the glare's afterglow. When my eyes reconciled the darkness, I spotted a black man, a kid really, his leather overcoat buttoned tightly from ankle to eye, the fringe caressing the tips of his freshly shined alligator shoes. He'd crossed through the yard of a vacant white house.

"Who the fuck is this guy?" I said aloud to myself.

He stopped just shy of the bumper, off to the side, so I

couldn't gun it and run him down. While he paused before his work, freeing the raincoat lapels, I heard a door slam and turned to spy through the tinted windows of the van's rear. An older fellow had stepped onto the street from the driver's side of the Honda he had just parked behind the Bookmobile. The headlights had faded, the engine silent.

The elder unzipped his duster and drew a hand to the HK machine pistol dangling beneath his left arm from a shoulder harness.

The kid fired first, raising the Uzi from beneath the tails of his duster and letting loose a few short bursts. I sunk into the floorboards when, after a brief calm, the two men switched to auto, peppering the cargo area and the cab with rounds as the van wobbled from side to side, tossing me back and forth against the seat and the floor pedals with each controlled burst.

There goes the new paint job, the stenciling and free advertising, I thought

In films, machine guns seem to never fail. Until their handlers release the triggers, they enjoy an endless and uninterrupted supply of ammunition. Not so in the real world, where gunpowder suffocates with its deathly stench and magazines only run to a thirty-round capacity.

The initial gunfire lasted maybe twenty seconds. Then came the attendant sounds following all brief and unintentional ceasefires, metal on metal, magazines replaced, hushed utterances heavy with expletives and threats.

Moonglow crept in through the dozens of holes that had ventilated the Bookmobile's hold. Strangely, the first editions remained undamaged and unmoved on their shelves.

One of the rounds had pierced the fuel tank and the

black plastic coverlet that ran the length of the van's interior had begun to fill, the pungent aroma inspiring thoughts of escape and retaliation. I glanced again in the rearview. The men now stood side by side behind the Bookmobile, stepping closer in synch.

Predictable and, whatever their fee, vastly overpaid killers.

Not sure how much they charged to murder me in Music City, but anything over gas money they surely hadn't earned.

That, or they simply underestimated this greasy white boy some soon-to-be regretful son-of-a-bitch had hired them to flatline.

Either way, the two erringly self-assured hard-cases had allowed me to slip out the passenger side, out of their gunsights. I fell flat on my ass, from the floorboard to the street, and saw my aggressors pulling open the rear doors.

At this period of my spiral into false confidence, I believed that, no matter how good their aim, it would take more than a few full leather jacket bursts to kill me.

I know now luck played a far larger a role in my bare survival.

As the two mumbled and gaped at the empty cargo bay, I kicked against the pavement, crawling backwards into the shrubbery and pressed the barrel of my HK between the bush's tiny branches. The gasoline had formed a small creek beneath the Bookmobile, flowing past the fuel tank, the transmission, and the engine, stretching toward the sidewalk beyond which I'd found cover.

I drew a bead on the elder. I could take him no problem; one shot to his brain stem and everything would go dark for the senior hit man. But then his apprentice could turn and let loose again with that Uzi. The bushes weren't bulletproof.

I turned onto my side and rested my forehead defeatedly against the grip of the useless pistol in my hand.

Then I remembered the Zippo I always kept on my person, a gift from Lex. He'd given me the lighter the day we'd cemented our partnership, when he agreed to help me kill my old boss and all his faithful minions before they could get to me and mine. Despite the fallout in Chicago, I'd kept the present, a rather flawed talisman against hard luck that had obviously lost its power.

I brought out the rusted souvenir, ignited the spark, and tossed my absent friend's token of future betrayal into the diminishing gas trail.

The partners were still staring dumbstruck into the empty van when the fire caught. The younger had time to back pedal a few feet into the road when the flames reached the gas tank.

The blast cut the elder in half, his upper torso fragmented into a dozen pieces. A hand, still aflame, landed on the top of the bush above where I hid. The dry leaves began to smoke and I rolled onto the sidewalk. I rose to see the surviving youth in flames, flailing and weaving miserably my way. He blindly triggered two final muzzle-flashes from the strangely untarnished machine pistol.

The gun clicked cold, but he kept pulling the trigger and howling like a castrated banshee. Just to silence the poor bastard's awful screaming, I raised my Heckler and Koch and blew a chunk of brain and charred flesh from the dying killer's skull.

As he collapsed like a burning barn, I caught first sight of the Lincoln Continental parked diagonally across the street as if to block off oncoming traffic and pedestrians from the macabre menace the two hired hands and I had made of the quiet suburban evening.

A few houses toward the street's dead end, an old maid looked on from a grassless front lot in her nightgown and curlers. Her husband in his thermal pants and undershirt stood behind her on the warped and bloated floorboards of the near lifeless couple's neglected front porch.

Across the roof of the Lincoln, from the driver's side, the crown of a leather watch cap appeared, but barely, indicating that the luxury sedan's chauffeur hadn't enjoyed many slam-dunks in his life of vertical challenges and Napoleon comparisons. The midget stepped forward, ducking as quick as he'd appeared behind the far side of the car's hood.

I backed away, squatting behind a row of mailboxes.

When the little fellow rose, he held the charred right hand of the elder killer who'd been nearly vaporized by the blast. In the severed extremity the machine gun remained firmly gripped, the dead finger within the trigger guard.

"Give me a break," I said.

Then I remembered the couple that had stepped outside for a better view of our violent little opera.

Witnesses, I thought, closing my eyes. If they'd stayed inside, and out of the window frames, they couldn't have gotten a very good look at the perps who'd turned their shitty street into a free fire zone. Why couldn't these poor assholes have been smarter?

When the machine gun burped yet again, I took little

comfort in knowing the shots weren't meant for me. The old lady screamed once then a second burst cut off the sound. I focused on the falling flaming pages of Yeats that drifted from the Van debris like hellish snows from the vengeful heavens. The mute midget had dropped the gun, the severed hand still holding on—a perfect setup. The little man was now on his iPhone, directing a beat cop on the Dixie payroll to speed over and arrive first to secure and try to stage the scene to the boss' liking.

The tinted window of the Continental's back door descended and Jimmy Dale Gibson's pallid, pockmarked visage appeared from the car's interior dark like a disembodied night terror.

"Was my dope in that fuckin' van?" Gibson growled.

22

Sitting at a booth in the Sweetwater, across from the gruesome, long-haired hillbilly mobster and his miniature driver, the hairless albino dressed in a chauffer's watch cap and the leather regale of an extra from "Cruising," I made a conscious decision regarding my personal life, one I probably should have come to long before stupidly informing Jimmy Dale about my guest in Nashville and her musical talents.

I would forego dating altogether if I were to survive Gibson and his Nashville ilk. And I would cease contact with Catherine. I considered what kind of a piece of shit would get two women killed, then, continuing with his lifestyle that had led to their deaths, involve another innocent female with the same masochistic cast of low creatures who had no problem dishing out death in random and unequal supplements.

"I assume that ridiculous vehicle of yours is traceable back to the book shop in Louisville." Gibson asked. His voice sounded like one of those quiet, slow farts that an old man of regular flatulence would emit without even noticing. "That means if my police can't clean it up before some good Christian Eagle Scout type arrives on…"

"We bought the van a week ago from a pretty desperate

junkie in a whole lot of debt to us," I said. "Neither me or my associates ever signed our name to anything when we paid cash for the Bookmobile and we've been so busy I hadn't gotten around to filing a salvage title on it. My laziness, for once, seems to have worked in my favor. The plates could trace back to the doper, if the junk heap was his to begin with and not his dead grandmother's or some shit."

"If it's stolen all the better. Anything else I should know?"

"That's it. I don't think anyone's going to make out our logo on the side after that fire."

"The plates won't be a problem," Gibson said. "If nothing else, I know my guy on the beat at the NPD can handle that much. But you didn't leave nothing else inside the van? You sure? I never understood men who claimed to enjoy surprises. There's absolutely nothing you left in that vehicle that we need to talk about?"

I thought for a moment. "You mean anything that could survive the fire?"

"I mean my heroin, you imbecile."

Jimmy Dale leered at the stage, through the growing crowd of standing fans, at a slightly elevated Catherine, standing between two pick-up players, a pedal steel man and young girl with a fiddle, my old crush's acoustic vibrating against her breasts as she sang, "I wasn't drinking to forget, I was drinking to remember." As if the line had helped Jimmy Dale reach a conclusion about her fate, maybe mine too, his grimace melted into a half-grin and he raised his glass, toasting the night's entertainment. "She is somethin'." He drained the decanter of Irish whiskey and slid it across the table for Pappy, his lawn jockey of a henchman, to catch. "Give us a minute, Pap. Go get yourself a drink. Another for me too, if you can fit it into your busy little schedule." I'd noticed that, when speaking to Pappy, Jimmy Dale always worked in a word that related to vertical ineptitude, *short, little, shrimpy.* So it wasn't really the sadism or the fact that he might've been one of the ugliest son-of-a-bitches I've ever seen in my life—I'm a Kentuckian so I've seen my sad share of grisly freaks—but rather his petty bullying that inspired the hope that someday soon Jimmy Dale would join the sad procession of ill-fated power moguls I'd seen come to grim ends, the Luthers and Lexes of the world.

As Pappy pounced away from the booth, bouncing from one foot to another like a wounded burlesque dancer, Jimmy Dale said, "Where are you right now, Catlett?"

"The Sweetwater Music Club." I forced eye contact with the sinister son-of-a-bitch. "Nashville, Tennessee. The United States of America. Planet fuckin' earth? Heard of it? I'd quote you the longitude and latitude lines too but I know you're a man of high parts, Jimmy Dale, and I wouldn't want to insult you with excess."

"I meant in a more metaphysical sense."

"Have you looked around? Hippies, pacifists, democrats for Christ's sake, and in Nashville, the South, to boot. I mean you're obviously a Republican, right?"

"I don't appreciate—"

"How more metaphysical can we get? We're stuck in the Sweetwater. Also, it smells like a goddamn menstruating poodle in this place."

I finally got the grotesque to grin at one of my asininities.

"I am not stuck anywhere."

"That's debatable, Jimmy Dale. I don't think the retirement plan for Dixie mafia ward bosses includes a gold watch and some 401(k)."

"No, you usually leave this line of work prostrate," he said. "Speaking of which, it's a good thing for you that those flames had that dope smell. At least I know you brought something down with you, that you didn't come to my town empty handed."

"You thought the explosion of my van, our crew's perfect cover into which I just pumped weeks of work and a ludicrous amount of cash—you thought I'd destroy the Bookmobile just to cover up a lack of inventory?"

"I've seen men smarter than you act stupider. But relax, I got a whiff of the crime scene."

"Relax? I wasn't exactly tense. You're not the first trigger-happy murderer I've met in this line of business."

"More like rusty blade-happy," he said. Dale's jack-o-lantern leer broadened. "You strike me as a man familiar, too familiar, with the sweet scent of opium."

"I believe I've shared quite enough with you about my personal life."

"My question now is, what wretched souls did the two bodies belong to who decided to try and kill you on my territory?"

"How do you know it wasn't someone trying to sabotage your set-up here in Music City?"

I already knew who'd tried to kill me. But I wasn't ready

to share this information with Jimmy Dale. It was worth a try to throw him off.

"You don't think very highly of me as an administrator, I take it."

"What about Ma and Pa Kettle?" I asked of the two senior citizens Pap had silenced with the dead contract killer's submachine gun.

"Unfortunate that they got such a good look at our faces."

"No, Mr. Gibson," I said. "Hemorrhoids are unfortunate. What Santa's little helper did to those people was heinous."

"The cost of doing business."

I'd heard that phrase so many times over the past year, I nearly regurgitated at the sound.

"Those bodies," Jimmy said, "the men we killed together, they were the ones ultimately responsible for the destruction of the product I purchased, not to mention your van, correct?"

I nodded. Catherine covered "You Belong to Me." For a moment, I wondered if she was trying to tell me something, then cursed myself for poor prioritizing, for the toxic levels of self-absorption and sexism that had so heavily influenced my descent into the underworld.

"Who were those men?" Jimmy Dale had followed my gaze, rolling his eyes at the sight of the cowgirl crooning, then shaking his head in professional disapproval at me still nearly drooling, jaw agape, head tilted over my shoulder as if flat-lining upright.

I didn't want to inform Jimmy Dale that a bent DEA

agent I'd pissed off in Louisville had likely hired the murderous duo.

That bastard Sexton.

I hoped I lived long enough to watch him die.

"Who they are is irrelevant. They're dead now."

"They destroyed the product you were bringing me."

"Actually, I'm the one that destroyed it. I had to. Otherwise I'd be dead and the cops would now have your dope."

"That doesn't still the cravings of my loyal customers."

"Now I make one call to the River City and get you some more first editions and we're back—"

"We..." Jimmy Dale clasped his hairy, hoary hands to my wrists and squeezed tight, applying enough pressure to force my head to the table, my jaw chattering as I mumbled stilted pleas for mercy, turning coward the only way I knew how, fast and without shame. "We are *not* back, Jon. And you won't be going *back* anywhere if we don't settle a few issues that most certainly *do matter* still. For instance, it *should matter* to you that I'm wondering why I'm doing business with a man who shows up to a meet with two dead niggers and his very conspicuous vehicle in flames instead of the dope I ordered."

"Joseph and Milligan vouched for me." My wrist bones felt like they'd turned to river silt. "They don't lie. They're solid. And you know what we bring you is better than anything you're going to find in the south. We deliver it..." I had to focus on my breathing a few moments to keep from breaking into tears. The man had a grip like a one-handed peep show regular.

"There you go, ol' boy. You've finally identified what doesn't matter." Jimmy Dale brought his face closer to the

Formica, his voice softening, like we'd just become BFFs, bonding through beastly torture. Pain was probably the only medium to express intimacy the Dixie boss understood. Lucky me. "You see your product's quality is no longer of consequence because it has joined the ether. And what if some other witness comes forward? Another welfare couple rubbernecking safely from behind their kitchen window? That's either a pay-off or another hit I have to contract out. I mean it'd be nice if we killed every retiree in that neighborhood, but that kind of thing can get out of hand real quick."

"Imagine how Stalin and Hitler felt. All that overhead just to exterminate a race of people? Jesus. I know, man."

"And what's more, you've brought along a possible witness. Why would you pick tonight, here, now, for a first date?"

"Mr. Gibson, my generation is really into the idea of multi-tasking."

"Are you smarting me?"

"No, I was simply trying to answer—"

"We'll see how smart you are when I glue your eyelids to your brow so you ain't got no choice but to watch me teach little puss 'n' boots with the guitar how to fit a Memphis white snake in her throat.

"She's a civilian. She's not in the game. She disappears and people will come looking."

"I can slaughter that bitch and lose not a wink of sleep. I'd control every aspect of the investigation. I own this police department. Believe that, Catlett. South of Cincinnati, I am the most powerful player in any black market you can imagine. Atlanta, Memphis, Biloxi, Birmingham, they all answer to me. I chose Nashville to lay down roots because, aside from shattering the wrists of closet homosexuals who botch business deals, I love country music more than anything on this shit planet."

"I'm quite a fan myself. Speaking of my wrists—"

He tightened his grip.

"Goddamnit," I yelled. No one noticed. The men were too busy mentally undressing the songstress on the stage while their girlfriends fantasized of cowgirl-clad voodoo dolls.

"Lower your voice or I'll break your wrists and drag you out of here by your dick."

"What is it with you and dicks?" I asked him, a shameful whine permeating every syllable.

"Then I'll replace you as the lady's escort for the evening, show her what a hot date I am. Some real musky, chicken-skin Southern hospitality."

"She doesn't know shit," I said.

"Yet," Jimmy Dale said.

"Can you just be straight with me?" I asked. "Is there any possible way to leave her out of this? Even if you have to take me and leave me face down in a cow pasture or whatever the fuck you Nashvillians have around here—"

"Probably a small body of water or in different pieces in dumpsters—"

"We both get the idea. I'm asking if you can spare her."

"I could spare both of you. I'm not promising anything, though. Not until I'm confident I'll have my supply by morning. And your life doesn't strike me as sufficient leverage. You don't seem like a man afraid of dying."

"I'm more afraid of your reputed talent with dull blades and pelvises."

"As you should be."

"That can't do for now, leverage wise?"

He finally released my wrists.

"Thank you, Jesus." I moaned quietly and tucked my hands beneath my armpits, softly squeezing the muscles the gangster had nearly torn. "Oh, thank you, sweet tender baby Rabbi Jesus."

"I'm astounded that you've survived this business this long." Jimmy Dale turned his alabaster face toward the dim bar of light that shone between the swinging fluorescents and the dance floor. "You're a shrewd negotiator. And you're also fortunate that I'm not in the mood for the expenses of hostages and blackmail. But believe this, if you don't get your crew and your operation under control by the time of our next meeting, I'll have to resort to the knife."

I somehow faked the courage to agree to Gibson's terms.

"You don't wish to seek my counsel?" Jimmy Dale said.

I shook my head. The minute Jimmy Dale found out a DEA agent was behind all this, he'd sever all ties with Louisville, using a rusty bowie knife to do so. "It's my problem. My territory. I'll handle it. Plus, to be honest, this is personal."

"You want to borrow my operating table?"

"No, thanks. I'm not one for flamboyance when it comes to my violence. I believe I'll just settle for the usual, shoot him in forehead then go home and see what's new on Netflix."

"Go home and get a good night's sleep."

"Yes, sir."

"You sure you can handle your city?" Jimmy Dale asked.

I hadn't been sure of that at any point in my life, of my city, the source of such ancient and everlasting wounds.

"I've been handling it for a few decades now." I rose from the booth. "Can you point me in the direction of a rental car agency that won't ask too many questions?"

"I'll do you one better," he said. "I'll send Pappy up with you. You can ride into town in style and he can ride back with my heroin."

Catherine said into the mic that this would be her last song.

I hoped just for the evening.

23

"So, you wrecked your van?" Catherine shook her head then appraised again the interior of the Lincoln in which we rode back up 75. Pappy hadn't spoken a word. He'd nodded noncommittally upon meeting Catherine in the back of the club as I'd loaded her guitars and pedals into the trunk that seemed to have been constructed for the sole purpose of transporting human bodies.

I'd grown tired of her incessant curiosity. Seeing two innocent senior citizens machine-gunned after murdering two men yourself, combined with the constant threat of a slow and torturous death, tended to wear down a man's patience. I remained thankful, though, that Pappy had taken an alternate route back to the highway, avoiding the crime scene. "I don't much feel like discussing it, hon."

"Don't fucking call me 'hon.' Treat me like a moron. The van disappears and all of a sudden you produce a chauffeur? You're into some bad business, Catlett. I've heard rumors. You look clean, but you act like a man on death row. What exactly did you leave out of that little confession you made on the side of the road?"

"I've been through hell this year. Can you lay off? And why are you so goddamn upset anyway? We're getting to ride back home in style."

"Because Irina warned me that you were a liar. And I gave you a chance anyway. You go and prove her right on our first goddamn date."

"Hon—" I couldn't help myself.

"Call me that again and I swear—"

"Would you rather I call you bitch, because I think I'm ready for that phase of intimacy."

"When we get back to the city, I'm never speaking to you again."

"Do I have to wait another hour for that to kick in?"

Pappy's reproachful gaze reflected at me from the rearview mirror.

"And how did you come up with this guy again?" She wagged a finger at our driver.

"Old friends," Pappy answered for me. "Apparently so old, my friend done forgot how to speak to a lady."

We arrived in Louisville well after midnight. The region's rhapsodic seasons had invited into the river valley a strange coupling of unpredictable river breezes and perpetual humidity. My Kentucky home had momentarily washed me clean with dim hope and sentimental wonder. But in the quiet moments that lacked sensory distraction, after Catherine and I had agreed on a frail truce in the patriotic hometown rhetoric we shared crossing the city limits, I returned to freezing.

Just past the Crittenden Drive exit, my cell vibrated.

Thomas' name appeared on the screen.

"I gotta take this," I told Catherine. "It might be about the store. Sorry."

She nodded for me to go ahead.

I answered.

"Listen very carefully—"

I couldn't talk in front of Catherine. "I'll have to call you back."

"I wouldn't hang up that phone right now unless you want a real unpleasant fucking surprise when you return to your store. If you're still with the broad, that's alright. Just listen."

I love it that he'd called Twice Told *my* store.

"Okay?" I said.

"This is serious. The big leagues, bub."

"Did you just call me 'bub?'" I asked.

"It's a Lexington thing. These cops from Lex were helping us on a—"

"Oh my God. It's fucking insane how deeply I do not care about anything you're saying right now. I thought you had something important to tell me. I don't have time for goddamn anecdotes."

"Catlett. This is the day that separates the men from the boys."

"Why have I not hung up yet?" I asked myself. I looked at Catherine and mouthed, "Paul," rolling my eyes.

"You can end up living off food stamps and smelling unwashed assholes in some half way house in Duluth," Thomas said, "or you can look St. Peter in the eye when you reach those glorious goddamn pearly gates and, when he asks what you did with your life that's so great, you can reply, with a white man's pride and certainty, 'Ever heard of Twice Told Books, St. Pecker? You're fuckin' welcome, bub.'"

"I'm failing to derive any meaning whatsoever from what you just said."

"Paul's wife is missing. That meaningful enough for you?"

I immediately hung up on Thomas. I couldn't hear anymore. Not now. Not with Catherine beside me and almost willing to forgive. The same night the hit on me in Nashville had failed, Paul's ex disappears? I needed more details, but I'd bet a thick wallet of American folded money that the two events were connected.

I wish now things had been so simple.

"Is everything okay?" Catherine asked, reading my expression that followed the shady phone call.

I blinked a few times and tried to evict the overwhelming dread from my soiled spirit. "Yeah. Just money stuff with the new store."

"Never a dull moment." Then she redeemed the cliché with one of those all-forgiving smiles of unadulterated joy and wonder that only a good woman can form, gracing me with such a moment toward which all men motivate their worldly toils. "Can one of us wave a white flag and officially end this petty little lovers' spat?"

"Lovers, huh?"

"I've decided you're worth more than one date and some irritation over compromised travel plans."

Pappy grinned at me in the rearview. Perhaps even psychopaths are humbled by the presence of love and genuine good will, both nearly extinct in the life I'd chosen, their absence creating a vacuum into which souls like mine and Paul's and Pappy's are forever lost.

* * *

"She went out for some dessert." Paul leaned against the foyer wall of the new West End branch. The store had been closed for four hours. Mad Dog and Thomas had come in at nine, an hour before shutdown, and ordered Myron to bring in the sandwich board and lock the doors. Our crew would remain on lockdown until we figured out how many adversaries we faced and how to deal with each without losing too much manpower and money. Myron had posted a few of his lieutenants in cars to stake out every entrance into the mall parking lot, just in case our enemy decided to come at us head on.

All were present. Thomas' team formed a strangely comforting circle, lining the walls of the store, a wavering womb within which Paul paced while the rest of us awaited further details regarding the disappearance.

While eagerly anticipating the culmination of Paul's account, I noticed Snyder in the corner leaning on one of the record bins. She gave me the shit eye for the duration of the meeting. We hadn't spoken since the no-star motel room tryst and I'd honestly believed she'd wanted it that way, a casual coupling with no guilt, shame, or, for that matter, joy and companionship to follow.

I suppose I'd been wrong. While I barely knew Snyder, I knew the look.

"You got a lot of nerve paying attention to any pussy but this one," she may as well have been screaming.

For a moment, I wondered how she'd discovered my date with Catherine across state lines. Then I remembered that Paul gossips like a high school girl and that a criminal organization isn't far above a fraternity or a pack of ado-

lescent punk rockers on the invisible ladder of social so-
phistication.

"She just never came back," Paul repeated. "She went
out for ice cream and three hours later, she's still gone."
He'd left Adam at the boy's grandmother's and lied that
Mom had called and was having car trouble in town.

At this point, we'd be insulting the boy to assume that
Adam did not know better. Why would his mother have
driven all the way into the city from the bucolic riverside
just for a pint of ice cream when there was a Kroger a few
miles down Rose Island Road? Paul had buttressed his
original lie with an even stupider one, that Eherler's tasted
better if bought from one of the chains, not some grocery,
pre-packaged.

Pappy entered the circle. He'd just returned from
dropping Catherine off in the Highlands and I wanted to
make the most out of a shit situation. While the night's
meeting would only serve to fuel Jimmy Gibson's suspicions that us Louisville boys couldn't handle our business,
at the very least, Pappy would get the promised heroin and
stand as a witness to my tale of dead senior citizens and
exploding book vans.

"Paul," I said.

My old partner looked my way.

I couldn't forget what he'd said earlier about gladly
allowing his ex to die at Luther's hands.

I needed to talk to Adam. If Paul had lied, I needed to
know why. I wouldn't put it past the bastard, as uppity as
he'd grown since he took ownership of the store, to have
initiated some long con.

I repeated his name before adding to his questionable

story what had happened to me, to our organization, in Nashville.

Before I began my account, I asked, "How do we know it's safe to talk here? Did anyone fucking think of that? Huh, Paul?" I mocked the circular wave of the index finger with which Paul had gestured in the Highlands store when I first came to town and he'd been worried that some federal judge had initiated a wiretap.

Mad Dog answered for Paul. "The probation and parole people stay as far away from work on weekends as humanly possible. As far as they go, there's no safer place for us right now. Also, our proximity to their office might cause our enemies to pause before trying to hit us at home. And I scanned the place for bugs. We're good. Also, I bugged both the homicide dicks' patrol unit and each of their civilian vehicles." Mad Dog tapped on the screen of his iPhone, which displayed a colorful GPS map. "We'll know with plenty of lead time if they're headed our way or tailing one of us."

"You bugged the motherfuckin' five-oh?" Myron yelled. "You fuckin' crazy, old man?"

"He knows how to get away with it," Thomas assured us. "And they'd have to tail us on their own time. The department ain't exactly liberal in handing out overtime and granting special investigations. They need all that drug money they confiscate for marble fireplaces and golf trips for the chief."

"Who did this?" Paul demanded satisfaction like a scolded child. "Who's after us? Chicago?" He turned to Myron. "Any trouble west of Roy Wilkens?"

Myron grinned. "Nah, man. Every niggah in the five-oh-two that ain't half retarded knows who's daddy on them streets."

Without going into what led to the mostly accidental invitation of Agent Sexton into our lives, leaving out Adam's track marks, Mad Dog nearly incited a breach in the sound barrier when he explained that our main local competitor happened to be a drug fed.

"A DEA agent?" Snyder cupped her face in her hands to muffle a frustrated grunt, then mumbled, "We're all fucked."

Pappy stood near the circle's center and held his palms upturned, indicating their obvious emptiness.

"Goddamn it." I had more pressing obituaries to write, bigger habits to feed, more people to kill. Instead, I had to cut off the clamor of questions that followed my Nashville story and take Pappy into the storage room where Thomas had stashed a few emergency bricks of dope for such an occasion. "Everyone is going to have to quiet down and silently reflect for a few moments." I nodded toward Pappy and explained, "Oswald Cobblepot here has pressing business to discuss with me. Don't worry. It will be a short transaction." I winked at Myron and his corner boys as they laughed at the sight of the pale gnome.

I didn't trust that Jimmy Dale Gibson hadn't sent Pappy along with explicit instructions to kill us all. How he'd accomplish such a feat, the odds stacked against him with nearly a dozen armed criminals to his one, I could not imagine. But since the little henchman closely resembled a freakish comic book villain (hence my reference to Batman's Penguin), and given the bum hand he'd been dealt genetically, a suicide bombing seemed genuinely within the realm of possibility.

Thomas and Mad Dog filed behind me as I headed down the short hall that ran alongside the checkout counter, on one side a cardboard stand-up of Richard Pryor cursing into his microphone, opposite him a vinyl listening station resembling a telephone booth in which customers could enclose themselves and enjoy the sweet sonic ecstasy of Miles Davis and Chuck Brown.

Paul entered my peripheral. I turned and pointed toward the broken circle of psychotics. "You," I said to him, "stay."

"Are you mistaking me for your fucking dog?" he yelled.

"Speaking of which," I said, "where is Irina?"

"Thank God you're not the father of a human being," Paul said. "She's locked safely in your bedroom office, you selfish shit."

"Cool," I said. "Great. If they toss a Molotov cocktail through the window, there goes my Irina."

"Your second," he said.

"You need to step away from me," I told him. "Right now."

"I don't answer to you anymore, remember? All this shit is under my name."

"And you're too emotionally distracted to conduct business." Thomas bumped Paul aside with his chest. The merc flared his nostrils. "You walk the circle a few times."

Paul took a step back and Thomas barked, "Walk it off, bro."

Paul pivoted back toward the rest of our confederates,

his head low and his shoulders slumped.

"Thanks," I murmured as Thomas passed me into the back room where I held the door open for my strange bedfellows, the dirty cop, the mercenary, and the albino midget.

Thomas ignored my gratitude and stopped short of a tin shelf nailed loosely to the unpainted dry wall and retrieved from within a cardboard box, one of many labeled "over-stock" in black magic marker, a late 1970s book club edition of Dickens' *Bleak House*. The dust jacket had been lost. The red leather boards concealed not knowledge and over-descriptive prose, but uncut Afghan fire, or, as those crazy West End kids loved to shout, "The Taliban." Thomas shoved the book into Pappy's open arms then stacked on another, *Moby Dick,* then more until Pappy could barely balance the pile.

Jimmy Dale Gibson could shut the fuck up now about his lost heroin.

"Now we're good," I told Pappy. "The highway awaits you."

"We're not done." Pappy tucked the books under his arm. "You're facing a serious threat to this entire operation and when Jimmy Dale finds out...The fucking DEA? We both know his favorite kind of response to adversity."

Thomas closed the door, turned the lock, and crossed his arms, blocking our Nashville guest's only escape route. We all realized the new gravity Pappy had brought to this exchange. He needed to be on our side or else we could not allow the little shit to leave the store alive.

I thought a moment, ignoring the scurrilous glares from my two associates, both wondering what Pappy and Jimmy

Dale might do to make a bad situation worse.

"I know that if your first inclination was to run south and tattle-tale, you wouldn't warn me first." I tried to lead the witness a little.

"I'm glad you're sharp enough for me to skip severing a few fingers to get your attention."

"You're outnumbered," I said.

"And you're observant," Pappy said. "But I guarantee I can take a chunk out of you, Catlett, before your butt-buddies can draw a bead or lay a hand on me."

"What do you want, little man?" Mad Dog asked. The lilt in his tone gravely downplayed the fatal straits in which we'd all found ourselves.

"A simple trade. A fair deal. I can help your men with strategy and manpower. It's what I do for Gibson. Of course, I'll need more specifics. But believe it or not, this wouldn't be the first federal agent I've bested. Not the first dirty one either. I just need to know how many people need to die."

I'd foreseen Pappy's end of the trade. "And you want to wear the Nashville crown without pissing off the Russians."

"The Dixie crown would be nice. But really, I just want Gibson gone. The things I've had to do for that man would keep you awake for the rest of your nights. I'd rather kill him than help him kill you and starve while we wait for the Russians to set up a whole new distribution network. We couldn't go to another supplier without incurring communist wrath. While we sit out the business, new operations will start up and I'll have to take care of all of them, from Murfreesboro to Nashville, when the Russians get us back up and running. It will be an orgy of blood and death I'd rather avoid."

"I have no problem with any of this." I'd already decided. Jimmy Dale could die the death of a thousand dull blades if it meant the survival of Twice Told Books and the only family I had left. We would need Pappy's reinforcements along with his wealth of piratic insights far more than Gibson needed to continue breathing.

And it looked like Pappy needed us too.

He couldn't take out Gibson on his own, for the Dixie syndicate and the Russians took great umbrage to such drastic changes in local management that didn't follow chain-of-command protocol. But Twice Told had become an indispensable cog in Barinov's plans and I was confident we could facilitate such a shift and quickly. A man like Gibson could be replaced easier than the most senile Walmart greeter. Now that we handled all the import south of Cincinnati, I could honestly say to Pappy, extending my hand to cement our new partnership, "You got yourself a goddamn deal, shorty."

"Extremely moving," Mad Dog said. "Now how do we handle the fed?"

"My turn to talk," Thomas crowed. "And thank God, because I've been waiting fucking forever to drop this bomb on you boys. You ready for some real genius, real genius?" he said to me.

Then he laid on us the plan he must've been concocting ever since he'd entered the dope game, the grand scheme he'd adjusted over the recent weeks to include Sexton, and now Pappy.

I soon better understood his joy.

"I love it." The demented killer jockey was the first to stamp his approval. "And I got just the men to assist in its execution."

Mad Dog then delivered more good news. He tapped his cell screen again.

Blacksican had been arrested, still slinging on some corner, still, unbeknownst to the arresting detective, working hard dealing heroin for a DEA agent.

"You'd think Sexton would've shot the bastard for leading us to him," Thomas said.

"Nah," Mad Dog said. "Sexton's too lazy to replace an employee. Blacky'd have to deep cock the fed's wife to get that junkie drug cop off his corpulent ass."

Blacksican was out on bail and wanted to make a deal.

And he'd only speak to Thomas.

24

"He gonna kill me," Blacksican wept. The flow of his teardrops formed tiny, jagged mournful creeks along the rutted landscape of his fattened flesh.

"And we'll kill you if you don't talk," Thomas said from the passenger side of Mad Dog's brand-new Buick, the old cop's only flashy purchase since I'd known him, a gift to himself after so many recent near misses.

"They'll kill me, man." Blacksican threw up his arms. "Or you all will or I'll catch me a stray round in the middle of this motherfuckin' siege or whatever you call what you crazy motherfuckers are planning."

I'd been silent thus far. I'd lost what little faith in humanity I'd salvaged after my brutal youth when my sweet Irina died in front of me. I clung to her corpse in a car trunk for a half hour awaiting my own execution, which Mad Dog thankfully prevented.

Still unsure how far I could trust Thomas, especially after I'd seen that mad glimmer in his eye when he'd proposed the outlandish raid on Sexton's strip club, I insisted on being present for this off-the-books interrogation. I didn't mind the possible death of Blacksican—shit, that kind of thing might have restored a small fraction of depth to the human gene pool—but I didn't want anyone jumping the gun before the fat waste of flatulence informed on his master.

I'd once again underestimated my associates. They'd remained calm and patient while I quickly tired of listening to the drug mule's whimpering.

"Your boss doesn't give a fuck about you," I said to Blacksican. "In fact, he's a cop himself, a DEA man moonlighting as a drug lord. And you're a liability to him now, catching a charge like you did tonight."

"Bullshit."

He could tell by our expressions that we didn't feel the need to lie. Then he probably remembered how we'd coerced his assistance before.

I stared across Third Street at the main library's marble steps from the vacant pay lot where we'd parked. The moon's dim and exhausted glow barely pierced the willow canopy that all but obfuscated the short avenue of tightly trimmed shrubbery and crumbling flagstone. Blacksican began again recounting the numerous scenarios that might work against his survival.

"Goddamnit." I drew the only gun I had left from the small armory I'd had Mad Dog find me. I'd had to dispose of my beloved HKs—I'd forgotten which I'd used to shoot my assassin—at the Two Rivers Campground outside the Nashville city limits while Catherine finished her set and schmoozed with her fellow entertainers.

I rapped Blacksican across the forehead with the black Beretta's butt. "Next time I'll use the gun as it was designed."

Thomas handed Blacksican a bandanna to still the flow descending his temple from the labial head wound.

269

"Spill," I screamed so loud the sound startled the two cold-blooded professionals who squeezed their faces between the front head rests to stare down our victim. "Listen you portly fucking cock-sucker…" I had to throw in the five-dollar word just to keep myself grounded in an ideal even marginally noble, the elegance of the English language, the last refuge for scoundrels. I made a big show of racking the Beretta's slide and placing the barrel against Blacksican's puffy, acne-battleground of a cheek. "Listen to me very closely. I know you know something big that's going down with Sexton and his stupid little gentleman's club. I know because you wouldn't be fighting so hard to hide it otherwise. You're not that good of an actor. You don't have any capacity for abstract thought and you possess the emotional depth of Telly Savalas. So please, for your sake and mine, start making some noise with your mouth besides whimpers and sobs. Anything, really. I'll even be happy with a hearty chuckle, you silly son-of-a-bitch."

"You want me to start laughing?" Blacksican appeared confused, yet willing to accommodate, so I forewent any further abuse and said that I didn't really want to hear him force some awkward tittering fit, but he got an A plus for enthusiasm.

"Listen again. Closely. I want to know everything about Sexton." Then I whispered, imitating Gary Oldman in *The Professional*, "Everything."

Blacksican did not disappoint.

25

The crestfallen drug mule's confession elicited a reverent silence from the front seat. After hearing the plan Thomas had fashioned, then Blacksican's story, one would almost have to believe in fate, or predestination, as if the cosmos had aligned the fat man's arrest with our earlier proposals.

Tomorrow morning, before dawn, the entirety of the Greenwood Crips, Sexton's secret allies and the city's deadliest street gang, would surround Playa's. Some of the members would wait on scooters and in tinted-windowed SUVs as guards against potential dope thieves while a select few would enter the gated lot behind the building for re-supply, loading Sexton's shitty Cincinnati heroin—Myron had cut off anyone he didn't know well from weighty Taliban purchases—into the trunks of two or three (I couldn't believe it) registered taxi cabs. Apparently, the Crips had grown disciplined enough to recruit ghost members who had a reasonably clean rap sheet and persuade the young upstarts to seek employment with River City Taxi.

"That's brilliant," I said.

"Cops never pull over taxis," Thomas agreed.

"They're a good company too," I offered.

Mad Dog just looked at me.

"What?" I asked.

"We can't," Mad Dog returned his gaze to the parking lot beyond his windshield. The older cop had already foreseen how the plan would decimate our already soiled and broken consciences. That was the strange thing about the American samurai with his lightning bolt streaks and Wyatt Earp moustache; he had limits. He had a heart. And he had a code. I walk the earth a lesser man as I was unable to comprehend this back then.

"We have to," Thomas said.

"I can't," Mad Dog said. "Those kids..." Mad Dog lowered his head. "I've been arresting those Greenwood Crips for years. They got a raw deal, all of them. Crackhead mothers. Abuse you wouldn't comprehend. You worked with kids like that when you ran the gang squad, Thomas. You should know better than anyone that they don't deserve to get caught in this crossfire. I'm not going to—"

"But we can save more of them," Thomas said. "These dozen or so..." He paused then asked Blacksican, "How many will there be?"

"Eight." Blacksican barely moved his mouth, already wishing he'd just let us kill him and probably realizing that he wasn't going to survive this despite spilling his guts. "Maybe nine or ten."

"Ten," Thomas said. "Ten in exchange for the hundreds the gang squad can save? Fair trade, you ask me."

"What?" I asked.

Mad Dog joined me in my awe. "You think..." Then Mad Dog laughed almost as insanely as Thomas, as if the madman's sickness was as contagious as the common flu. "You think if you raise enough hell in the ghetto, they'll give you your gang squad back and you and the other narcos can have your little office and work with those short skirted social workers and do God's will the right way?" He laughed harder. "Your way."

"Don't cross me on this, Milligan." Thomas swiveled his head and gaped at his old bunkie then shouted for Blacksican to exit the vehicle. "*Now!*"

Blacksican waddled out and dragged himself toward the alley that ran alongside the library.

Thomas rolled down the passenger side window, produced a Glock from under his seat, and shot the poor, overgrown street child in the back four times. We were out of the parking lot and headed toward Old Louisville before Blacksican had even collapsed.

"At least he doesn't have to worry about Sexton killing him now," Thomas joked.

"Nice," I finally said. I looked down at the gun in my hand. If Thomas were not an infamous policeman, I would have clipped him then and there. "Leave a body in front of the public fucking library. Smart. Let me out of the car, Chad."

"You two pussies need to realize something," Thomas yelled, flooring the accelerator. "I have more man power than either of you. My troops will slaughter you and leave you, in your dying moments, to wonder what will become of your women." Thomas looked over at Mad Dog, and added, "And your kids." Then he whispered, "And your precious little daddy's girl Snyder, the one you like to imagine as the grown baby your last ex-wife aborted without telling you before she took off with one of your snitches—you know how easy it would be to command my street contacts, to make a true whore of your precious little angel? They'd love nothing more than running a fifty-hour train on a nice little white girl with a sassy mouth, especially if they had police protection."

"I'll kill you," Mad Dog said.

"And I'll help him," I said.

"You really believe you can get to me before I make Snyder disappear? I have her wired for sound and I got a tail on her twenty-four seven. Even if you got to me, by the time you found her, she'd be bleeding from—"

"Stop it," Mad Dog said lowly but with a deathly earnestness that quieted his tormentor.

"Then you better say something or nod and let me know we're all on the same page."

Mad Dog shook his head and murmured, "Sure, sure, Thomas."

"I'm not going to ask Catlett to give me the same assurance because I already know he's such a coward he won't risk taking me on."

"That's a relief," I said. "I'm glad you have so much faith in me, Thomas. I really feel like we've connected since we started working together, you know."

I wanted to cut his heart out and serve it for dinner to the families of all the innocent people he'd yet to kill.

"You son-of-a-bitch," Mad Dog said to the man who'd been his friend just this morning. Then Milligan softened his tone and implored, "Please, son."

"I'm not your fucking son," Thomas said. "And never wanted to be, you pathetic, delusional old man. You're not cut out for this anymore. You still believe there's a code of conduct, that there really are good thieves and honest killers, cop or otherwise. You think there are rules we are supposed to play by. Not anymore. Everyone rats. Everyone's out for their own."

"You really can stop this," I said. "We'll have Tennessee in our pocket soon. There must be another way to take down Sexton. He's not worth this."

"Shut up." As the lights of West Louisville twinkled through the dirty windshield like dying stars in the closing distance, Thomas turned and glowered at me between the head rests and said in a cancerous hiss, "You really want more dead women on your conscience, or whatever's left of it. It may be kind of hard to get a date if you keep on with this bad habit of getting girls killed."

I sunk into the leather upholstery and covered my mouth, whatever life I had left draining quicker than a lanced abscess, hollowing my cheeks and withering my posture like a dying daisy.

"If I find out you've taken as much as a step against me," Thomas said, "I'll have that Catherine cunt whored out in River Park for a month before I drown her in the Ohio. I already have a man outside her house. If he doesn't get a text from me every hour on the hour, he knows which hole to stuff first."

Mad Dog said, "We're not these kinds of men. This is a business, not a Holy War. We do not have to forfeit what's left of our souls just so you can get a promotion and corner the dope trade, you goddamn hypocrite. You're not the only one the system short changed. This is America and we always knew we served the biggest gang in town, those fancy bastards at city hall. You really want to be like them, sending other people's kids to die for you the way they did you when you went to the desert? Thomas, please. No one riding in this car has the right to lead those boys to their deaths."

"That's what you don't get." Thomas hung his head, as if it honestly hurt telling his old departmental rabbi these hard truths the elder had never wanted to face. "I'm driving this car. I'm not a passenger. I'm in charge. You know why? There will come the day when you're unwilling do what your adversary isn't and that will be the dawn of your undoing. See, I'm here to tame these badlands, to tame these streets for good. The madness can be contained. It can be channeled. And I will soon be the captain of the chaos that took our cities and our homes. When it belongs to me, you'll see peace restored to the streets where your children and brothers and sisters used to walk free. But a sacrifice must be made. Anything worth saving is worth dying for."

Then he looked at me in the rearview while Mad Dog continued to whisper, "Please" and "Don't" like the desperate mantras of a man dying alone with his failures.

"What they don't tell you," Thomas said, "if it's worth dying for, it's worth killing for."

26

In fear, Mad Dog and I drank.

It was my first shot of alcohol in nearly a year and I felt that I'd betray the universe if I didn't give into my own fatal illness while allowing the day's events to progress. We drank by the river, our asses wet with silt and sludge. We'd lost any concern over appearances.

Mad Dog couldn't stop dictating exactly what kind of travesty we'd done nothing to stop. We sat there watching the sunrise from the riverbed while the slaughter commenced. "They're tearing them to pieces as we speak," he said.

Thomas had never cared about profit, and for that I could almost respect the man. But he'd committed a sin that, in its boldness, had cast hellish shadows on us all, Paul, me, Mad Dog, even Myron. He believed he was the alpha and the omega, that his will had long been aligned with that of the cosmos, and that anything he did to bring about the reinstatement of his precious little unit had been pardoned from jump street by the creator himself.

Right now, behind Sexton's club, Pappy's Nashville street hoodlums were massacring the Greenwood Crips as they arrived to load the agent's heroin. Thomas' own troops, Snyder included, were perched on rooftops to snipe any of the gang members who might arrive from the flank. All eight or ten teenagers would be dead in about five minutes.

With the help of Mad Dog's smartphone and Google, I'd done my research. The average Louisville Crip didn't even live long enough to drink legally.

We were complicit in the murders of children.

Around this same time the massacre commenced, Pappy would hand-deliver Jimmy Dale Gibson's heroin and watch as the leering, long-haired Dixie mob czar tested the product, digging out a bump with one of his rusty blades and snorting straight off the dull tip. Then the midget would stab the ward boss repeatedly in the kidney, liver, and heart, entering downward through the arm pit as the dying man raised his hands in supplication.

Gibson was found dead in the office above a pawnshop he owned, his face buried in a gram of heroin.

Ironically, back in Louisville, a few hours later, Sexton was found the same way.

"That's how he gets us off killing a DEA man," Mad Dog explained yet again after a long pull from his flask. "The first on the scene will see the dope, see that Sexton's dirty. And something will have to be done."

Paul had remained with Myron at the Broadway store, said he had to await word on his former lover's fate. He didn't seem to care what we did about Sexton and Nashville and keeping the Russians happy.

This should've worried me more.

It was Snyder who got Sexton.

Holed up in his office, his puppet of a manager firing down the upstairs hallway, warding off assailants, the two security men already dead at the bottom of the darkened steps.

Bilotta snuck around the side of the building and cut the lights.

Sexton couldn't see to get his fix, to snort a bump of the sweet powder that might calm his rioting nerves, so he had to open the window that looked out onto Seventh Street.

From the attic of a vacant Victorian, Snyder fixed her sights, allowed the man his last snort of Cincinasty, his new brand name for the product he believed could compete with the Afghan.

Then she relieved him of all worldly concerns, along with the top half of his skull.

27

By mid-day, as Mad Dog drove me drunkenly to Paul's mother's house where I planned on having a little talk with my godson, news of Sexton's corruption and a detailed map of his entire operation were recounted on local NPR and TV news. The mayor, panicking over his poor polls, announced the reformation of the now infamous gang squad, an act of public contrition that might please policemen and frightened white people. Ultimately, nothing would bring back the nine dead teenage Crips some "new and still unidentified street gang" had murdered in broad daylight. But the Mayor assured that, "These moralless culprits will be brought to justice and prevented from further dirtying our fine city's national reputation."

"To stop gang violence," Mad Dog slowly slurred, "we had to make some more of it. Shit, Thomas made up a street gang. He created it just for job security. Creative motherfucker, ain't he?"

I ran my hand through Irina's blonde hair.

The dog looked up at me from my lap. We'd retrieved her from the bookstore office. She'd be my present to Adam. My last gift to the world, maybe. If Paul didn't like it, fuck him. Chances were none of us would live long enough to watch the self-righteous prick steal anymore of his son's joy.

The dog looked up at me with eyes free of judgment or comparison or hate, the things that had placed me and Mad Dog in the seats in which we now rode like helpless passengers on a runaway train.

The worst part of it was that Mad Dog's son had gone to school and worked hard to become a social worker. "He probably knows some of those kids." Mad Dog had driven himself to tears, a miracle if I'd ever seen one.

I remained silent. It seemed better to say nothing than to offer empty comfort.

Then I remembered Scott.

Once this went public, if my name were thrown in the mix, my oldest friend's career would be over. He'd told all his friends about his brilliant college running buddy who'd risen from poverty and opened his own bookstore. I texted him, "I'm sorry," and tossed the burner out the window. What more could I say? Everything I touched withered and died.

Milligan dropped me off at the front steps of Mrs. Frank's, Paul's birth mother, and my surrogate over the last five years.

I almost cried along with Milligan, when, in his cracked voice, he called me *son*. "Walk away from all this. Don't look back. If you keep on, you'll just pile up more bodies. You'll just..." He had to stop and breathe. "Either that or buy a suit. You'll need one for all the funerals. And you'll need one for your own, which, if you don't heed my warning, will be sooner than you could ever imagine."

I like to think that Milligan gathered all his illicit profits, wherever he'd buried them, and retired to a life of lesser evil in some enlightened Western European beach town.

I can't believe that he threw himself off some bridge somewhere or that they found him dead of a self-inflicted gunshot wound in some Tijuana brothel.

I can't believe that, although it's probably the truth.

Adam was high again.

"I'm sorry," I said to Mrs. Frank as she paced before Paul's old room where the boy now nodded off. I stared at him through the open door. Irina had jumped onto the twin bed and begun licking the kid's hand, making her way up his arm. He began to come out of it and laugh. The laughter made me think of the child Paul and I had stolen from this world.

Mrs. Frank threw up her hands in surrender to the God that she'd credited for getting her and Paul through the suicide of her alcoholic husband, through the welfare checks and her rise from the slums into a middle-class neighborhood, a small frame house, and a salary position with benefits at the Veteran's Administration. She ran her hands through her thick gray curls, straightened slightly by the bandanna tied at her hairline.

"I'm sorry," I mumbled again.

"What's the dog's name?" she asked.

"Irina," I said. Mrs. Frank hadn't followed my criminal exploits. She didn't read the papers because she didn't trust the businessmen that owned them. And she hadn't met any of my lovers. Paul had spared her that. He didn't want to

JONATHAN ASHLEY

get the poor lady attached to a girl who might disappear any moment.

"Where'd you get that name?" she asked playfully, elbowing me. "Some exotically beautiful Highlander that fell for your charms?"

I laughed, but could no longer disguise my sadness. "She was someone very beautiful, Mrs. Frank. I think you would've liked her a lot."

The old woman patted my cheek.

"You were always a good boy," she told me. "You got nothin' to be sorry about. Maybe the puppy will bring him out of this. Maybe you can help. I don't know what I did..." She went weak at her own perceived failures. "If I'd been around more for Paul maybe..."

"Don't." I pulled her to me and she fell apart in my arms.

I nearly apologized again. Instead I simply said, "It's okay...I promise Everything will be fine," some of the biggest lies I've ever told

28

The sapphire sunrise over the verdant rolling hills of LaGrange deceptively welcomed me to my new country estate. I'd walked from Mrs. Frank's backyard to the Highlands branch where I'd left my car. The drive to the country had taken half an hour, too much time to think with so many demons dancing and singing their songs in my head. Long before I searched the farm grounds, before I checked under the porches, through the weeds and woods that ended somewhere past the property line, before I even hit the half-mile gravel drive, I knew exactly what awaited. To check the garden last may have been a subconscious decision, for that would be the most obvious burial spot for a novice killer like Paul. I didn't want to believe that a man I'd called my friend, my partner, had recently, and for no reason that furthered our business concerns, murdered his ex-wife and buried her on my property, just in case trouble came down on us and he needed a patsy ripe for framing.

As much as I wanted to hate my old friend, this morning I couldn't force enough ironic disdain for the universe to absolve myself of the part I'd played in all this death and loss and societal degeneration.

Intellectual pride would be the downfall of Paul Weddington Frank. Thinking his son naïve enough to believe Paul's story about his mother's disappearance, the same day Adam had told Paul about my farm, the same evening Paul's ex-wife had decided that she would move her son up north to be closer to her parents and their money.

Paul had taken the news calmly, asked if he could speak to Renee in private, at which point Adam retired to his room where he broke down and banged his emergency dose, the shot some drug addicts were disciplined enough to keep around just in case they needed a relapse.

When he came to, Paul was downstairs, but Mom was missing.

I found her in the dying garden of watermelons and cucumbers the previous owner of my country retreat had planted.

After digging into the dampest plot of soil with my bare hands, after uncovering the brittle, bloody fingers, the cheap ring that Paul had left on her—probably a final act of disdain, leaving Renee with the Bosnian's wedding band—I decided that I would be damned if my old friend remained in blissful denial of what he'd done and why, nor of the hell that was coming.

My phone buzzed. It was Thomas.

"Get over to the West End store," he told me.

A level of reason that had long eluded me returned and before answering the call, I'd hit record on the smart phone app.

Since Thomas was high on a sense of self-satisfaction, he'd be more likely than usual to say something stupid on an open line. "In the store room, there's a drop piece taped under the top shelf. When you see what your goddamn friend Paul has done—"

"And what exactly has Paul done?"

"Are you being real?"

"I'm in the middle of something." I knew getting aggressive would weaken Thomas's equilibrium. Then, for good measure, I lied, "And frankly, you handsome bastard, I don't appreciate you speaking of my friend in such a reckless manner."

"I don't give a fuck what you appreciate," Thomas screamed, as I knew he would. He did surprise me with some bad news, throwing my act off a bit. "Your dumbass friend, about an hour ago, went to check on his degenerate junkie son."

"So now we're finding out how you really feel about the disenfranchised street people I thought you wanted to help."

"Fuck you, Catlett. Paul found his son stoned. He found the baggie, saw that it was the Afghan and went back to the West End store. Paul shot Myron."

"No..." I closed my eyes. "Shot him...like..."

"Like there's a freshly dead Nubian laying behind the front counter of your Broadway branch."

"No...no..." was all I could say.

"He's cleaning up the mess, but he wants you to help dispose of the body. Now, I want you to listen carefully..."

Thomas explained where I could get some lye without leaving a paper trail, then how to spread it over Myron's body.

"And once Paul has helped you dig the grave, leave two bodies in it."

"Don't you think you've killed enough people today?" I asked, leading him like a poorly coached government witness.

"I served the Commonwealth today, Catlett," Thomas said.

Then he hammered the final nail in his coffin. "Did some scumbag Greenwood Crips have to perish so that we could make way for a better tomorrow? Sadly, that's how it works sometimes. That's the job."

"Funny," I said, "I must've missed that LMPD recruiting add."

I hung up on him and saved the recording.

I called Mrs. Frank and asked for an address. I felt not a small bit of shame and remorse for what I'd helped do to her family. But ultimately, the lesser evil would be to leave Adam in his grandmother's care.

I mailed her and my Godson the key to the safety deposit box I'd bought, where I'd placed nearly a hundred thousand dollars.

Then I headed west to kill my best friend.

29

Thomas didn't tell me Snyder would be there.

Her eyes never left us as Paul and I loaded Myron's corpse, wrapped in a blue tarp, into the trunk of the Saturn she'd stolen for the job. She wore a London Fog overcoat with an assault rifle concealed beneath.

I hoped I didn't have to kill her too.

"This is ridiculous," Paul said. He didn't act like a man who'd just murdered an ostensible intimate in cold blood without much evidence for the killing's motive.

"Yeah, I agree," I said. "Shooting our own people, not the best business plan you've ever presented."

"I'm talking about burying him on your farm," Paul said. "With those two murder cops bringing so much heat down on you and yours."

"They don't have metal detectors for bodies," I said. "I know exactly where to put him. A cop could walk right over the grave and not notice because the entire floor of the barn is loose dirt."

"They do have technology that can help them find buried bodies," Snyder corrected me. "But they're not going to waste that unless they know someone *very* important is missing and there's a 99.9 percent probability he or she is dead."

"Excuse the hell out of me," I said. "I'm not up to date on all the CSI shit out there. I just started killing people less than a year ago, so I'm a little green. Still, we're in agreement—what are they going to do, dig up every acre of my land on the off chance I might've killed someone there? No. They're wanting to link me to a drug ring and no one's going to know there's a body to look for, *period*, especially if we stop bickering and head east."

"Aren't you forgetting something?" she ordered from the driver's bucket.

Paul had fallen asleep in the back.

"What?" I said.

She meant the gun, the one Thomas had specified.

"Is there anything special about this something?" I referred to the gun in question.

"Just get it."

In the inventory closet, I used a rag to shield my fingerprints from the revolver's grip. The piece was still hot, probably used in the siege on Sexton's compound. I would be found with two in the head and a gun recently used in a mass murder.

This way, Thomas could put the bookstore behind him and focus on his new career as the LMPD's answer to Agent Sexton, the cop who'd hypocritically persecuted drug dealers, eliminating the competition while he cornered the market.

"Shit," I said, thinking of the raven-haired sexpot in the passenger seat of the stolen car parked behind the loading dock.

I dropped the warm wheel gun in my pocket, then drew my Beretta and checked the clip's load. Fifteen shots plus the one in the pipe. If I couldn't take her and Paul with sixteen rounds, I deserved whatever was coming to me.

I cursed aloud again then spoke Snyder's name. "I'm sorry, love," I said.

And I was just starting to like her.

Inside the sagging barn facing the garden where Adam's mother had been buried, before I dug her up and dumped her in the river chained to cinderblocks—the fashion of my first corpse disposal—between smelly bales of hay, Paul and I took turns digging our grave, the story of our lives.

He'd yet to speak since we'd hit the gravel drive and the bumps in the road woke him from his nap. He'd murdered his own wife and a dear friend and slept like the peerlessly just.

I didn't want to hear any of his excuses anyway. I could've recited his arguments before he even spoke them. We shared the same disease. His had just progressed quicker.

I rose from the grave first. I looked down at Myron's body, the left half of his face all skull and muscle. "You deserved better," I said to Myron.

Paul must've thought I'd been speaking to him. "What?" He looked up from the shallow hole.

I drew the Beretta instead of the revolver.

"What are you doing?" Snyder asked. She stepped from the barn door against which she'd been leaning.

"Thomas said to kill him," I told her.

"What?" Paul shouted.

"Which I have no problem with," I continued, the gun

290

aimed at Paul, my stare at Snyder. "But I'm doing it for me and those fucking children we killed and Myron and the woman this piece of shit buried in my fucking garden."

"What?" Paul repeated himself, tossing the shovel aside.

"I'm not having an innocent found buried in my garden," I told Paul. "I have to draw the line somewhere. You and Myron—that's one thing. But your ex-wife? That could get me the chair. Two killers might get me ten years. What did you think would happen? They'd think I killed her if they ever dug deep enough?"

I trained the gun on Snyder for a moment and told her to drop her rifle. She didn't respond. And I did not want to shoot her. Sadistic and dead-eyed, she still seemed the most reasonable of all the psychopaths I'd encountered this year.

Paul laughed, punched the walls of the hole he'd dug, kicking the mud at his feet, further ruining his suit pants with utter abandon. "None of it matters, you dumb whores."

"What?" I stepped back, now leveling the gun in a more general direction. This way I'd have a chance of shooting whichever one tried to draw first. Paul had yet to dispose of the piece with which he'd murdered Myron.

"You're all going to prison," Paul said.

Shit.

"No..." I said to him.

"That's right. I was the smart one, Catlett. Me. Not you. In the commonwealth, the cops and the DA always award the get-out-of-jail free card to the first asshole willing to testify. I saw the writing on the wall and I took my opportunity."

He wasn't just a killer. He was a rat too.

He told his own story now, giggling like a circus clown. He told of how Catherine had been pressured by Neil and Bob to wear a wire, thus the trip to Nashville. She had even planted a bug under her seat. The possible connection between Twice Told and this new brand of heroin nicknamed "The Taliban" had turned enough federal heads for the two detectives to get a wiretap authorization in no time.

"Catherine..." I said.

"For what it's worth, Neil said she cried like a baby when she finally agreed."

"Why?"

The detectives and a few narcos who had it in for Mad Dog had come together and convinced a judge to release Catherine's surviving junkie brother from LaGrange if she helped build a case against our crew.

Neil and Bob weren't as stupid as I'd thought. Now who possessed the worst ego?

While the bug in the van had burned up in the Nashville fire, the LMPD knew that the tracker had lost signal in a close vicinity to a quadruple homicide that occurred the same evening Catherine and I had our music city rendezvous. With Catherine's testimony and the wire she'd worn, the honest narcotics cops had enough to begin to build a case.

"Why am I not in handcuffs already?" I said.

"Catherine backed out of the deal," Paul said. "They wanted her to get you to admit everything on the wire. She said 'no.'"

I smiled for the briefest moment.

She'd liked me after all.

The detectives then approached Paul, putting the screws to him with the recordings, explaining that if they made a case against me for murder, they would offer me a plea bargain if I gave up our crew. They gave Paul a chance to testify first, an opportunity he'd accepted once they agreed to his terms. Immunity and witness relocation in exchange for a full confession.

"Did they bother telling you about Adam?" I asked.

"What?" Paul's laughter ceased.

"The cops knew Adam was using before any of us did. They were the ones that told me. You fucking idiot. They played you like a fiddle. And they didn't care to let you know about your kid because the last thing they wanted was for you to do something stupid and blow up their case. Ruin their chances of making headlines and earning some promotions. I suppose, like that dick told you when he first called before I came town, they never thought much of your parenting skills. They figured you'd never notice that your son was starting to look like a concentration camp regular. They sure underestimated you."

"You're goddamn right, they did." Paul was fuming. He knew now that he'd not escaped the noose. We'd all been used. Everyone but Thomas. That is, if Paul had included the cop's name. "They always underestimate me."

"You're right, Paul. They never thought you'd murder the mother of your own son and then ice one of the key players in our little hick town cartel. I'm sure they were looking forward to arresting Myron, maybe getting him to flip on the real brains behind all this."

"You're just mad that I was smart enough to screw you first," Paul said.

"Did you tell them about everyone?" I asked.

"No." Paul's smile reappeared and widened. "Didn't want to burn all of my bridges here in town. Figured I might need a few friends like Thomas and Dog. No. It was all going to fall on you. Then I thought maybe Thomas could get you clipped while you were in lockup. Maybe I could keep helping out with the business under the safe umbrella of the federal government."

"You're out of your mind," Snyder said. "You think Thomas would ever trust an informant?"

"He's done worse," Paul said. "You were there this morning, sugar." He winked at the murderess.

"Wait?" Snyder asked. "If you made a deal, why are you even here right now?"

Paul, still quite amused with himself, said, "Whuh-what?"

"Why?" she said. "If you're sitting pretty with a plea deal, why have you returned to enemy territory?"

I knew I liked her.

She pulled back the skirt of her raincoat and leveled the AK at the laughing man standing in the grave.

"The deal wasn't final." I was the one laughing now. "Who's smart now, Paul?"

The feds probably needed a little time to okay the arrangement with a judge. And I'd bet all the fortune I would never get to spend that Neil and Bob and their federal friends had even advised Paul to lay low. But he hadn't informed them of his many sins, his many interests that needed tending to before he left Louisville. They'd also underestimated the power of the megalomaniac's overly sensitive and perpetually wounded pride.

"I didn't..." Paul stated again.

"He never stutters unless he's lying or he's been caught." I thought of the time the clever little shit had drunkenly hit on Irina then denied it. I'd forgiven him for that as I would for all his trespasses.

Like I'd forgive him for this once there were some layers of dirt between us.

"Well..." Paul realized his mistake, that his gift for the gab had been the beginning of his end. "They were gonna meet with me today."

"But the shootout on Seventh Street," I said. "You hadn't counted on that. On Neil and Bob having their hands full with a murder investigation involving a dozen teenagers and a DEA agent. Kind of put you on the back burner, didn't they? The narcos too since it's a drug case. You also didn't envision your son's junk habit. Junk he bought from *Sexton*. Myron had nothing to do with it. Your boy loved Myron. I did too. But this, all of it, is on you and me."

I turned my head to Snyder. "He hasn't signed anything."

"Or else this piece of shit would already be in Arizona or fucking Carthage, Ohio in Wit-Sec."

"Wait..." Paul sadly attempted to talk his way out of this, grinning only a moment before I shot him in the face.

He went for the pistol grip sticking out of his waistband and had his hand on the gun but collapsed before he could pull, his arms and legs jerking spastically as he choked on the blood pouring down his cheeks from the mashed mess where his left eye had been.

I holstered my piece and dropped to my knees.

"You gonna kill me now?" I asked Snyder. "Go ahead."

"What?"

"Are you going to kill me? Don't insult me and act like this all wasn't a set up."

"I didn't want to."

"And I understand."

"Honestly," she lowered her gun and said, "I was hoping I found a good enough reason not to kill you and to bury Thomas instead."

Snyder admitted to seeing Bilotta leave his sniper's perch and engage one of the Crips trying to ride away on a scooter. "He was using a revolver. I thought it was weird at the time. Didn't put it together until Thomas insisted you use the gun on Paul."

I was humbled by the plan's genius.

"And all of this masquerading would have satisfied investigators." Snyder understood now the grand design we'd all unknowingly helped implement.

"If Thomas is silencing potential objectors to his power claim..."

"His own troops," Snyder said, "are not exempt."

The phone call I'd recorded had been Thomas' one glaring mistake. That and neglecting the potential X factors, Mad Dog's conscience, Paul going murderously rogue, Adam's dope habit.

"Let's review options." I told her about the phone and reminded her that we now also had a gun used in the Seventh Street massacre. Plenty of evidence to ruin Chad Thomas.

"And I know the name of his best man in Afghanistan," Snyder said.

"That'd be a federal case involving the military."

"And it would make some lucky local cop's career."

I thought of Scott. Maybe I could still save his job.

"We might be the ones to fire the real money shot." I winced. I hadn't meant to make a porn reference. She had caught my lecherous slip and we both took a moment from the dreadful conversation to laugh together.

"What about Bilotta?" she asked. "What about the rest of them?"

Her fellow killers. She held a blood bond with them that I respected and understood. "Sadly, angel, soldierly loyalty doesn't translate well onto the streets of Louisville. We all knew the risks when we signed on. Plus, from what Paul said, the heat's coming. Enough of Thomas' co-workers have it in for him. And, apparently, they've united, those homicide detectives, the narcos Paul talked about. Whoever doesn't run or try to offer up a true evil architect like Thomas, well, they're on the chopping block. That ain't on you or me. Thomas, if he hangs, it'll be his choice whether to rat out the Russians. If he does, he'll wish we'd killed him instead."

She looked down at her combat boots.

"Thomas promised," she said lowly, "no more children after Afghanistan." She couldn't speak directly of the teenage vagabonds she'd watched die in the streets of her own country that morning.

"Well, he lied."

"I only see one way out."

"You know with Thomas, it's a matter of time until you only have a few choices. When it's either him or you."

"I know."

"Whatever you decide for now, if you kill me and hit the road or if we get this evidence into the hands of a district attorney or a reporter or the right cop, I need you to promise me something." I asked if she would leave some more of my money on Mrs. Frank's front porch, a sizeable amount. I told her where to find my other go-bag of quick cash and that she could keep some for herself as long as Paul's mother got the lion's share. It was the least I could do after killing her son and risking the life of her grand-child. "Or you can give the rest to the Salvation Army," I quoted Johnny Cash. I'd be okay with those last words. But I had a little more to say after she agreed to my terms. "Or we could use our money. Get out of town. Maybe you know someone who can make us passports, huh? We could leave the Feds enough rope to hang Thomas and we could run. We could run before they come for us. And maybe we could live a little for a while longer."

"They'd probably get us eventually."

"Eventually, they get us all."

She smiled and agreed with me again.

"It's up to you."

I threw my pistol into the grave.

And I was ready, no matter what she chose.

Jonathan Ashley is the author of *Out of Mercy* and *The Cost of Doing Business*, both of which will be reissued by Down & Out Books in 2018. His work has appeared in *Crime Factory*, *Out of the Gutter*, *A Twist of Noir*, *LEO Weekly*, *Kentucky Magazine* and *Yellow Mama*. He lives in Lexington, Kentucky.

OTHER TITLES FROM DOWN AND OUT BOOKS

See www.DownAndOutBooks.com for complete list

By J.L. Abramo
Chasing Charlie Chan
Circling the Runway
Brooklyn Justice
Coney Island Avenue

By Trey R. Barker
Exit Blood
Death is Not Forever
No Harder Prison

By Eric Beetner
Unloaded (editor)
Criminal Elements
Rumrunners
Leadfoot

By Eric Beetner
and Frank Zafiro
The Backlist
The Shortlist

By G.J. Brown
Falling

By Angel Luis Colón
No Happy Endings
Meat City on Fire (*)

By Shawn Corridan
and Gary Waid
Gitmo

By Frank De Blase
Pine Box for a Pin-Up
Busted Valentines
A Cougar's Kiss

By Les Edgerton
The Genuine, Imitation,
Plastic Kidnapping
Lagniappe
Just Like That (*)

By Danny Gardner
A Negro and an Ofay

By Jack Getze
Big Mojo
Big Shoes
The Black Kachina

By Richard Godwin
Wrong Crowd
Buffalo and Sour Mash
Crystal on Electric Acetate

By Jeffery Hess
Beachhead
Cold War Canoe Club

By Matt Hilton
Rules of Honor
The Lawless Kind
The Devil's Anvil
No Safe Place

By Lawrence Kelter
and Frank Zafiro
The Last Collar

By Lawrence Kelter
Back to Brooklyn
My Cousin Vinny (*)

(*)—Coming Soon

OTHER TITLES FROM DOWN AND OUT BOOKS

See www.DownAndOutBooks.com for complete list

By Jerry Kennealy
Screen Test
Polo's Long Shot (*)

By Dana King
Worst Enemies
Grind Joint
Resurrection Mall

By Ross Klavan, Tim O'Mara
and Charles Salzberg
Triple Shot

By S.W. Lauden
Crosswise
Crossed Bones

By Paul D. Marks and
Andrew McAleer (editor)
Coast to Coast vol. 1
Coast to Coast vol. 2

By Gerald O'Connor
The Origins of Benjamin Hackett

By Gary Phillips
The Perpetrators
Scoundrels (Editor)
Treacherous
3 the Hard Way

By Thomas Pluck
Bad Boy Boogie

By Tom Pitts
Hustle
American Static

By Robert J. Randisi
Upon My Soul
Souls of the Dead
Envy the Dead

By Charles Salzberg
Devil in the Hole
Swann's Last Song
Swann Dives In
Swann's Way Out

By Scott Loring Sanders
Shooting Creek and Other Stories

By Ryan Sayles
The Subtle Art of Brutality
Warpath
Let Me Put My Stories In You

By John Shepphird
The Shill
Kill the Shill
Beware the Shill

By James R. Tuck (editor)
Mama Tried vol. 1
Mama Tried vol. 2 (*)

By Lono Waiwaiole
Wiley's Lament
Wiley's Shuffle
Wiley's Refrain
Dark Paradise
Leon's Legacy

By Nathan Walpow
The Logan Triad

(*)—Coming Soon

Made in the USA
Middletown, DE
02 August 2017